THE HOPES AND DREAMS OF LIBBY QUINN

FREYA KENNEDY

Boldwood

First published in Great Britain in 2020 by Boldwood Books Ltd.

A CIP catalogue record for this book is available from the British Library.

Paperback ISBN 978-1-83889-909-7

Ebook ISBN 978-1-83889-903-5

Kindle ISBN 978-1-83889-904-2

Audio CD ISBN 978-1-83889-910-3

MP3 CD ISBN 978-1-83889-907-3

Digital audio download ISBN 978-1-83889-902-8

Boldwood Books Ltd
23 Bowerdean Street
London SW6 3TN
www.boldwoodbooks.com

For the original Grandad Ernie who left us with so many magical memories.

PROLOGUE

Once upon a time, there was a little girl called Libby who travelled to a hundred different worlds and lived a thousand different lives just by opening the pages of a book and discovering the magic in the pages.

'There's no greater gift that you can give someone than a love of reading,' her grandad, Ernie, had told her.

She blinked up at him as she sat on his lap, the wool of his much loved and worse for wear cardigan scratchy against her bare arms.

'Where were we with this one?' he asked her, flicking through the yellowing pages of the latest book he had picked up in the charity shop for her.

He believed that books should be loved. They should look loved and lived in. He loved folded down corners, and broken spines. He loved notes scrawled in the margins. Signs that a book had been pored over, read, devoured.

'I think,' Libby said, using her small hands to turn the pages herself, 'we were just about here...' She pointed to a page with a fresh fold at the top.

'I think you might just be right, Libby,' her grandad laughed, 'right at the point where Mr and Mrs Twit are about to get their comeuppance!'

Libby felt a swell of excitement. She couldn't wait to find out what happened next. She couldn't wait to see the awful Twits with their awful ways come undone.

'When we're finished,' she said, 'can you tell me one of your stories? From when you were wee?' Libby may well have loved the stories in these books, but she loved her grandad's stories just as much.

'Actually,' he said, 'I was thinking we could go to the bookshop and see if we can pick up a new book or two?'

She wrapped her arms around his neck and kissed his stubbly cheek. 'Can we really?' she asked.

'Of course,' he said. 'Can you imagine, Libby, if we owned a bookshop? How amazing would that be? All those books.'

'I'd never ever leave it, ever,' she said.

'No, I don't think I would either.' Her grandad smiled. 'Maybe one day we will. But first let's find out what happens to the Twits.'

Libby nodded, lay her head against her grandad's chest and watched his finger move along under the words on the page as he read to her. And the story came to life before her eyes.

1

GREAT EXPECTATIONS

Libby hadn't slept at all well. A fizz of something – excitement or nerves, or maybe both – had kept her awake most of the night.

She was finally doing it. Chasing her dream. The dream she had shared for years with her beloved grandad. Her heart ached a little when she thought of him, but she knew he wasn't really gone. He was still beside her. He always would be.

She'd assured herself of that as she reached for her very battered copy of *Great Expectations* and started to read through it. She could almost hear his voice as she read, remembering the first time he had opened the book – which was already well-loved, its spine broken, pages yellowed – and read it to her. Inviting her into the world of Pip and Estella and the incomparable Miss Havisham.

Nodding to the picture of her grandfather, Ernie, which sat on the dresser of her childhood bedroom, Libby stopped reading long enough to whisper: 'We're doing it, Grandad. We're finally doing it.'

When she eventually put the book down, still much too early for any right-minded person to be getting up, she stepped into the shower and allowed herself to mentally run through the to-do list in her head.

First of all – pick up the keys. That was the most important bit. That was the bit that made her stomach somersault. That was the bit that allowed her to push all and any worries about what she might find when she finally opened the doors to her new property on Ivy Lane aside.

Sure, the shop didn't look like much now. In fact, it looked, from the outside, as if it might be better to knock it to the ground and start again. But Libby could see past the chipped rendering, the peeling paint in the window frames and the yellowed newspaper lining the inside of the windows of the corner-plot premises. She could even see past the broken downpipe from the upstairs flat, and the overflowing guttering which looked like it housed its own ecosystem. She could close her eyes and imagine what it could be.

As soon as her best friend Jess had called her, telling her the shop she had often dreamed of owning was finally up for auction, Libby had known exactly what she wanted to do with it.

She wanted to do exactly what she had always talked about with her grandad. What they'd always said they'd like to do 'someday' but never really thought they could – not when life became more about being sensible than taking risks.

Libby Quinn was tired of being sensible. Of never taking risks. There was a yearning for something more inside her and this was her chance to try and find it. She'd turn the ramshackle shop into her very own slice of heaven – where the heady smell of books would mix with the warm aroma of coffee and cake – and a welcoming atmosphere for everyone who crossed her threshold. She'd create an oasis of calm in this little side street for book lovers just like her.

The timing of Jess's phone call couldn't have been better.

Libby had been tending Grandad Ernie's grave and telling him all her news, as she did every week. She'd been asking him for a sign about what to do with her life next, when her phone had buzzed to life.

Tears had pricked at her eyes as Jess spoke, and Libby had felt goosebumps rise on her skin. 'It's our shop, Grandad,' she'd said, once she'd ended the call. 'The one we said would make the perfect bookshop!'

And it was, it was the very building, replete with original stone fascia and cornicing, wooden framed windows that they had said would be ripe for loving redevelopment. Ivy Lane was coming back to life, thanks to the growth of the nearby university campus but also the increased numbers of visitors flocking to Derry each year to soak up its history and culture.

Grandad Ernie had called it. He'd said it would come into its own and he'd been right. Libby could see that. It mightn't be just there yet – which had to be a good thing when it came to the price of the shop – but it was well on its way.

And now she had the means, and the drive, to see if she could make it work. The guide price had been comfortably within her means. Well, it would be, Libby had figured, once she sold the terraced house she had bought as soon as she'd been able to scrape together a deposit and had lovingly restored. Added to the generous inheritance Grandad Ernie had left for her, and the redundancy package she'd just received after thirteen years of dutiful service to an insurance company now intent on going digital, she'd realised she stood a chance.

So, she'd wasted no time in getting the house up for sale. Thankfully, the market was in her favour, and in a matter of just days, she had a cash buyer lined up and was making plans to temporarily move back in with her parents.

She'd marked the day of the auction of number 15 Ivy Lane in her calendar and didn't allow herself to think too much about what would happen if she was outbid. She had to believe it was meant to be hers.

She'd half expected her parents to tell her she had lost her mind. But they hadn't. 'Well, I think that's just perfect,' her father had said, growing misty-eyed as she outlined her plans for the shop. 'It's exactly what Grandad would have wanted for you.'

He'd reached his hand over to hers and given it a squeeze, while her mother had dabbed at her eyes with a tea towel. They were both still grieving themselves, Libby knew. Grandad Ernie had lived in the Quinn house for thirty of her thirty-four years, her dad intent on making sure his father never wanted for anything, most of all company.

'I wish we'd done this when he was still here,' her dad had said, and she'd watched her mother lay a hand on her husband's shoulder to comfort him.

'Now, Jim. Come on. We've always said things happen when they're meant to happen. Let's just focus on how happy the old fart will be, sitting up there watching our Libby chase her dreams!'

Although Linda Quinn had a selection of choice descriptions for her late father-in-law, there was a genuine affection in her voice when she spoke of him.

'It will be hard work, mind,' Linda had told her only daughter. 'You'll have to get those hands of yours dirty.'

'Sure, I'm not afraid of getting my hands dirty, Mum,' Libby had quipped. 'Didn't I take on that house and get stuck in?'

'I've a feeling, love, this shop of yours will be a bigger job than that house. And I'll imagine you'll want to turn it around quicker than you did that house too.'

'She'll have me and the boys to help her,' Jim had said. 'And I know you can be handy with a mop and bucket too, Linda.'

'No rest for the wicked,' her mother had said, rolling her eyes, but Libby had spotted the warmth in her father's expression when he'd turned to his wife and reminded her: 'And even less for the good.'

Now, in the shower, however, Libby was starting to panic about just what might lie behind the peeling paint and cracked render of number 15 Ivy Lane.

She took a deep breath. The stars had aligned to get her to this point, she reminded herself. She just hoped they were up for an extra bit of aligning over the next weeks and months.

The property had been bought sight unseen, a bold move, Libby knew. But her dad had walked around the outside of it, tapped the walls, looked up at the exterior with an eye only a builder could have and had told her it had the 'bones of a good building'.

But, regardless of her dad's keen builder's eye, she felt increasingly nervous as the big moment neared. In a little over two hours, she would have the keys to her future in her hands. She would open the door to her big investment and see exactly what she was facing.

Ten years was a long time to lie empty. God knows what leaks and infestations may have set in in that time. She shuddered. The word 'infestation' made Libby Quinn sick. If there was one thing in this world guaranteed to reduce her to a quivering wreck, it was little furry creatures scampering across the floor. She wouldn't even bring herself to say the 'm' word.

'Focus on what you do know,' Libby reminded herself as she rinsed the shampoo from her shiny chestnut-coloured hair. 'Accentuate the positive,' she said aloud. Pest control were only ever a phone call away.

And Jim had called in favours from all his building pals. A spark would be over later to check on the electrics before she dared to switch anything on. Allegedly, the water supply was still live, but if there were issues, a plumber was on call to look at them. He'd be round at some stage to check the pipes anyway. 'You can't be too careful with old buildings. Could be lead piping, or asbestos in the walls. A full survey will give us a full picture,' her dad had said, adding that he wouldn't be surprised if the damp course was compromised. But she wasn't to worry, he'd said, on seeing her stricken face. He knew people. He could get mates' rates.

And she had to remember, she'd got the shop for less than she had been willing to pay. She had more money than she'd originally thought to play about with, but still her budget was by no means unlimited. She'd be doing a lot of the work herself. Getting her hands dirty, just like she'd told her mother. She looked at those hands now, as she towelled off after her shower, the soft pink gel manicure she'd had done just the week before wouldn't last much longer. She'd be saying goodbye to such fripperies over the coming months.

But, she sighed, no matter what the cost, she was doing this. Libby Quinn was doing it! She was taking an unused, unloved shop on the corner of Ivy Lane and fulfilling not only her dream but that of her grandad. She wouldn't fail. She couldn't fail.

* * *

Libby knew the bag for life at her feet, crammed with cleaning products, would be just as woefully inadequate for the task ahead as a spoonful of Calpol would be to a woman in labour, but still she insisted on bringing it with her. She'd use everything in it, and more – much more – over the coming months, but bringing it with her gave her a sense of making the place her own before she even picked up the keys. Her plan, after all, was to move into the flat upstairs as quickly as possible so that she could work on the refurb morning, noon and night. A teeny, tiny, hopelessly optimistic part of her held on to a glimmer of hope that the flat would be a stylish time capsule of a home, ready to move in to bar the flick of a duster and a quick spray of Zoflora.

'Are you sure we can't come with you?' her dad asked as they sat around the breakfast table. Just like Libby, both Jim and Linda Quinn had been unable to lay on in their beds and had been fizzing with a sense of shared excitement.

'I need to put on my big-girl knickers and do this myself,' she told them. Which wasn't exactly true. Her boyfriend of eight months, Ant O'Neill, was going with her to pick up the keys from her solicitor's office. An accounts manager for a nationwide banking chain, he exuded an air of calm and professionalism which none of the Quinn family seemed to be in possession of at that moment. He would be able to help her keep her emotions in check and not sob all over the young solicitor who had finalised the paperwork for her. 'You can meet us there in a bit,' she said. 'When I've had a moment to adjust. Maybe eleven or so?'

Jim nodded. 'Of course, pet,' he said. 'Your grandad would be very proud, you know,' he said, his voice cracking, and Libby was forced to wave him away, unable to say anything else for fear of her own floodgates opening.

Thankfully any chance of an emotional breakdown was tempered by the sound of a car pulling up outside and the loud beep of a horn.

'My chariot awaits,' Libby said as butterflies danced in her stomach.

'Before you go,' her mother replied, 'we have a little something for you.'

Libby knew by the look on her mother's face that she was

about to endure an emotional ambush and she placed her hand softly on her stomach as if to settle it.

'It's just something small, for the shop,' her mother said, handing over a small paper bag folded over on itself.

Libby carefully unfolded the bag, and shook the contents out into her hand. Through tears, she glanced down at the picture of her and Grandad Ernie encased in a plastic keyring looking back up at her. She was, maybe, eight or nine in the picture and they were both grinning at the camera. Her heart constricted with love and loss.

'I love it,' she croaked, just as another loud beep grabbed her attention.

'You'd better go,' her dad said as she kissed them both on the cheek.

'I'll see you soon.'

* * *

'You all set?' Ant asked, smiling widely – a twinkle in his eye. The kind of twinkle that sent Libby a little weak at the knees at the best of times – never mind when she had been too nervous to eat and her blood sugars were most likely sliding downward anyway.

'I don't know whether to scream with joy or throw up,' Libby said, placing her bag on the back seat, where she noticed a bottle of champagne and a card with her name on the envelope waiting for her.

'It's just a good luck card,' Ant said, following her gaze. 'And a little something to help us toast your new digs? As much as your parents have a lovely home, it isn't the best for getting you on your own.' He smiled, just as her stomach flipped.

Ant O'Neill was as incorrigible as he was insatiable, and Libby couldn't help but smile as she climbed into the passenger seat beside him. 'That sounds like a plan,' she said, reaching over to kiss him. She intended for it only to be a peck, but he pulled her closer and kissed her in a way that made her tingle.

She pulled back and laughed. 'Anthony O'Neill, none of that carry-on. There is work to be done. And lots of it.'

'Yes, ma'am,' he replied with a salute. 'I'm at your service. Now, let's go and pick up some keys!'

Her grin was so wide, it almost hurt, but she couldn't have stopped smiling if her life depended on it. There was certainly no going back now. Come hell or high water, or even little furry creatures, she was to be the proud owner of a unique fixer-upper and she would work her hardest to fix it up.

2

OF MICE AND MEN

Ant had helped her draft a business plan. He was good like that. He knew facts and figures, whereas Libby was more inclined to lose herself thinking about just what books she would stock, how she would make the space welcoming for readers and writers alike.

She had a very clear vision of what she wanted to create. A shop which sold vintage books alongside new titles. A shop which housed a small café area selling coffees and teas and hot chocolate with melting marshmallows, so that people could make book buying a luxurious experience. She wanted to create a hub for book lovers. Little working spaces where writers could hot-desk, book a couple of hours of uninterrupted writing time among the smell of ink and paper. She wanted a shelf which stocked the books she had fallen in love with on her grandfather's knee when she was a little girl. Roald Dahl's fanciful tales. *The Little Mermaid* and *The Secret Garden*. Fairy tales and, as she grew, works of great literature made accessible by the soft voice of her grandfather and his unending patience with her many questions.

Even though the book trade was more competitive than ever –

and people were more inclined to download the latest title or toss it into their trolley along with their weekly shopping in the supermarket, Libby remained hopeful she would make it work. Even Ant was enthusiastic about some of her moneymaking ideas. Including a coffee bar and rental space for writers and writing groups would definitely help, he'd said. If she wasn't mistaken, he'd looked quite impressed.

And that had given her the confidence to share her plans with her parents. While they were always supportive, she knew they worried about her. Especially after she had taken Grandad Ernie's death so hard.

'You do know your Grandad just wanted you to be happy,' Jim had told her, after Libby had outlined her plans. 'It's a big job.'

'Well, you've always told me to dream big,' Libby had said. 'And I don't want to spend my whole life wondering what if. This is my chance, Dad, to do what Grandad and I always talked about.'

Jim had nodded. 'Then I'll do whatever I can to help,' he'd said and she'd known he meant it.

She just hoped he wouldn't change his mind when they finally saw inside her brand new property.

* * *

'Well,' Ant said, standing on the pavement outside number 15 Ivy Lane. 'She's all yours. What do you think?'

Libby blew out the breath she had been holding in for what seemed like forever. Was it her imagination or had the place fallen into even further disrepair in the few days since she had last visited or was it just the case that reality was starting to set in?

She nodded and looked at him. Tears pricking her eyes. It was all a bit overwhelming, she realised.

'You can do it, you know,' Ant said. 'I know it's scary, but it's not beyond you.'

'What if it's falling to pieces inside? Like really falling to pieces. Rotting from the inside out. Unsalvageable,' she said. 'Oh God, have I been really stupid? Throwing all my money in a cash sale on a building I've not even looked inside of?' Panic started to nip at her heels.

Ant placed his hands on her two shoulders. 'Libby,' he said, 'look at me.'

She focused on him. On his chocolate brown eyes, on the wrinkles around them. Laughter lines which gave him an air of George Clooney-like charm.

'Don't freak out. Whatever we find, it's fixable. You can do this. You've just got to be brave.'

'And put my big-girl pants on,' she said, reassuring herself.

'Are they the ones I like?' Ant asked, with a cheeky grin. 'With the lace and...'

She swiped him away, laughter rising up. 'Not now,' she said. 'There's work to be done.'

They both turned and looked again at the peeling green painted exterior.

'Let's do this,' Libby declared, managing to keep the tremor from her voice.

She found the key on the red fob – the one with 'shopfront' written on the label in blue biro – and took a deep breath.

'This feels momentous,' Ant said, grinning.

'It does!' Libby agreed, slipping the key into the mortice lock and, with a little persuasion, she managed to turn it. She had to put her shoulder to the door, heft a good deal of her weight behind it, to push it open. 'Check for furry things,' she whispered, closing her eyes, half expecting to hear the sound of little rodenty feet scurrying across the floor. All she could hear, though, was the thumping of her own heart.

'None that I can see,' Ant said. 'But it's dark in here. When did you say the electricity was being turned on?'

'It might be on now, but I'd rather not check until the electrician has had a look around.'

'Ah now, either it'll work, or it won't,' Ant said, and she opened her eyes just in time to see him reach up for a switch close to the door and flick it to the on position. She had visions of the shock of electricity sending him hurtling across the room, but there was no such drama. Just a momentary pop of light which died almost as soon as it had come to life. 'Fuse will be gone,' Ant explained. 'Hope the spark isn't too long getting here.' He took his phone from his pocket. 'We'll have to make do with what we have,' he said, switching on the torch and shining it around the interior of the shop.

Libby followed suit. Although the smell should've given her an idea of what was in store for her. It was a glorious mixture of damp and decay, stale air carried dust motes, quite probably containing some sort of deadly virus, around the expansive interior.

'I'll tear down some of this paper,' Ant said, walking to the window and doing his best to pull the long-adhered newsprint from the glass panels. What did come off left traces of long-forgotten news stories in print on the panes. Some of it just remained resolutely stuck. 'We'll need to soak it,' he suggested, standing back and wiping his hands on his cargo pants. Two black handprints left their impression on his light-coloured trousers.

'You didn't really think through your attire, did you?' Libby asked.

He looked down and smiled. 'I suppose not. But clothes can be washed. I'm sure these stains will come out in the machine.'

Libby wasn't so sure. This looked like the kind of grime that held on for dear life. She needed more than a bag for life filled with spray bottles of antibac and sugar soap to even begin to lift it.

She was glad she'd worn her oldest jeans, a grey oversized T-shirt she'd borrowed and never given back from an ex-boyfriend and her comfiest trainers. Her hair was tied back from her face with a red bandana. It was much less likely to collect spider webs that way.

Yes, the smell was inhuman. And the grime was thick and black. The electricity was shot and the window frames looked like they might actually be rotting, but that didn't stop the panic in the pit of her stomach being replaced by pure, unadulterated joy.

She was grinning wildly as she walked the length of the shop to where an abandoned drapery counter still stood, complete with a battered old cash register. Walking behind it, she looked back across the entire expanse of her new kingdom. She could see more than grime and grot and crumbling plaster. She could see it as it would be.

And it was going to be magnificent...

That was her last thought before a mouse, and two of his friends, ran out from under the counter and between her legs in a furry convoy that made her scream at the top of her lungs and jump on top of the aforementioned counter.

'I'll call pest control, will I?' Ant asked, while Libby tried her damnedest to stop hyperventilating.

* * *

Her breathing had slowed to near normal by the time they were back outside the shop and staring at the door which provided an independent entrance to the flat.

'What're the chances that this will actually be the frozen time capsule of perfect fifties vintage style I've been hoping for?' she asked, eyeing the tarnished brass number plate.

'The what?' Ant enquired.

'You must have seen it on the internet. Every now and again one of those clickbait sites posts a story about someone uncovering a perfectly preserved home, with all original fixtures and fittings.' She chewed her lip.

'You did see inside the shop, didn't you?' he asked, and she nodded. 'And you do know the same person or persons who owned the shop owned the flat and left it to rot for the last ten years?'

Libby did know that, but the owner hadn't been from Derry. He lived in Scotland and had inherited the shop after a lengthy search for any living relatives of the very eccentric old lady who had run the drapery store and who had died in 2009. Said relative had most likely never even been to Derry – he had put the shop up for auction as soon as the papers were signed to him.

'You never know though. There's a chance,' she said, her optimism decreasing by the second.

'I admire your go get 'em attitude. Never change, Libby Quinn,' Ant said. 'The world needs more pure souls like you.'

'Nothing wrong with a bit of hopeful optimism,' she said, looking through the keys on the battered red fob again until she found the one marked 15A, even if she wasn't quite feeling as optimistic as she stated.

It took a bit of work to fit the key into the old rusted lock and she needed Ant to put his strength behind it to help her turn it.

Even then, when the lock had turned, she found the door itself didn't seem to want to shift easily.

Still she persisted, the wooden door moving slowly as if something was blocking its path. That something turned out to be a mountain of yellowing junk mail and free newspapers piled just short of the letter box and which, by the stench, had made for a great litter tray for some animal. Probably multiple animals and definitely creatures bigger than mice, she thought, looking at the size of the droppings and the way some of the paper had been shredded.

'Are those teeth marks?' Ant asked, and Libby looked at him, eyes wide, but nostrils firmly pinched shut. His cool exterior was, finally, starting to crack.

'Pest control will sort it,' she replied with forced jollity. Reminding herself to focus on the positive, she looked up, taking in the full picture in front of her.

The fairly bleak full picture.

A set of steep, threadbare stairs, poorly illuminated by a dirty window at the top, provided her with a completely underwhelming vista.

She touched her hand to the discoloured wallpaper inside the door and was disheartened to find it more than a little damp.

'It might just be condensation,' Ant said, but glancing up, at the yellow staining and cracked plaster of the ceiling, Libby could see that it was much more serious than that.

Between that and the stench of animal urine, Libby felt tears prick at her eyes. Breathing in (but not so deeply that she inhaled any more of the foul odour), she steadied herself.

'The ceiling can be fixed. The carpet can be lifted,' she said, optimistically. 'I can re-floor if necessary. And sand down the stairs – put spotlights in, some stained glass at the top. It can be gorgeous.'

'Hmmm,' Ant murmured, his voice flatter than it had been. 'I admire your vision.'

She bristled. She needed him to buoy her up now, not start to waver.

'We've still to see the flat. Maybe it will be okay?' she said, her secret hope of a perfectly preserved cosy turnkey home all but disappearing.

'Hmmm,' Ant said again, perhaps with even less enthusiasm this time.

'Shall we go in?' she asked. Originally, she had harboured a little daydream that he would carry her over the threshold, but given the risk of slipping on rodent droppings, and his insistence on keeping one hand firmly clasped over his nose to mask the smell, that seemed unlikely.

Libby led the way upstairs, paying attention to any creaks and keeping her eyes and ears open for any furry friends.

She was, of course, deluded to think that the flat would be anything more than a fairly rotten shell that looked as if it had been much longer than ten years since anyone had lived there. It was so much worse than she had imagined. The décor could only be described as decrepit and it wasn't a look she wanted to go for.

The smell had not improved either. Now there was a certain 'possibly a dead body somewhere here' aroma added to the mix.

Ant had gone a distinctly green around the gills colour.

'I'll air the place out,' Libby said, walking to the sash windows in the living room, which overlooked Ivy Lane, and rattling them violently until they screeched open, inch by painful, sticky inch, letting in a rush of fresh air which she gulped at. Plastering a smile on her face, she turned around. 'There's potential here,' she said, looking back at the cherry blossom trees, which were in bloom just across the street. They offered a hint of something beautiful that wasn't visible inside.

'It's a huge job though, Libby. Bigger than I anticipated.'

She looked around. It was a huge job. Mammoth. There was little to instil confidence. The peeling wallpaper was from the eighties, and the carpet, sticky underfoot, was probably from the seventies. The paintwork was peeling and yellowed. The kitchen held together by grime and probably little else. An old, ugly and quite possibly dangerous gas fire hung from the wall in the living room and in what Libby assumed was supposed to be the bedroom, there were just a few bolts of psychedelic fabric, soggy cardboard boxes and a mannequin, which looked as if it was pleading for someone to put it out of its misery. Libby wasn't feeling brave enough to look in the bathroom just yet, and by the expression on Ant's face when he walked out of the small room, she was glad to leave that for later.

'It's doable though. I mean, it has to be. I've sunk too much in now to do anything other than plough on,' Libby said, while realising she still very much wanted to plough on. This place, even with its faults, still felt like it was meant to be hers.

She just wasn't sure where exactly to start. The one thing that she did know was that she was going to need a hell of a lot more than a bag for life containing disinfectant, cleaning cloths and Febreze. She knew she'd have to start small.

She fished in her pocket for the new keyring her parents had given her, and replaced the battered red fob with it. 'There,' she said, 'it already looks better.'

'It does,' Ant replied with a smile. 'And it will only get better from here. My advice is to get a skip here stat. Pay someone to rip everything out. Get it all down to the bare bones and then you can start rebuilding.'

Libby thought of her budget, which she had realised was going to be tested more than anticipated, and sighed. 'Skip hire, I can do. But I hoped maybe to rope in a few strong men, or women, to help me clear as much as possible? I have to start as I mean to go on, Ant, and do as much of this as I can myself. My budget is finite, you know that.'

'I'll help out with the cost,' he said, smiling. He was a successful businessman, who had known just where and when to invest his money over the years. The result was, he was exceptionally wealthy, and generous with it. He'd yet to meet a problem he couldn't fix by either throwing money at it or by launching a charm offensive.

'Ant, I have to do this on my own. Moneywise, I mean. Actual elbow grease I will accept, always. Same with soothing massages afterwards.' She winked. Trying to flatter him into agreeing to throw his toned, Gaelic-football-playing physique behind her plans.

'I don't do the heavy work,' he said. 'You know that. Can't risk an injury on the field. And I would only hold you back – you know. You're bound to find someone to be able to help out, and if you won't accept my help financially, then maybe you have to compromise a little?'

By the way he spoke, you'd think he played for the national team not his local club, and increasingly on a friendlies-only match basis.

Libby felt dejected.

'Libby, now don't be cross with me,' he said, pulling her close to hug her. 'But we have to be sensible.'

His phone rang and he stepped away to answer it, gesturing to her that he was taking it outside. He pinched his nose and pulled a face to emphasise the fact the smell was getting to him. When she eventually followed him back outside, he was unloading her cleaning materials from his car. For a moment her heart leapt just a little. Had he come round to the idea of helping her after all?

'Look, I have to go. Work emergency. I've called pest control and the guy will be round soon. I'll get on to the skip hire people too. You take some time to get a feel of the place yourself. Without me breathing down your neck. And when you're done playing shop, come over. I'll make us something delicious to eat and we can crack open that bottle of champagne and celebrate in style? And give you that massage?'

Libby doubted she was hiding the disappointment from her face very well, but she didn't want to make a scene. She didn't want to mar this momentous day with a petty argument with Ant. Maybe he was right? She'd be better off without him making her feel uncomfortable about just how much of a job this was going to be.

'Dad will get the skip hire sorted,' she said. 'He knows people. But, yes, go on. I'll see you later. Get that champagne in the fridge.'

She forced a bright smile on her face and he pulled her close, kissing her forehead. Despite having been together for the past eight months, they weren't quite at the 'I love you' stage yet, but he did whisper that he believed in her, before he, quite gleefully, got back into his fancy car and drove off.

Puffing up her chest, Libby looked back at the shop. Her shop. Infested as it was with furry friends, and smelling as it did, like a toilet, it was hers and hers alone. She owned it outright and she would make it work.

Still, she couldn't help but breathe a very audible sigh of relief when she saw her parents' car turn into the street, her father with a look of pride and excitement on his face that made her heart soar.

3

LES MISERABLES

'It's not as bad as all that,' her father said. 'I mean, once we get the trades in, we'll get it sorted quick smart.'

'You really think so?' Libby asked.

'Yes. Absolutely. Well, maybe not quick smart, but it will get done. Patience, my pet. And maybe rethink that proposed opening date?'

Libby's heart sank. She didn't want to delay the opening date. She had chosen the fifth of August, which was a mere ten weeks away, for a reason. It was her grandad's birthday.

'Your grandad will understand,' her dad said, putting his hand on her shoulder.

'Of course he would,' her mother said, her voice soft, but Libby wouldn't. It was all part of her plan, to open her shop on what would have been her grandfather's eighty-seventh birthday.

'We'll see,' she told her parents. 'I'm prepared to do as much work as I need to. I don't have anything else to take up my time and if we can get people on board...'

She noticed the look pass between her parents. The look that said she was reaching too far, but they were underestimating her determination.

'We'll do whatever we can to help,' her father said. 'You know we will. We just don't want you setting yourself up for a fall.'

'I appreciate that,' Libby told them. 'But just give me a chance.'

Just as she said that, a large crash interrupted them – a crash that turned out to be the cracked yellowing ceiling plaster in the hallway to the flat finally giving up the ghost and bringing a nice flood of sludgy brown water with it.

Libby was doing a brilliant job of not giving into despair. She focused on the good things. There was a water supply to the shop. She wouldn't risk drinking it, but it would be good enough to clean with. The pest control people had been efficient in laying traps and searching for any possible entry points. They'd be able to get it under control, they'd told her, and it shouldn't take too long.

Her dad had been true to his word and had arranged the first of many skips, and had been able to shore up in the joists in the hallway and cut off the supply to the leaking pipe. She had shooed her parents away eventually, knowing that she really could only make limited progress that day and also knowing that she really, really wanted to have some time alone with her thoughts, and her memories of Grandad Ernie, in the shop. She allowed herself some time to dream a little more – to close her eyes and imagine the transformation this place could undergo. The exposed brickwork she would make use of, copper light fittings, comfy chairs, repurposed bookcases. She wanted to give it a sense of always having been there, but also offering every-thing the modern reader might want.

It was enough to light a new little fire in the pit of her stomach and she decided to make a start on putting her own mark on the store. First of all, she liberally sprayed the old drapery counter with sugar soap and set about scrubbing it down – revealing a lovely soft varnished finish underneath the layers of grime. When it was done, she stood behind it, and allowed herself a little role play – chatting to imaginary customers, hitting the buttons of her cash register and grinning like an eejit at the thought of this shop coming to life.

She'd been so engrossed in her task, she hadn't noticed the change in the weather outside – blue skies now gone and replaced by ominous clouds. She only realised when she moved on to her next task – that of beginning to tackle the windows – that it was starting to rain, but not even a deluge of rain could dampen her spirits.

The shop's many window panels were one of the things she loved most about it, but she didn't like the matted newsprint stuck to them, or their general state of disrepair. Some of the wooden frames were slick with mould, and that was when they weren't rotting due to the damp air. Then, of course, there were the panes of glass which had been broken and long since boarded over. She had already booked a glazer to come out and measure up the following week, but for now she scraped off the newspaper and poured copious amounts of window-cleaning cream onto a cloth and rubbed it in large circular motions over the glass. Nothing said 'this is a place undergoing a transformation' more than windows obscured by large swirls of pink gloopy cleaner.

Arms aching, T-shirt long since dirt-splattered and damp, Libby decided to step outside to look at her handiwork – and only cursed a little when she heard the click of the door to the shop closing behind her as she stood in the now much heavier drizzle and tried to look through the obscured windows to where her keys – to both the shop and the flat – sat on the counter, right beside her mobile phone.

She rattled the door, as if the action would jolt the lock to open and let her in. She contemplated kicking the door in – but she doubted she had the brute force needed and it would only be an extra cost she would have to cover.

Looking around her, Libby tried to think of a clever solution to her problem, but the only thing she could think of was taking her damp, dirty and probably very smelly self to the bar across the road and trying to ask a hopefully friendly barkeep if she could use a phone to call for help. She'd given her parents her spare set of keys and if she could just get them dropped round to her, she could possibly save the rest of this day.

The Ivy Inn looked like a fairly amiable spot from the outside. It didn't look like an exclusive wine bar, but nor did it look like a student drinking den.

Since they were going to be neighbours, she figured it was a good thing to say hello and introduce herself anyway. Although she would have much preferred that she was looking slightly more presentable than she currently was, she left her pride in a puddle at the door of the bookshop and crossed over the road.

With its hanging baskets, resplendent with multicoloured blooms, The Ivy Inn had a welcoming air. It promised a beer garden to the rear, and Libby was relieved she didn't have to walk through the plumes of second-hand smoke as she pushed open the heavy wooden door and walked in.

It was already busy for early evening – groups of friends sat around chatting over glasses of wine and half-drunk bottles of craft beer. A few family groups were enjoying an early tea – children colouring in with stubby crayons or lost on their tablets while mum and dad had a medicinal drink to get them through to bedtime. The bar had once been three houses, which had now been knocked together, so it was filled with little nooks and crannies where the most reclusive drinker could escape for some peace and quiet. The entire atmosphere was warm and welcoming, just as she hoped it would be.

Libby was conscious of leaving wet footprints on the slate floor, so she walked quickly to the bar, where a tall, dark-haired barman was deep in conversation with a couple of perfectly preened ladies.

She shivered, even though it wasn't that cold, the wetness of the rain having soaked through her clothes, and waited for him to notice she was there.

And waited.

Eventually, she tried a polite cough, which went unnoticed, and she was forced to attempt an impression at something more consumptive. That got his attention – and a rather disgusted look from the two blondes, who clearly didn't make much of Libby's drowned-rat appearance.

'Are you okay?' he asked, his expression warm. 'Can I help you?'

'Yes, well I was hoping you could. I'm Libby Quinn,' she said, reaching her hand out to shake his – and then instantly regretting moving her arms from covering her chest which, thanks to the rain, had given her the look of a wet T-shirt competition entrant.

He gave her hand a cursory, but firm, handshake but didn't offer his name.

'Erm, I've just bought the shop across the street.'

'I'm sorry for your troubles,' he said with a cheeky smile, but Libby was not in the mood for humour. She already felt protective of her new home, and even though she knew it required a lot of work, it made her feel uneasy to have anyone else suggest this to her.

'Actually, it has loads of potential,' she replied. 'Or it would, if I could get back inside it. I stepped out, and the door shut behind me – and my keys and phone are still inside.' She sniffed, and shivered a little. 'So I was hoping, as my new neighbour, you might be so kind as to let me use your phone to get someone to bring over the spare keys?'

'Well, I suppose it wouldn't be very neighbourly of me to say no, would it?' he asked, his tone light.

'It really wouldn't,' she said through chattering teeth.

'I suppose I'd better then,' he said, walking to the end of the bar and lifting the hatch to gesture to her to come through.

Libby smiled at him (it took all her effort to do so) and followed him through to a back office, where he pointed to a phone on the table.

'You can leave 20p by the phone for the call,' he said, and while she was fairly sure he was joking, she wouldn't have been surprised if he wasn't.

'When I retrieve my purse from the shop, I'll be sure to do so,' Libby said, as she watched him walk back towards the bar – leaving the door open. Did he want to listen in? Or did he think she would make off with whatever mess of letters, invoices, empty Coca Cola cans and scrunched-up crisp wrappers that were lying on the desk?

She dialled her parents' home number first, swearing when it rang out. She didn't know either of their mobile numbers off by heart. In fact, there were only two mobile numbers she did know by heart – and one of them was her own. The second belonged to Jess. Glancing at her watch, she saw it was late enough for Jess to be done with her surgery for the day. She wouldn't have dared call her if she had still been seeing patients. Tapping the number in, she waited for her friend to answer.

'Hello?' Jess answered gingerly, not recognising the number that had flashed up on her phone.

'Jess, it's me, Libby. I need your help.'

'What's up? I've been hanging for news from you all day,' Jess said. 'Are you at the shop? Do you have your landline up and running already? When can I come over for a nosy?'

'As it happens, you can come over right now,' Libby said and pulled the phone away from her ear while her best friend squealed with delight. 'But I need you to do me a favour first. Can you call round to Mum and Dad's – see if they're home yet? I've tried the landline, but no answer. But you know them, they never hear the blasted thing anyway. I've managed to lock my phone and my purse inside the shop and I'm standing here soaked to the skin. Mum and Dad have the only spare pair of keys,' she explained, regretting that she had handed them over just a short time before. 'Oh, and Jess, can you bring me a change of clothes too – my skinny jeans and a sweatshirt maybe? I'm in The Ivy Inn – you know the pub just across the street?'

'Ah, that explains the strange phone number then,' she said.

'It does,' Libby replied, peeking out of the door just in time to catch a strange woman, red hair tied up in a messy bun on her head with a pencil stuck through, staring right at her. She jumped back and felt herself step on something. Something furry – and now very upset, it seemed. A loud yelp, followed by a volley of barks, made Libby drop the phone and yelp in surprise herself.

'Oh God, I'm sorry. I'm sorry,' she muttered at the big border collie, who was now jumping on her. Was this how it would end? Mauled by a rabid dog in the back room of a bar?

'Paddy! Down, boy! You can't eat the neighbours – we've talked about this!' a female voice called out – presumably belonging to the redhead who had frightened her so much in the first place.

The dog stilled immediately and backed away from Libby as the woman walked into the room, before sitting at his owner's feet and looking suitably ashamed of himself for his outburst.

'I'm sorry,' Libby said, scrambling to reach the phone but daring not to break eye contact with Paddy, who had now adopted the look of a very docile and friendly dog and not the wild beast she'd been terrified of. 'I stood on his tail. I didn't know there was a dog here.'

'Did Noah not tell you about him? I could swing for him!' the woman said, crouching down and ruffling the fur around Paddy's neck, which was adorned with a red bandana, not dissimilar to the one Libby wore in her hair. 'Most people around here know Paddy. He's part of the furniture and, honestly, you might not believe this, but he wouldn't hurt a fly.'

Libby stared at them both, her heart only just returning to its normal rate, before the sound of Jess's distant voice cut through her thoughts. 'Libby? Libby! Are you okay?'

She lifted the phone to her ear. 'I'm fine. I... Can you just get here as soon as possible? Thanks,' she finished, before ending the call.

Of course, by fine she meant absolutely and completely mortified, but she wasn't going to say that on the phone, or in front of her new neighbour who probably already thought she was a few sandwiches short of a picnic.

'I haven't hurt him, have I?' she asked, her face blazing.

'He seems fine,' the woman replied, as Paddy wagged his tail playfully as if to prove the point. 'Say hello to the lady, Paddy.'

At that, the dog plodded over towards Libby, plonking himself at her feet and raising his front paw for her to shake it.

Libby couldn't help but smile. 'Well, hi Paddy. I'm Libby. Nice to meet you.' She looked up at the woman. 'I've just bought the shop across the street,' she said, 'but locked myself out.'

'Yeah. Noah was telling me. It's nice to meet you. I'm Jo and, for my sins, I'm assistant manager of this place.'

'Nice to meet you,' Libby said, before she shivered once again. 'I don't suppose you have a towel or something I can dry off a bit with? My friend is coming, but she'll be a while.'

'Oh God, of course. I'll get something for you now. Did Noah not offer? Honestly, that man!' Jo smiled, a broad smile that lit up her face, and went to fetch a towel.

4

THE STRANGE CASE OF DR JEKYLL AND MR HYDE

Libby had done the best she could in the ladies' toilets with the towel Jo had given her. She still looked like a drowned rat, but her mascara was no longer running in rivulets down her face and her hair was no longer dripping. She was assessing the damage in the mirror when Jo walked in, a T-shirt in her hand.

'Why not change into this, for now? It's one of the ones we normally keep for the quiz winners. It won't win any fashion awards and, I'm afraid, we've only a size XXL left, but it's dry and warm.'

Libby could've cried. 'Thank you so much,' she said, before walking into one of the cubicles and peeling off her T-shirt, as well as her sodden bra. She slipped the supersized T-shirt on and felt instantly better as she walked back into the warmth of the bar.

'You can wait over by the fire if you want?' she heard a male voice say. She looked around to find Noah nodding towards the far-left corner of the pub. 'The table's free, if you're quick.'

Her sodden T-shirt and bra folded into a tight bundle in her hands, Libby weaved her way through the tables to where a small open fire had recently been lit in the hearth. It was just warm enough not to be overwhelming but to compensate for the falling temperature.

Libby lifted a copy of a newspaper that had been left on the table. It would be a good way to pass the time, and indeed to hide from any prying eyes.

This was definitely not how she imagined making her first impression on her neighbours. If she'd had it her way, she wouldn't have met them until the shop was looking shipshape – with its own hanging baskets of flowers outside, its quirky little writing nooks set up and ready to go, and the freshly ground coffee she was planning on serving filling the place with a delicious, welcoming smell.

She'd planned to drop handwritten invitations to all the nearby shops, bars and restaurants and invite them in for a launch with wine and cheese and maybe a little music or poetry reading. She'd even planned to wear the gorgeous Pinko strappy maxi dress she had splurged on with her redundancy money before ploughing everything else into the business.

Mucked to the eyeballs and with not even enough money on her for a cup of tea, or even a phone call to her best friend, had most definitely not been part of her plan.

To distract herself, Libby faked an interest in whatever celebrity scandal was masquerading as news and hoped the traffic gods would be kind and Jess would get there quicker than expected.

She was surprised when, just a couple of minutes later, she heard a soft cough. When she looked up, she saw that Noah was stood beside her table, a large cup of coffee in his hand and Paddy dutifully at his feet.

'Jo asked me to drop this over to you,' he said, and Libby could see the redhead give a thumbs up from behind the bar. 'She says it's on the house. And Paddy here wants to know if he can sit with you?'

Libby raised an eyebrow.

'Actually, that's not strictly true. This dog hunts out any heat source and plonks himself down in front of it. It would take a better man than me to try and stop him.'

'Very kind, I'm sure,' she said. 'My friend should be here soon and I'll be out of your hair – and able to leave you your 20p by the phone. I'm opening a coffee bar in the shop. You can tell Jo there'll be a free coffee waiting with her name on it when we open,' she said.

'So, that's your plan for the old place?' he asked, sitting down opposite her, while Paddy padded to the front of the fire and lay down on the slate flooring, just as Noah had said he would.

'Not as such – it's just a small part of it. I'm opening a bookshop.'

Noah sucked in air through his teeth. 'A bookshop in this climate?' he said. 'I admire your courage.'

'People will always read books,' she answered, unable to keep the irritation from her voice. She'd had this same conversation a hundred times since she'd started sharing her plans. Only her parents and Jess really believed in her. Ant, well, he made a good show of it, but she wasn't overly convinced. 'It's going to be something a bit different, anyway,' she continued. 'More than "just a bookshop". A creative space, a place for writers and readers to meet and chat about their work, have a quiet space to work in *and* get great coffee.'

'Well, I wish you the very best with it – that old place could do with a bit of love. I always thought it had character – deserved someone to give it a bit of a boost. And anything that gives this street a boost is okay by me,' he smiled.

Libby shifted in her seat. 'Well, that's the plan. As soon as I can get back in, of course.'

'Well, if you need anything – coffee, T-shirts, phones, whatever – feel free to call over. Either Jo or I are generally about most of the time. The other staff aren't too bad either. I look forward to seeing what you do with it.'

A call from Jo for Noah to come and help out ended the conversation and Libby couldn't say she was upset to have him leave and go back to his duties. She lifted the newspaper and returned to hiding behind it while waiting for Jess.

Jess arrived thirty-five minutes later. Thankfully, she had in her possession a bag complete with change of clothes and a set of spare keys, which she rattled in front of Libby.

'I don't think I've ever been as glad to see you as I am now,' Libby said as she stood up to kiss her best friend on the cheek.

'I like your T-shirt,' Jess smiled – as she stood back to admire the black cotton shirt emblazoned with 'The Ivy Inn' right across the chest.

'The very height of fashion,' Libby deadpanned. 'Now, let's get out of here before anything else goes wrong.'

'Libby Quinn, we'll see you around!' she heard Noah call, as they headed for the door.

All eyes, including those belonging to Jess, turned to look at him, before they looked back at Libby. Libby bundled her friend out of the door and raised her hand to wave a silent goodbye.

'Who, in all that is holy, is that?' Jess asked, as she peered over Libby's shoulder and tried to catch a further glimpse of the man with the deep voice.

'Noah. He runs the place. Along with the redhead, Jo. Did you see her?'

'No. I didn't. They run the place? Together? Are they a thing?'

Jess asked, as if her future happiness depended on a negative answer.

'No idea. Possibly,' Libby shrugged.

'I bet they are,' Jess said, even though she had only caught the quickest glance of Noah and no glance at all at Jo. 'I know my luck when it comes to romance. They'll be a thing. Probably married. Probably one of those couples who can't keep their hands off each other and call each other "babe".' Jess Hutchison, or Dr Jess Hutchison as she was known to her many patients, had become cynical when it came to matters of the heart. Libby knew all her friend really wanted was someone to go home to at the end of the day, but so far any possible happy ever after had eluded her. And while Jess was a successful, strong, independent woman in many ways, she was also not afraid to admit she craved the security of a relationship.

'I'm sorry,' Libby said. 'I'm sure Mr Right will make himself known to you sometime soon.'

'I'd be happy with Mr He'll-Do-For-Now, to be honest,' Jess said morosely as Libby jiggled the spare key in the door to try and open it. 'We aren't all lucky to have Ant O'Neill on our arm. Speaking of which, wasn't he supposed to be helping out today?'

'Erm, he went back to his to cook a special celebratory dinner for us,' Libby muttered, embarrassed that he was not with her, sleeves rolled up and mucking in. 'Actually, I should probably call him,' she added as she nudged the door with her shoulder as hard as she could. For a door that had closed so easily behind her, it was a nightmare to get open. It was pushing six thirty now and at this rate it would be half past eight at the earliest before she would be able to get to his house. Just as she was running over the logistics in her head, the door gave way. 'Ta-dah!' Libby declared as she gestured for Jess to go in.

In the dullness of a rainy May evening, it looked even more

depressing than it had done that morning, despite all of Libby's hard work on the counter and the windows. The cream cleaner would hide what was going on in the shop, but it didn't help showcase the potential of the interior at all. An electrician would be out the next day, she'd been assured by her dad. She'd have some form of power at least. Light would help, she hoped.

'You have to imagine how it will look,' she said to Jess. 'And, you know, how it will smell. It will definitely smell better than this. And imagine the sun shining in the windows and the aroma of coffee and baked goods.'

Jess put her hand to her chest and for a moment Libby wondered if her friend was actually going to be sick. She watched as Jess looked around her, shook her head, her hand still clutched at her chest. She felt her optimism falter yet again.

'Oh Libby,' Jess said. 'It's going to be amazing. Grandad Ernie would've loved it. I can just see him now, smiling down. I mean, he'd also be telling you what books to order and to make sure no one bent the spines, but he would be smiling. He'd be so proud. I'm so proud,' Jess said, pulling her friend close and hugging her.

This was just the reaction Libby had needed her friend to have, and she hugged her back tightly. 'He would love it, wouldn't he? And you know full well he'd already have at least one book order in. Multiple copies of *Great Expectations*.' Libby wiped tears from her eyes with the back of her hand. 'I can't think of a name for it yet,' she said. 'I want it to honour him in some way, but not in a super cheesy way. I want people to take me seriously.'

'Hmmm,' Jess said, looking around. 'I'll get my thinking cap on. But if you're hoping to launch in ten weeks, we don't have much time. You'll want to get your branding right.'

Libby knew that. Ideally, she'd already have the shop name sorted, but trying to choose made her head and heart hurt. 'I'll do it this week,' she said, and nodded as if to reassure herself that she was absolutely in control.

'Good woman,' Jess said. 'Now, show me around – I can already see this place has bags of potential. Where will you put the writing nooks? And the coffee station? And will you have little wrought iron bistro sets out on the front street in the nicer weather? Have you thought of a colour scheme?'

Libby was only too happy to oblige her friend with answers. Both for the shop and the flat upstairs. After changing out of her wet jeans into the dry pair Jess had brought with her, Libby gave Jess the full tour. Thankfully, her friend managed to be positive about everything, even the flat, despite the fallen ceiling and the general air of decay.

'The main thing is that the space is good. It's all there. And even the yard to the rear could be useful,' Jess enthused.

At the moment, the yard to the rear looked as if it was moonlighting as a landfill site.

'The skips arrive tomorrow. And the plumber, and spark. And a joiner too. Dad is getting a full survey done as well.'

'Hurrah for your dad!' Jess said with a smile. She was almost as fond of Jim Quinn as Libby herself was – having spent a great deal of time in her teenage years in the Quinn household. The Hutchison home had been warm and friendly but overpopulated and always noisy and Jess quite frequently escaped to her friend's house to study, or watch TV, or help Linda bake, or listen to music. Sometimes she just escaped there because spending another five minutes in a house with six younger brothers and sisters might have resulted in murder.

Libby looked at her watch and swore.

'What is it?' Jess asked.

'I told Ant I'd be with him for half eight. I still need to get home and get my car. And get freshened up. And changed.'

'How about I drop you off and you grab a shower there. You have a change of clothes at his, don't you?' Jess asked.

'Just spare underwear, and I'm not sure this inviting ensemble I'm currently sporting will endear him to me,' Libby said, gesturing to her clean but well-worn jeans and Ivy Inn T-shirt.

Jess bit her lip before her eyes brightened. 'New frock!' she squealed.

Libby rolled her eyes. 'If we don't have time to drive back home and pick up clean clothes, we'll hardly have time to indulge in a little late-night shopping.'

'No. You eejit. I have a new frock. In the boot. It will be lovely on you. I bought it in the spring sale, but it didn't suit me. I was going to charity shop it, but, looking at you, it's obvious. It would be lovely with your colouring. Actually, it would be perfect for you. I don't know why I didn't think of you before.'

'Dr Jess Hutchison,' Libby said, 'I love you.'

'You can love me even more when I tell you I have my emergency make-up kit in my handbag. You can give yourself a quick transformation.'

'What would I do without you, Jess?' Libby asked, grateful for her exceptionally organised and equally generous friend.

'It works both ways,' Jess said, squeezing her pal's arm. 'We keep each other right, don't we? Now, let's get going or you'll be late anyway.'

Libby smiled as she climbed into the passenger side of her friend's yellow Mini Cooper, allowing herself a flush of pride and excitement at finally owning her very own bookshop, even if it didn't yet have books, electricity or even a name.

5

SLEEPING BEAUTY

By the time they reached Ant's house, which overlooked the golden sands of Lisfannon Beach, just ten minutes across the border from Derry into Donegal, the muscles in Libby's body had started to seize up. Her arms had taken on the feel of lead weights and there was a crick in her neck that would take some serious quantities of Deep Heat to relieve. In addition, she felt exhaustion descend on her, as if the journey in the car had allowed her to relax for the first time that day. She also realised she was hungry, and that she hadn't eaten since breakfast. This never happened. Libby Quinn had never missed a meal in her life.

She hoped against hope Ant would have the dinner he'd promised her almost ready for serving. He'd texted her earlier to say he was making his signature dish – slow-cooked stroganoff. Her mouth was watering at the very thought – creamy, rich sauce, tender strips of melt-in-the-mouth beef, served on a bed of rice with tender stem broccoli. She was so hungry, she'd have to keep a real check on her manners so she didn't make a show of herself by shovelling the food into her mouth and licking the plate after.

'Here you go, my love,' Jess said as they pulled up the gravel drive to Ant's house, a modern build on the hill, with floor-to-ceiling windows enough to give the lucky residents unmatched views of the waves crashing to shore. It was minimalist and pristine, and Libby didn't even want to think about how much it had cost him to build it.

'You're a total star,' Libby told her friend, who, she realised, would be driving home to her riverfront apartment, where she'd eat her dinner – no doubt something healthy and full of superfoods which she didn't really like, but felt compelled to eat – alone in front of re-runs of *Sex and The City*. Hardly the ideal way to spend a Friday night in your thirties. She felt a wave of guilt wash over her that while she was about to enjoy a lovingly prepared home-cooked, delicious feast washed down with a couple of glasses of wine, her friend was not. The joys of an Irish Catholic upbringing – there was always a dose of guilt on offer, even for things which were in no way your fault.

'Why don't you come in and join us? You know Ant – always makes way too much food, even for my appetite. And there's never a shortage of wine. I'm sure he wouldn't mind.' Okay, so actually Libby was sure Ant would mind, but he would be polite enough not to say anything.

'I don't think so. I wouldn't want to be a third wheel,' Jess said, but there was a hint of a waver in her voice.

'You'd hardly be a third wheel and you've been a lifesaver today. You two are very important to me, you know.' Libby meant every word and it pained her that Ant and Jess had barely gotten to know each other over the last eight months.

Jess raised a perfectly shaped eyebrow. 'You're very important to me too, sweetheart. But I'd feel awkward. I'm sure Ant has plans for you both. Plans that most definitely don't involve me and, quite frankly, I'm okay about that.'

Libby laughed. 'Oh God, the way I'm feeling now, there will

be no shenanigans tonight. I ache all over and am wrecked,' she said, hoping Ant would understand why her libido was out of order for the evening.

'Well, sure,' she said, making a 'shoo' movement with her hands. 'Get out of my car and into his dreams or some other such muddled clichéd nonsense.'

Libby looked at her friend, still uneasy at leaving her, but she could hardly put a gun to her head and force her. And the more time passed, the more she realised just how much she needed a shower and a glass of wine.

'You're sure?' she said.

'I am,' Jess replied, a hint of frustration in her voice. 'Don't forget the dress from the boot. I'll catch up with you tomorrow. I'd love to come and help out. I can be there first thing.'

Libby reached over and kissed Jess on the cheek, told her she loved her and then resisted the urge to groan loudly as she stood up. She took the dress from the boot of the car and started to walk towards the house in time to see Ant open the door – looking fresh as a daisy (a very manly daisy, of course) and grinning at her.

'I'd advise you not to inhale too close to me,' she said. 'I'm not at my most fragrant.'

'I like your T-shirt,' he said, glancing at The Ivy Inn logo. She was suddenly acutely aware that she wasn't wearing a bra, and felt the need to cross her arms. 'Pretty sure that wasn't what you were wearing when I left you,' he said.

'Long story,' she said with a grimace, 'but it can wait until I'm clean, sat at the table and sipping some lovely red wine. Would you mind if I jump in the shower?'

'Actually, I would,' he said, placing his hands on her shoulders. Her heart sank. Please let him not want to have sex – not now anyway, she thought. 'Because I have run you a big bubble bath and I've poured a glass of wine. I've even been a good metro-sexual and lit some candles for you because I thought you might like them. So, if madam would like to climb into the tub, I'm sure I could help you relax.'

She was so grateful, she could cry, and climbed the stairs wearily, stripped off, pulled the bandana from her hair and slipped beneath the bubbles in the claw foot tub. The soft warmth of the water made her muscles start to relax and she exhaled loudly as she closed her eyes and inhaled the musky scent of the bath oils Ant had used.

She smiled at him when he pushed the door to the bathroom open and walked in carrying two glasses of wine – handing one to her and sipping from the other as he perched on the chair beside the bath. This room was one of Libby's favourites. It was luxurious and at least double the size of her bedroom, never mind her bathroom. The height of the house on the hill allowed Ant privacy enough to install clear glass windows so Libby could stare out at the evening sky while she let her troubles melt away.

'Dinner will be ready in about thirty minutes – do you think that's enough time to get yourself suitably relaxed,' Ant spoke, cutting through her thoughts.

'Hmmm,' she purred contentedly as she sipped from her wine glass. 'It just might.'

He stood up and moved closer to her. 'I might not be the best at mopping floors and scrubbing windows, but if you hand me that soft sponge, I'll help soap you down?'

In her newly relaxed state, Libby found it easy to acquiesce to his wishes so she sat forward, pulling her knees to her chest as he knelt beside the bath and sponged her back, before tenderly washing her hair. She groaned with pleasure as he massaged the shampoo into her scalp. She could get used to this

– to feeling pampered and cherished. The fact that he didn't even try to cop a feel once during the process earned him extra brownie points.

By the time she was dried and dressed in the very pretty floaty summer dress Jess had given her, her dark hair brushed, tousled and hanging damp around her shoulders, she felt like a new woman.

Libby padded into the kitchen, where the aroma of cooking smells made her tummy gurgle in anticipation.

'I hope you're hungry,' Ant said, putting food enough for four on the table.

'I told Jess you always cook too much and invited her to join us,' Libby quipped as she sat down and watched Ant refill her glass.

'She didn't want to stay?' Ant asked.

'Didn't want to be a gooseberry.'

'Hmmm,' Ant answered. 'Probably a good thing. I prefer when it's just the two of us.'

He smiled as he served up dinner – but was unusually quiet while he ate. If she had been less tired, Libby might have asked what was on his mind, but she was so exhausted that her brain was struggling to form coherent sentences – plus, she was so hungry she didn't want to stop eating. Not even for a few seconds. She simply wanted her dinner and an early night – which she hoped didn't clash with Ant's plans too much.

As it happened, when she said she really just needed to sleep, he nodded that he understood and wished her sweet dreams. It felt strange to climb the stairs to his bedroom on her own – stranger still to curl into his king-sized bed without him. She was sure, however, that being a light sleeper, she would wake when he came up to bed and they could at least indulge in some light spooning.

She was shocked, therefore, to find the sun was streaming in through the windows when she woke.

Libby turned over to see Ant, fast asleep and snoring softly, in the bed with her. Even in his sleep, he had the look of an Adonis about him, dark lashes brushing his gently sun-kissed cheeks, a five o'clock shadow giving his strong features an even more manly look. She took a moment to enjoy just looking at him, before she turned back over and grabbed her phone from the bedside table. It was shortly after seven and if she was to be at Ivy Lane in time for the spark and the plumber to arrive, she didn't have too much time to waste. Especially as she still didn't have her car and needed to rely on Ant to drop her home before she could go to the shop.

Shifting in the bed, trying not to wake Ant as she did so, Libby sat up and looked out the floor-to-ceiling windows, which provided an enviable vista of the beach and the water of Lough Foyle gently lapping at the shores. She could already feel it was going to be a warm one and that before the morning was out, the beach would be busy with walkers and families on day trips. She might have felt envious of them if she didn't have the shop to go and work on.

Quietly, Libby padded down the stairs into Ant's open-plan kitchen and living area, pulling open the French doors which led to the well-tended (by a gardener) garden outside. She put a pot of coffee on – and decided she would take Ant some breakfast in bed. It was the least she could do after being such poor company last night.

First, though, she wanted to take a minute just to breathe in the crisp early-morning air, smell the salty tang of the nearby sea, let the warmth of the sun beat down on her face and touch base with what mattered to her most. Those simple pleasures.

Grandad would have loved it here, Libby thought, with a

regretful sigh. He loved walking along the beach, or building sandcastles with her. They'd collect stones and bring them home to make artwork, using plaster to stick them to the outside of jam jars or photo frames. The bigger shells he would hold to her ear and ask if she could hear the sea. Then they'd read *The Little Mermaid* together. Again. She still had the very book they would read, with its cute Ladybird logo on the front. It was one of her most treasured possessions. Just thinking about it brought a lump to her throat.

Libby wondered if she would ever be able to think of him again without feeling a huge sense of loss. It had been two years. Surely it should have gotten easier.

She inhaled deeply again, and vowed she would not cry – not today. Not this weekend. Not when she was working so hard towards achieving their dream.

'Books will always be your friend, Libby,' he'd said. 'They will transport you to a thousand different worlds. Different times. Mythical creatures, magical monsters, good and evil, scary and funny. There's no situation so bad that a book can't help you feel better, even if just for a little while.'

Libby wasn't so sure she believed that – no book in the world had helped her when he was ill, no book provided comfort when he had died. But she wanted to believe it. She really did.

Even though Libby had made him his favourite breakfast, and then had climbed into bed afterwards and had her wicked way with him, Ant was prickly when she asked him to drop her home.

'It's Saturday morning,' he said with a pout – that wasn't particularly becoming on him. 'We always spend Saturdays together. Usually in bed. Or walking on the beach or going for a boozy pub lunch, followed by more time in bed.'

She knew Ant liked their weekends together. They rarely saw each other during the week due to Ant's crazy work hours, but surely he knew she had to devote as much of her time as possible to the shop now that she had the keys in her hands. She'd also be working to the timetable of the tradespeople, knowing that getting the right people in for the job was vitally important.

Her relationship with Ant would have to go on the back-burner until it was all under control. She'd hoped he'd understand that, but by the petulant look on his face, it wasn't something he was happy about.

'We've talked about this,' she said. 'I know we usually spend the weekends together, but you do understand, don't you? There's so much to be done. More than we thought. It will be worth it, though, when it's all done. The shop and the flat. We'll be able to make up for lost time.'

'If you say so,' he said, his voice dejected.

Libby leant across to kiss him softly on the lips. 'Don't be cross, Ant. You know you're important to me. You know how much I like you.'

'I like you too,' he replied, kissing her back. 'That's why I want to spend so much time with you.'

'We'll be able to do that. Still. You could always come and help out?' she asked.

His face clouded a little. 'Well, I was thinking, if you're going to be working, I might as well do the same. I've a lot to catch-up on.'

He was huffing. She knew it.

Well, she thought, he'd just have to learn to live with their new dynamic.

Libby nodded, told him it was okay. Kept any hint of disappointment from her voice. 'It's not forever,' she reassured him. 'But I really should get ready,' she said as she glanced at the clock. 'I can get a taxi back if you want to get on with your work,' she added, in the hope it would appease him a little.

'No. It's fine,' he said. 'I'll drop you home.'

'Thank you,' she told him, kissing him gently before she got up and jumped in the shower.

Jess was waiting outside the shop when Libby pulled up. She was leaning against the window, arms crossed, dungarees on and her blonde hair pulled back in a messy bun. For all intents and purposes, she looked like she had just stepped out of a soft drink commercial – and not like her usually perfectly groomed GP persona, rarely seen out of pencil skirts and three-inch heels.

Against the shop window sat two large shovels, brushes and a bucket containing sponges, cleaning materials and rubber gloves.

'I know you said you had people coming to do a proper clear out, but look, every little helps, doesn't it? And I've brought some dust masks. You never know what moulds and spores might be flying around in there.'

That was Jess, Libby thought. Always a doctor, even on her time off. Health was her primary concern, but even with her over cautiousness, Libby was so grateful to have her friend by her side.

Jess continued: 'I've a spare set of clothes in the car, plus a flask of tea and sandwiches. And by "flask of tea", I actually, on this occasion, mean actual tea and not wine, like that time we went on the train. Although I figured if we got finished up here early enough, we could enjoy a late lunch with your new neighbours across the street.' She gestured to The Ivy Inn – and Libby cringed.

'I'd rather not,' she said, the passage of time doing nothing to lessen her embarrassment at having stood on Paddy's tail, scaring the life out of the poor creature, not to mention turning up looking like something out of a horror movie. The Creature from the *Black Lagoon*, perhaps.

'It looks like a nice place, and that barman looked like a very nice barman. Please, Libby?' Jess pleaded.

Libby felt a little guilty. She knew her friend was dying to get a closer look at Noah, and she also knew she'd have to make an effort to get along with her neighbours as she had plans to be a fixture on Ivy Lane for a long time to come.

'Okay. We'll see how we go, sure,' Libby said, before a white van pulled up and a man, who introduced himself as 'Terry The Spark' as if it was his actual given name, said hello.

Libby had no sooner let Terry The Spark in than another van arrived. This time, a short, squat man in jeans and a white T-shirt that didn't quite cover his rounded belly, arrived. 'Are you Jim's girl?' he asked, without introducing himself.

'I am,' Libby said.

'Grand so. He asked me to have a look at your pipes,' the man said.

Libby heard Jess splutter and laugh behind her.

'You're the plumber then?' Libby asked, doing her best to ignore Jess's wiggling eyebrows.

'Well, what else would I be?' the man said, sniffing and hoisting up his jeans. 'I'm Billy O'Kane. Your da's a good man,' he said. 'So anything Jim Quinn wants, Jim Quinn gets.'

'That's good to hear,' Libby replied, and she turned to find her father getting out of his own van and walking towards them – his hand outstretched to Billy to shake it.

'Cheers for doing this,' he said. 'It's a big deal to us, you know. Our Libby here, taking on her grandad's dream.'

'Another good man there,' Billy said with a nod. 'Ernie was a character.'

As a lorry rattled loudly into the street, carrying a large skip, Libby felt a buzz of excitement at the lane coming to life. And all of it was to help her dream become a reality.

As she turned towards Jess, she saw her friend hastily brush a tear away. 'This is brilliant,' Jess said. 'Really brilliant.'

'You might not think that so much when you see the number of traps the rat catcher left!' Libby laughed, but she did feel it was pretty special all the same.

* * *

She felt it was a little less brilliant several hours later when her T-shirt was damp with sweat, her skin itching with dust and the electrician was outlining his plans to rewire the place.

The bill was staggering, and that was without any bespoke work in the shop such as extra outlets and wiring in her new lighting. It was just to make sure the power (which was on, to be fair to him) was up to code, safe to go for the foreseeable, and both her shop and her home would be future-proofed.

'I mean, it's not the worst I've seen,' Terry The Spark had said. 'You'd get away with less, but it's only a matter of time before the whole lot needs rewiring. You're better doing it now when you're ripping the bones of the place out anyway.'

He was right, of course. As was the joiner, who priced replacing some rotting joists and the rotten window frames and hanging fireproof doors. And the plumber, who said there was little of her current arrangement that was salvageable and she'd be better updating the pipes as well as the fixings.

Libby tried to remain positive throughout, but her smile became more and more of a rictus grin as the morning wore on. Finally, when her father talked of re-rendering the shopfront, after tackling several patches of rising damp that had eaten away at the plaster, she allowed a small moment of panic. She was doing the sums for the project internally, and it was starting to scare her. Her contingency fund was going to need a contingency fund all of its own.

'Sweetheart,' her father said, 'this is the big cost bit. The scary bit. Yes, we hoped it would be better inside than it is. But it could've been worse. And these guys, they're giving you a good rate – and I can stand over the quality of each and every one of them. It's best to do it right first time.'

Libby nodded. Her dad was right. Just as he always was.

'And, darling, you're not to stress out. Your mum and I, well, we have some money put by. We'd be happy to invest in making this dream come true for you.'

Libby felt a lump form in her throat and she couldn't speak. All she could do was shake her head. She didn't want her parents dipping into their savings.

'I don't want an argument, young lady,' her father said. 'You forget that you're our little girl even though you're a grown woman, and we want you to be happy. We believe in you and this shop. And,' he added, his voice cracking, 'he was my father. I want to do this for him too.'

Libby pulled her father into a hug, and could feel the slight tremor of emotion in his frame. They both missed Ernie Quinn terribly, but her parents had already given up so much. Her grandfather's money had gone to her, with her parents' blessing, to follow her dream. Asking for more wasn't fair, but then it was almost as if she could hear Grandad Ernie in her ear whispering, 'You didn't ask. Your dad offered.'

* * *

By early afternoon, Libby felt calmer. She at least knew what she was facing and her father had assured her that while her ten-week turnaround would be tight, it wasn't impossible.

Ant had even texted to say he was sorry for being grumpy, and had arranged for a specialist team to arrive first thing on Monday morning to clear out the yard and help strip out the flat and dispose of all the waste. It was his 'treat' to her, he said, and after a morning of pulling up damp and rotting carpet, she was too tired to argue with him or refuse his generous offer.

'I could murder a cup of tea,' Jess said, pulling her dust mask down. 'I think it might be time for a break.'

'I say we grab that picnic of yours and walk up to the lawns at the university. We can pretend we are living the uncomplicated lives of students and soak in a little sun too,' Libby said.

'Not to mention dodging whatever deadly diseases lurk in here. No offence,' Jess said.

'None taken,' Libby replied, knowing that not only would she wash her hands thanks to the reconnected water supply, but she'd also make liberal use of the medical-grade hand sanitiser Jess always carried with her.

They left the shop, Libby thankfully remembering her keys this time, and chatted as they walked up the hill towards the Magee Campus of Ulster University.

'So, how was your evening with Ant?' Jess asked.

'Quiet! Thankfully. I was so tired. He was really lovely, you know. Made a great dinner, didn't mind when I went to bed early, alone,' Libby replied. 'He was a bit funny with me this morning though. He seemed annoyed that I'm at the shop, even though I've only just got the keys and there's so much to be done. I'd sort of hoped he'd want to come in and help, but no.' She noticed the look of concern on Jess's face. 'But he did text me to say he was sending some people on Monday to help with the clear out. I know Dad's friends have already made a start, but many hands make light work and all that...'

'That's nice of him,' Jess said. 'To arrange that.'

'Yes. It is. And it makes up for yesterday and him bailing on me at the first sign of doing any actual heavy lifting himself.'

'You should have known he'd not be up for that. Have you not noticed he's a clean freak? I've never so much as seen a hair out of place on his head, and his car isn't filled with empty Diet Coke cans and crumpled receipts like ours are. In fact, I don't think I've seen it dirty on the outside, never mind on the inside. And his house? He's a man who lives alone and his house is show-home perfect. No Xbox controller. No toothpaste residue on the sink. How many single men do you know who live like that?'

Jess had a point, Libby acknowledged, although she hadn't really given Ant's fastidious attention to detail and cleanliness much thought. No doubt Jess was doing her Dr Jess routine again and was almost ready to jump in with an OCD diagnosis.

'You've got a good one there, Libby. He's not perfect, but he's far from the worst. Unlike any man who seems to show an interest in me.' She sighed and Libby looked at her. It was unlike Jess to get downhearted about anything – let alone her love life, but lately something had changed. She seemed more fragile, more in need of someone to love than she ever had before.

She'd had her share of relationships – some of them long term – but they had pretty much all been on her terms and she had been the one to break them off. She seemed to relish her independent life. But, thinking of it now, it had been a while since she had been out with anyone for more than one or two dates and she had frequently called Libby after to talk about how disastrous they'd been. After her mention of looking for Mr Right outside the pub, Libby wondered had she not been clued in to how her friend was really feeling.

'Oh, sweetheart. I thought you were happy on your own. For now anyway.'

Jess sighed. 'So did I, but I don't think I'm happy with it any more. Maybe it's just us getting older – everyone is settling down. God, Libby, some of our friends are on baby number two and I've not even met anyone who I could ever see myself sharing my Netflix password with. The older I get, the smaller the pool of available options is. I'm afraid I'll become one of those older women who gets increasingly outrageous in her behaviour trying to bag a younger man. The signs are already there. I mean, there's this twenty-nine-

year-old male nurse started at the practice and he's, you know...
God, he's gorgeous. I found myself wearing a slightly shorter skirt
when I knew I would be working the clinic with him. Now, I've
control of it all for the moment – but I'm afraid of what I could do.'

She looked so serious that Libby felt a little guilty for stifling a
giggle at the thought of her friend becoming a fully-fledged man-
eater. Nothing could be more unlike Jess.

'We need to find you someone nice then,' she said, 'before you
get a reputation as a Dr Feel-Good.'

'If you could, that would be great. Although I'm starting to
think there's a definite lack of hot, available men about. They
don't call this the Maiden City for nothing.'

And she was right. Derry had long since earned the title of the
Maiden City. While the official explanation was something to do
with the city's walls not being breached during the Siege of Derry
in the 1600s, it was often said it was now more likely to be
because the female population outnumbered the male population by a ridiculous (and quite possibly false) amount.

Libby laughed, but at the same time she tried to think. The
two women knew a lot of the same people and that didn't help.
'Maybe when the shop opens there will be a steady stream of
single, available and attractive men coming through the door. I
can offer a discount if they take you out.'

'It's books you'll be selling, I'd say you're more likely to get a
steady stream of old ladies, and mums looking for something for
their teething toddlers to slobber over.'

'Now now,' said Libby. 'Readers come in all shapes and sizes,
and ages and marital statuses! And don't forget the writing
nooks,' Libby added, defensively. 'We might get a real arty type in,
all poetic and beardy and ridey.'

It was Jess's turn to stifle a laugh. 'Knowing my luck, if you got one like that he would have some unsavoury habits, like writing sci-fi erotica, or not washing or something.'

'Well, I can't help you if you're going to be fussy.' Libby laughed, suddenly putting her hand to her tummy as it rumbled loudly. 'Time for tea and sandwiches, I think,' she said. 'This spot will do nicely.'

Jess nodded in agreement and pulled a picnic blanket from the bag and spread it on the lush green grass. Reaching in to her insulated picnic bag for the flask of tea, she swore. 'Oh for the love of God, this is just great.'

Libby, who was now feeling almost faint with hunger, had a feeling this 'for the love of God' was not a good 'for the love of God'. Her fears were confirmed when Jess lifted one sodden hand out of the insulated bag.

'I mustn't have sealed the flask properly,' she said, reaching in and picking out sandwiches which had turned to mush in their kitchen paper wrapping. 'I don't think these will be edible – and what's left of the tea – which can't be much given the crumby tea soup in the bottom of this bag – has gone cold.'

Knowing that Jess was feeling a little emotionally fragile that day anyway, Libby plastered a 'ah well, never mind' smile on her face, even though she felt a little emotionally fragile herself at the thought of the lost lunch. 'We'll just eat something else,' she said. 'It's okay, Jess. Don't worry about it. It's the gesture that counts.'

'Not when we're starving with hunger,' her friend countered. 'But I suppose we could always go to the pub for lunch? Just think of it – something warm and tasty and a dirty big chocolatey dessert after?'

'Are you feeling quite well?' Libby asked. 'Lunch and dessert?'

'Pre-menstrual,' Jess said. 'I might even have a starter. Don't judge me!'

Ah, so that explained Jess's extra emotional behaviour.

Jess blinked her large, blue eyes and a single, self-pity filled tear rolled down her cheek. While Libby had hoped not to darken the door of The Ivy Inn again until her wet T-shirt introduction had been well and truly forgotten, she thought of how Jess's face had lit up on seeing Noah the day before. And, if she was honest, she also thought about how hungry she was.

'Okay,' she said. 'Let's go and get fed.'

Jess smiled so brightly that Libby couldn't help but smile too as they packed up the wreckage of what had been their lunch and started to walk back down the hill towards Ivy Lane.

The buzz of conversation and the delicious aroma of lunch greeted the girls as they walked into the bar. Unlike the day before, the bar was completely packed – with each and every table filled with happy punters enjoying their day off.

Libby looked to Jess and shrugged her shoulders. 'Seems we won't get a table,' she said, partly relieved that she had a legitimate reason to leave and partly disappointed because the food smelled so incredible.

She noticed Jess was looking all around, standing up on her tiptoes to add some height to her 5'4" frame so that she could see as much as possible. 'Looks like that table over there is almost finished,' she said, nodding to a family of four who were tucking into bowls of ice cream. 'We could just take a seat at the bar and wait? Or eat at the bar?'

At a prime spot to make small chat with Noah, Libby realised. Even though Libby didn't want to – Jess had already grabbed her by the arm and was dragging her towards the bar, where, to her huge relief, Noah was nowhere to be seen.

Instead, two women, neither of them Jo, were serving; smiling and chatting happily with customers. Libby relaxed a little and pulled herself up onto a bar stool, while Jess ordered two glasses of red.

'This will have to be it,' Libby said, clinking her glass with her friend's. 'We're both driving.'

'More's the pity,' Jess sighed. 'When was the last time we had a nice afternoon drinking session?'

Libby tried to think back – it had been a while. Possibly even pre-Ant, she thought with a degree of shame. Had she become one of those friends who suddenly became unavailable when there was a man on the scene?

'When the shop is up and running, we'll make it a priority,' she said.

'Or just get a taxi next time we finish working across the road? In a few weeks you will be living there anyway – no excuses then.'

'I suppose,' Libby conceded – but also wondered how she would balance Ant's need to have her each and every weekend to himself, Jess's increased loneliness and the work that needed to be done in the shop. Taking a large gulp of her wine, she vowed to actually put all of it out of her mind to enjoy her lunch and this time out with her best friend. Living in the moment – isn't that what it was called? It was something Grandad Ernie had tried to encourage her to do.

'Most of us never know what's coming, petal,' he had told her. 'So make the most of every moment. Don't waste them worrying about the next.'

'Let's choose what to eat before I faint with hunger!' she said to her friend.

Jess lifted the menu from the bar and scanned it. 'It all looks so good, I'm just not sure what to choose.'

'I'd definitely recommend the warm chicken salad, followed

by the chocolate fudge brownie with home-made vanilla ice cream,' a deep voice said from behind them.

Libby jumped – and her glass wobbled perilously close to the edge of the bar. Noah's hand reached out and steadied it.

'Sorry,' he said with a smile. 'Didn't mean to startle you.'

'It's in danger of becoming a habit,' Libby said drily.

He laughed. 'I suppose so. I'll try harder. Sorry. Another hectic day?'

Libby was suddenly acutely aware that she probably looked almost as dishevelled as she had the day before. At least she wasn't soaked through this time.

'What gave it away?' she said, forcing a smile. 'The dust in our hair, the dirt on our clothes?'

'Maybe the grotty smell,' Noah said, and Libby blushed. Between the dirty carpets and the sweaty lifting work, she probably did smell less than fragrant. 'Oh, I'm only teasing,' Noah said. 'Honest. You don't smell that bad.' He laughed and Jess laughed too. One of those forced laughs that was a little bit too enthusiastic and screamed that she clearly fancied Noah and his sense of humour. It reminded Libby that she hadn't introduced them yet.

'This is my friend, Jess,' she said. 'She's been helping me. We're just doing some clearing out before the heavy lifting starts on Monday. We were going to have a picnic, but there was a bit of an incident with a flask of tea.'

Noah raised an eyebrow and reached his hand out to shake Jess's. 'Nice to meet you,' he said. 'If you aren't too traumatised by whatever the incident was, we also do serve tea here.'

Jess shook his hand and smiled. 'I think we're good with wine for now,' she said.

'And I think we're more traumatised by the loss of our lunch, so we really do want to order something to eat.'

'Well, I'll leave you to peruse the menu. But as I said, warm chicken salad and the chocolate brownie afterwards.' He made a chef's kiss gesture. 'Just wave when you're ready to order or speak to one of the girls.'

'Thanks,' Jess said as he turned to walk away.

Libby muttered a quieter 'thanks' too, before turning her attention back to the menu. She didn't know why, but she felt rattled. Quite possibly because she felt as if she was one beat behind with his sense of humour.

'Well, he's lovely. And, he's not wearing a wedding ring, although I know in this day and age that doesn't mean anything,' Jess said. 'I wonder, is that other barmaid working – the red-headed one?'

'I don't see her,' Libby replied, not raising her head to look around.

'Hmmm,' Jess said, her attention going back to the menu. 'You know, I think might just go with his recommendation.'

'Because you fancy him?' Libby asked, raising an eyebrow. By the blush that immediately coloured Jess's cheeks, she knew she was right.

'Not just because of that,' Jess answered. 'It does sound appealing.'

Libby had to agree that it did and they both put an order in, adding a portion of chips to share as well because they figured they'd earned it with all their hard work.

* * *

Libby's parents were watching TV when she got home – perched on their usual spots, side by side on the sofa, holding hands. They were lost in some Saturday night drama in which, from what Libby could see, there was a scandal breaking in The White

House and the President was gearing up for a press conference. On hearing Libby walk into the living room, her father paused the TV.

'Hello, love,' he said. 'You look worn out. Are you feeling more settled about everything?'

Libby reached up and rubbed her neck. 'I think so,' she said. 'But I ache in places I didn't know I had. We made a good start though, and Ant is sending in a crew on Monday to help rip all the old stuff out.'

'That's very kind of him,' her mother said with a warm smile. Linda Quinn was a quiet woman, content to be a home bird and to tend to her nest. She loved having her only daughter under her roof again, even if Libby herself found it a little claustrophobic to be back with Mammy and Daddy after years of living on her own.

'It is,' Libby told her, with a smile.

'Shame he won't get his hands dirty himself,' her father interjected.

'Ah now, Jim, come on. Not everyone's as good with their hands as you are. The man works long hours in that fancy job of his. He probably wouldn't know the first thing about working on a building site,' Linda said.

'It doesn't take a degree to work out how to use a brush,' her father replied, and Libby couldn't help but snort. She loved watching her parents banter like this. Between this and her exhaustion, she suddenly found herself getting a little tearful. Libby knew she was lucky, in so many ways.

'Are you okay, pet?' her dad said, cutting through her thoughts.

She looked at him, could see how much he resembled his own father, more so now than ever. Maybe it was the greying hair, the glasses that he needed to wear more and more these days, or maybe the slightly more-than-middle-aged spread, but he was looking more and more like the man who had raised him single-handedly after her grandmother had passed away. Libby's breath caught in her throat.

'I'm fine, Dad,' she said. 'Maybe a bit overwhelmed. But fine.'

'Go get yourself a nice bath or a shower,' her mother chimed in. 'I'll iron some fresh pyjamas and leave them on your bed. Get a good sleep and you'll feel better in the morning.'

Libby smiled and nodded. That sounded perfect. She was suddenly grateful she had no plans to see Ant. All she wanted to do now was curl up under the covers with a good book and lose herself for a while.

THE WONDERFUL WIZARD OF OZ

After her shower, Libby selected *Little Women* from the rickety bookcase in her room. The bookcase Grandad Ernie had lovingly made for her. He'd been so proud the day he carried it up to her room. He told her that he'd buy her a book a month until there was no space left on it. And he was true to his word, filling the dark wooden shelves with a selection of classic tales.

It was now among her most treasured possessions – with each book not only containing its own story, but also holding a memory of when and how and why they had chosen that particular title together. It was a library of her childhood as much as it was of the classics.

Grandad Ernie was a man who had been both her nearest and dearest childhood friend and her hero, rolled into one. She loved him as much as she was in awe of him – with his larger-than-life personality. He had the ability to spin stories into something truly magical and to turn the most seemingly mundane of tasks into wonderful adventures. The walk home from school was never simply a walk – instead there would be imaginary monsters to outrun, streams to cross, mountains to climb and horses to climb on and ride – skipping up the street and shouting 'Wooooaaahhh there, horsey' without caring who was looking on and laughing. Time in the garden turned into lessons in botany, mixed with stories of fairies and little folk and the making of a fairy door to pin to a tree so that any of their cast of mythical friends could visit.

As Libby grew up, she outgrew many things, but she never outgrew spending time with Grandad Ernie. If anything, they became closer. How she loved spending time with him – listening to the almost lyrical way he would tell his stories. Playing draughts with him. Confiding in him about her crushes and her broken hearts. Simply sitting side by side in silence sometimes, eating an ice cream at the beach or enjoying a cup of milky tea.

After he died, Libby's father had told her how it was her birth that had softened her grandad – made him believe in love and good things again. He had closed his heart to happiness after the death of his wife, when Jim was just five years old.

'It wasn't that he didn't show me love as a child – he did – in his own way, but so much of my childhood was spent watching him grieve for your granny. It was like he didn't want to get too close – even to his own child because, I suppose, he was afraid he'd lose me too, the way he lost her. He did everything he had to do to care for me – there wasn't a child in the world cared for more, he never let me down in terms of my physical needs – but with you? It's like he was the person he was always meant to be – the soft, silly, loving bear of a man who made your childhood magical.'

There had been no hint of bitterness in her father's eyes – but her heart had ached all the same for the man who lost his mother at a young age, who had missed out on the innocence of a childhood.

As if he saw her thoughts, her father had said: 'Don't you feel sorry for me, girl. My heart was healed watching the two of you together.'

But as they had sat and talked, the two of them knew that both their hearts were broken.

Back in the present, Libby read until her eyes drooped, then reached to put the book on her bedside table. Her eyes caught sight of the photos in the frames which sat on it. A selfie with Jess, both in oversized sunglasses, brandishing ice cream cones and grinning at the camera. One with her parents at her graduation. Another when she was just a child, standing, smiling proudly beside her grandfather in the garden she had loved so much. They made her smile.

Just as she was drifting off, her phone pinged with a message. Squinting in the darkness at the screen, she saw it was from Ant.

I missed you today. Missed our sexy Saturdays. I need to see you soon. I need to have you soon.

While normally she would feel her very core tighten deliciously at a suggestive text from Ant, this time she just sighed. She was not in the mood for a booty call. He hadn't even asked how her day had gone and that nipped at her. Did he really not get how important this was to her?

Missed you too x

She'd typed back – hoping it would be enough to settle him, then she switched her phone off altogether and fell into a deep sleep.

* * *

After a Sunday spent totting up all the quotes so far, talking over the best options with her dad, and trying to ignore any attempts from Ant to get her to forsake work and come and see him again, Libby was itching to get back to Ivy Lane on Monday morning. Yes, she felt guilty fobbing Ant off and, yes, he was being generous with his help, but she couldn't just down tools and run to him. Not now. There was simply too much to do.

This was a fact she was reminded of again when she unlocked the door to the shop at just after eight. The sun was gloriously warm already, and the stale, malodorous smell greeted her as she walked in. She therefore made a decision to leave the door open to let some fresh air seep in – and perhaps to let some of the bad smell seep out.

Pest control were due just after nine to check the traps and lay more bait if necessary. Libby didn't want to think about what might, or might not, be filling the traps they had laid on Friday. Ant's team were due to arrive at ten, and Terry The Spark was due to arrive 'around ten' himself – bringing his own labourers to help get the basics in place. Libby had, rather optimistically she now realised, arranged for a shopfitter to come and look around the place at 10.30. That was before she realised it would be quite a while yet before the shop would be ready for finishing touches, such as shelves and floors and counters.

'Don't cancel him,' her dad had said. 'Just take it as having more time to talk about what you really want. Get him to do a good design job for you.'

'That's the bit I'm looking forward to most,' her mother said. 'All the wee knick-knacks.' Libby had smiled indulgently at her mum. It was as if Linda had some sort of transformation fantasy in her head. An image of Libby dancing around the shop singing 'A Woman's Touch' from *Calamity Jane* and the place magically turning from a bomb site to a boutique. Libby realised this was probably not too far from the fantasy she'd held herself, until she'd first laid eyes on the interior of the shop and the flat.

Making a mental list of all she wanted to achieve that day, Libby yawned and realised she would really love a coffee. Yes, she had already downed a large latte on the drive over, along with a bacon bap for extra energy, but the efforts of the weekend were catching up with her and she felt fuzzy-headed. There was a small convenience store just down the road, a few doors down from The Ivy Inn. It was one of four other shops on the lane, including a butchers, a florists and a charity shop. It was the only one however, apart from her own, which looked as though it was caught in a time warp. Faded decals advertising long-defunct newspapers still gripped the windows and everything inside looked faded, as if it were behind an Instagram filter which gave everything an eighties vibe.

She decided to take her chances and walked to the shop, pushing open the door to hear the tinkle of a bell. The inside of the shop, though meticulously clean, had a dated feel. Each item was still priced with a sticker from a gun, the shelves stocked with every kind of household essential from fresh bread to Brillo pads. A poster hung on the wall with ice lollies from the eighties on it and by the looks of it, the till on the counter was older than the one in the bookshop.

Libby was starting to lose confidence that there might be a coffee machine here ready to dispense a large latte with caramel syrup. She walked around the small shop on a reconnaissance mission, and was greeted by an elderly man who had appeared as if from nowhere and was now behind the counter.

'Ah, it's yourself,' he said. 'The new girl from the old drapers. I hear it's a bookshop you're opening – we sell a few books here,' he said, pointing to a lone shelf of fairly tattered romances complete with bare-chested hunks and wanton maidens on the front, along with a few sporting biographies. 'But I bet you'll have a better selection, won't you?' He laughed. 'And those e-book yokes too, I bet. Why anyone would want to read off a computer is beyond me. Paper and print – that's what it does. Technology will be the end of independent businesses, so it will. Libby, isn't it? Jo from the pub told me. I'm Harry.' He finally took a breath before extending one soft clammy hand for her to shake. As he did so, he broke into a wide smile, the glint off his sparkly white dentures almost blinding her. She put him at maybe seventy, or seventy-five. Slightly younger than her grandad had been, perhaps. She wondered why he was still working at his age, but she'd guess this shop marked his life's work. There was something proprietorial in his stance. A pride in his surroundings.

'Nice to meet you, Harry,' she said. 'Yes, I'm Libby – Libby Quinn – and we won't be selling e-books or e-readers. Print all the way. I'm a lover of the classics. I just thought I'd pop in for a coffee before the day starts properly.'

'Ah, I suppose it will be a latte or a cappuccino or something you'll take. The machine's over there,' he said, gesturing to the back of the shop. 'Hard to believe there was ever a time when people came in for a cuppa or a coffee, and I just boiled a kettle up and stuck a teabag in a polystyrene cup for them. They wouldn't go for that these days.'

'I'm sure your teas and coffees made from the kettle were as nice as any of these new ones,' she said, internally delighted to find she had been wrong and there was a coffee machine after all.

'Oh God, no. They were rotten. My Mary always told me they were fit for nothing but down the sink.' He laughed. 'But still, more innocent times. No health and safety and fancy coffee shops getting in the way of things.'

'Indeed,' Libby said, as she located the machine and pressed the button for an extra-large latte. She decided it was best to avoid telling Harry that she had plans to open a coffee bar of her own in the shop. She might not get out of there alive if she did.

'That's why it's nice to see some new life coming into this street,' Harry's voice carried from the front of the shop. 'And a bookshop too. It's traditional values, isn't it? Stories. Getting folk to read. Better than sitting in front of those Gameboy things,' he said. 'We've a grandson – well, he's twenty-five now, but he's constantly on one of those gaming things. Hard to get a conversation with him at all. A nod if you're lucky.'

The poor grandson probably couldn't get a word in when he tried, Libby thought as she carried her cup to the front of the shop.

'Things have definitely changed,' she said, 'but, as you said, hopefully we can keep a bit of life in the street. I like it here. Near enough to the town centre to get some footfall but not to be rammed with parking and buskers and the like.'

'Don't even get me started on buskers,' Harry said, crossing his arms over his rounded tummy – the buttons on his striped shirt straining over his white vest. As he took a deep breath and started to talk, Libby had a feeling he was getting started anyway.

What she had intended to be a quick two minutes to the shop and back ended up more than twenty – but Harry had given her a free packet of near date Ginger Nuts as a welcome to the area, pressed them into her hand, saying there was no need to say thank you and had smiled that dazzling smile again at her. She could see that, in his youth, he had probably been a very handsome man, and by the way he talked – and talked, and talked – she sensed he was lonely. That he enjoyed being at the heart of the community. She wondered if he and Grandad Ernie would have gotten along. She imagined they would have, although how either of them would ever have managed to get work done would have been a mystery.

As she sipped the latte, felt the caffeine surge into her blood-stream, she vowed she'd make a point of getting to know Harry a bit better. To keep a wee eye out for him.

Libby smiled as she crossed back over the street and unlocked the door, pushing it open again. She sat at the counter, on the stool she had brought with her, and sipped her coffee, doing her very best to practice positive visualisation. She even allowed herself to crack open the Ginger Nuts before she could mentally hear Jess's voice warning her about the many free-floating germs in the shop.

So, instead, she put the biscuits in her bag and opened her Pinterest account on her laptop. Smiling broadly, she looked at all the pictures she had pinned. Rich green walls. Copper light shades. Polished wooden floor. Vintage upcycled desks and chairs. Prints of classic book covers she would frame and hang around the shop. Reusing old shelving units – repurposing – that was the word, wasn't it? It would be quirky – different – homely. Exposed brickwork at the coffee bar. Plants trailing ivy leaves. Quirky sundries for sale at the counter. She could fix the old glass-front drapery unit to stock pins and postcards, tote bags and badges. A bibliophile's dream.

She was high on the thought of it, until pest control arrived and confirmed that, yes, all but one of the traps they had set contained vermin. Rats and mice. Double joy. The man laughed when she asked if he thought that was all of them, then?

'Not likely, my love,' he said. 'But we've an idea of where they're getting in. Hate to say it, but all this refurb work is likely to bring them out of hiding for a bit. My advice to you would be to let us lay the poison, but be prepared that we might need to work at this again and again until the heavy lifting is done and we can seal off any and all entry points.'

Libby's skin crawled at what she now imagined as an army of

furry friends scuttling between the floorboards and in the cavity walls.

'I've seen places in worse states,' Mr Pest Controller said. 'You wanted to see it when that old derelict factory beside the Craigavon Bridge went up in smoke. It was the bloody Pied Piper of Hamelin on the Foyle Road. Hundreds of the wee bastards running for cover.'

Libby shuddered.

'Yours is nowhere near that.'

'I suppose that's some reassurance,' she said, although she felt anything but reassured.

Libby pondered over the fact that the rat catcher was exceptionally cheerful for a man who spent his day chasing vermin and infestations. The thought made her mildly nauseous – but she suppose it took all sorts. She made a mental note to invite him to the grand opening. She needed cheery people around – as long as he didn't reference the scuttling vermin to her guests.

Next, Ant's handymen arrived, complete with a second large skip, which caused Harry to peep his head out from his shop and offer her a big thumbs up as it landed with an unceremonious clunk on the road outside the shop.

'Hard to beat a good clear-out,' he shouted, before disappearing back indoors.

The men started on the yard first, clearing all sorts of detritus in super quick time.

Libby sent Ant a text, thanking him and telling him the men were doing a great job. He sent a smiley face back and a simple:

You can thank me later?

Libby rolled her eyes, but she was feeling positive, so it was in a playful way. She didn't normally see Ant on a Monday, but just maybe she could make an exception and take a very quick visit to his that evening.

See you after work?

She typed back, and was rewarded with a grinning face emoji as a response.

When the shopfitter arrived to discuss her plans, she was positively glowing with excitement. She wasn't even fazed when he told her that while he could help with design, fixtures and fittings, including the stockroom, and with the coffee bar, it might be worth scouting some vintage markets or auctions herself for the older pieces she wanted.

'We could work on getting you some stuff – but, to be honest, it would be more economical for you to go with some reproduction stuff. A similar look for less money,' Craig, a tall, skinny redhead with a thick Glasgow accent said.

Libby pulled a face. Maybe he was right, but she had fallen in love with the idea of bits and pieces which had stories of their own.

Craig noticed the look on her face. 'If you have your heart set on the real deal, and you want the best deal – then shop around. I can get you a list of upcoming markets? I think there's one in Belfast soon that tends to be good. You probably have an idea of what you want, but I'd recommend looking at ercol furniture. I think it would suit the look you're going for. It's pricey – especially the mid-century stuff – but it's hard to beat, quality wise.'

Libby smiled. Shopping around was something she could do.

She liked Craig, she decided. There was something about him that made her feel reassured that not only was he on board with her vision for the shop, he was also not going to overcharge and underwork. His enthusiasm for the project was obvious.

They were leaning over the counter, scrawling sketches of what they thought the shop could look like when Libby was distracted by the sound of someone coming in through the door. She looked up and saw Noah walk through the door, with Paddy trotting dutifully behind him, sniffing the air.

9

THE OLD CURIOSITY SHOP

'Ah, Libby,' Noah said. 'Paddy and I just fancied a nosy. Given that the door was open. It's already looking better in here.' He nodded towards the newly cleared floors of the shop and where some of the old plasterwork had been stripped out.

He dropped Paddy's lead and the dog padded over to Libby and rubbed his head against her leg, his tail wagging furiously.

'He remembers you!' Noah said. 'And I think he's forgiven you for stepping on his tail.'

Libby blushed. She didn't want Craig to hear about that entire sorry episode. 'Well, it wasn't my fault...' she began before Noah laughed.

'I'm only teasing. Honest. But he does like you.'

Libby looked down into Paddy's big brown eyes. She imagined that dog could get anything he wanted with just a glance. She reached out and patted him, tickling him under his chin.

'Noah! It's you!' Craig said. 'How's it going?'

'It's going well, mate. Can't complain anyway. I saw your van outside and wondered if it was you or one of the other fellas. How's things?'

'Busy, you know. But that's not a complaint,' Craig said. Libby gave Paddy another pet and then looked pointedly at Noah, hoping that he would leave and she could get on with chatting things through with Craig.

It seemed Noah had other ideas. 'We're looking to do a little work to the rear bar area and beer garden and I'd been meaning to give you a call. I hope you're not too busy to have a look at it for us.'

Libby wanted to say that, yes, actually, Craig was too busy because he was here with her, talking about her shop and he didn't have time to discuss an upgrade to The Ivy Inn just now. She didn't though, much to her chagrin. She needed to be more assertive.

'I'm sure we can work something out,' Craig said. 'Might be six weeks or so though. With summer coming, that mightn't suit you.'

Noah nodded. 'I see what you mean. I suppose when we have a full idea of what we're looking at we can make a proper decision. Let me know when you're free to call over.'

'Well, I'm in the neighbourhood now,' Craig said, 'so how about I pop round when I'm done here. We can get the ball rolling at least.'

'Great,' Noah said, enthusiastically. 'Perfect.'

Libby expected that to be the end of the conversation. It was not. She anticipated that Noah, and Paddy, would leave the shop and she and Craig could go back to their discussion and preliminary sketches, but this did not happen.

Noah just changed the topic of conversation. 'Are those your ideas for here?' he asked, nodding at the notebooks on the counter. As if they could be anything else, Libby thought.

'Yes. Early stages, you know,' she said.

'Do you mind if I have a look?' Noah asked as he edged closer to the counter.

She fought every instinct to pull the papers to her chest. Was it churlish that she felt so protective over her plans? Especially at a stage when they were a mess of ideas and perhaps half-baked dreams? Would he think it all very twee? Her little writer nooks? Her ideas for fairy lights and copper framed terrariums, funky prints and vintage coffee cups? Her plan to use repurposed shelving units and vintage desks – creating a book lover's haven?

Noah turned the notepads towards himself, and glanced at the open Pinterest board on her laptop. She blushed as he took it all in.

'These are for writers?' he asked, pointing to the four dedicated workspace areas she had planned.

She nodded. 'A desk-for-hire kind of thing – a place to work among the books, with their own desks, coffee on call, et cetera.'

'For hire? But if any writer can just lift their laptop, go to Starbucks or any coffee shop, plug in and write among the coffee beans for the price of a latte – why would they pay to hire a desk here?'

'Well, it's a bookshop. It will have its own ambiance. A creative vibe.'

'The noise of customers coming in from outside? Will you have a radio playing? Will the coffee machine bubble and fizz? Will people look over their shoulders as they sit there writing? Could it take on a zoo-like feel? I mean, I'm sure you've considered all this, but...'

It was Craig's turn to cough uncomfortably while Libby felt her anger growing, and more than that, she was shocked to feel tears prick at her eyes.

'The spaces will be quite secluded, behind shelves, but with natural light from the windows. The hire charges will be minimal – with the chance to have their work featured on our social media pages and promoted through our mailing lists. I've been talking to a few literary magazines about accepting submissions or coming to the shop for events. The same with published authors. I have thought this through – you know. I've done my research. I'm not clueless. It's about building a community.' She was annoyed at herself when she felt a small tremor in her voice. Who was he to hint that her plans hadn't been fully thought out? Clearly he underestimated her.

'Oh God, I'm not suggesting you're clueless. Sorry! Shit. I just know how brutal it can be setting up on your own. We had a false start when we took over The Ivy Inn. Pitched it wrong,' he said, looking apologetic. 'We had to make big changes, fast. Costly changes. Sorry, I must sound like an arrogant asshole.'

Libby choked out a small laugh. 'Well...'

'Sorry, I worked in financial management in a previous life. Proper rat race stuff in London. I swear I still have PTSD from it.' He laughed a little, but there was something in his expression that told her he wasn't that far off the mark. 'I have profit margins drilled into me and sometimes they come out again. You've your head screwed on if you're already thinking about community though. I think that's what makes or breaks a new business these days. And it's what really matters.'

Libby flushed, with pride this time. Actually, she felt a little dizzy from the roller-coaster of emotions she'd been through in the last ten minutes alone.

'If I could offer one suggestion, and you can feel free to tell me to get stuffed, but from the pub, I know people do like privacy,' Noah said, clearly not wanting to extract his nose entirely from her business. 'I imagine that's even more the case when writing than when drinking in a pub. We created our nooks just for that – with Craig's help to design them. When we were going over ideas, we looked at curved stone walls – about four feet high – tonnes of character. Do you remember that, Craig?'

Craig nodded. 'Yes, I think I still have some pictures of where it was done elsewhere… hang on,' he said, logging into his iPad and scanning through. 'That's a cracking idea actually – just the right amount of privacy – maybe not stonework here, but something – reclaimed wooden cladding? It wouldn't add much to your budget, but it would be quite effective.'

When Craig showed her the pictures, Libby couldn't help but think that Noah may just be onto something. She knew, despite her bravado about having done her research, it would still be a battle to give the spaces the edge – especially for impoverished writers. All the marketing in the world couldn't change basic economics. This would make the spaces extra cosy – secluded – away from distractions but close to a creative buzz.

'Actually, that's not the worst idea,' she said. 'Thanks.'

'No worries, Libby. Sure, we're all in this together, aren't we? Trying to keep our businesses going? Trying to make Ivy Lane a place people want to visit and be a part of? It's in our mutual best interests to work well together – all of us traders.'

'You're right,' she said. 'I'm going to introduce myself to some of the others later. I've already met Harry.'

Noah's face broke into a wide grin at the mention of Harry's name. 'He's a legend,' Noah said warmly. 'He's the very heart of Ivy Lane.'

* * *

A full skip was lifted just before five and when Libby walked around the flat, it was little more than a shell of bare floors and walls. The old kitchen and bathroom suites had been pulled out

and it was the very definition of a blank canvas. It felt bigger –
already expanding with potential before her eyes.

Despite the long day and how busy she had been, Libby had a
spring in her step as she locked up and climbed into her car and
headed for home. She was still smiling as she showered and
changed into a strappy summer dress, tousled her hair and
sprayed it with sea salt spray to give it a relaxed look, and slipped
her feet into a pair of bejewelled flip-flops. Spritzing some of her
favourite Jo Malone perfume on her wrists and neck, before
slicking some gloss across her lips, she looked in the mirror and
realised that her smile, her happiness, went right to the heart of
her. She could see it shining out of her, could feel it in every pore,
and it felt so very good. The worries and stresses of the last few
days – God, from the last few years since her Grandad had died –
seemed to be fading and for the first time in a long time she could
see herself start to emerge again. Only better. Stronger. More
confident. Less likely to put up with nonsense.

She smiled at her reflection, called a cheery goodbye to her
parents and jumped in her car, windows down and radio blaring,
to drive out to see Ant. She smiled when she thought of his broad
shoulders, his toned arms, his sly smile that seemed to be able to
set her very core fizzing. She longed to kiss him – to let him feel
how happy she was after just one day of making real progress.
Imagine how happy she would be when it was all done and she
could leave the shop each day knowing that she had enjoyed
another great day living her dream?

She thought of how she had simply been going through the
motions in the PR company, writing copy and blog posts that
didn't fire her imagination. Yes, she did them well. She was given
free rein – but you could only be so creative when writing about a
new product on the supermarket shelves or a new colour of
lipstick. If she did her job well – and the company got the

coverage online and in the glossies they wanted – it wasn't even as if she would get to bask in the glory of it. She would simply move on to the next task. After thirteen years, it had become mundane, repetitive – it didn't ignite the same passion in her that it had when she had first started. When the redundancies had been announced, she had almost been relieved to find that her department was being restructured. Without the push, she was unsure whether she would have had the guts to jump – but it felt, at the time, that it was a sign from her grandad that the timing was right to start to dream big and live big.

While some people wanted to travel the world, splash the cash on designer bags and shoes, Libby allowed herself to believe that her dream wasn't unattainable. It had been scary – it was scary and it probably always would be scary – but as she drove along the coast road – the wind whipping her hair and the smell of the sea in her nostrils – she allowed herself to sing at the very top of her lungs, and it felt good.

She was still singing when she drove up the hill to Ant's house, treating him to one of her best high notes as she parked the car.

He smiled broadly when he saw her – standing up from where he was sat at the bistro set at the front of house – perfectly positioned in the luscious green gardens to catch the sun in the evening. Whoever had designed the house had considered the rising and setting of the sun perfectly. The garden was a suntrap and it was blissful to sit there and relax, breathing in the smell of the lavender and jasmine.

Libby slipped out of the car, pushed her sunglasses up on top of her head and walked to him, allowing him to pull her into a deep embrace before tipping her head back just slightly and kissing her, full and deep, on the lips so that she could barely wait for her body to intertwine with his.

No one had ever made her body respond the way he did – he knew how to make her giddy with lust with just one brush of his lips, one flick of his tongue, one gentle stroke of his finger on her sun-kissed skin. As he kissed her there, in the garden, she felt herself start to tremble, her heart race, and she knew she wanted him.

'Let's go inside,' she breathed and he was only too happy to oblige, leading her by the hand to his room.

* * *

'If I knew hiring you a skip and a couple of handymen would provoke such a reaction, I would have done it a long time ago.' Ant laughed as they lay together in his bed afterwards. 'I mean, most women like flowers or jewellery, but if skips are your thing…'

'Hey, I don't mind flowers or jewellery either.'

She sat up and lifted her dress from the floor.

Ant sat up too and kissed her softly on her shoulder. 'You freshen up and meet me downstairs. How does a cold beer sound?'

'It sounds blissful, but I'm driving,' she said. 'No sleepovers on school nights, remember?' she said, quoting his own 'rule' back at him. He worked such long hours normally that it was never really an issue.

'Sometimes I hate myself,' Ant said, and laughed. 'A soft drink it is then.'

Libby noted that he hadn't suggested an exception that night.

* * *

By the time she met him downstairs, he had prepared a Caesar salad served with slices of a fresh tiger loaf for them both. He held a cold beer in his hand, while a glass of fizzy water with a slice of lime sat beside Libby's plate.

'Today went well then,' he said, as she sat down and lifted her fork to eat. She was suddenly ravenous.

'Better than well,' she said. 'Oh, Ant, I know there is a lot of work to be done, but I can see it all coming together. It's going to be so good. Craig, the shopfitter, has some amazing ideas. He suggested I go and hunt through a vintage market this weekend, source some of the items I want for the shop. He said they normally have some really great pieces – you know, desks and the like for the writing nooks. Once I get some, I'll really be able to imagine what it will look like when it's done.'

'This weekend?' Ant said, his smile faded.

'Yes, it's only an occasional thing. So thank God I found out about it. The next one mightn't be for months.' Libby could see that Ant wasn't sharing her enthusiasm on this one, but she had a card up her sleeve she was yet to play. 'I was thinking you could come with me,' she said, giving him her best puppy dog eyes and using every trick Paddy had taught her. 'It's up near Belfast, so we could maybe even make a night of it. I thought we could book into the Merchant or somewhere else a bit quirky like that?'

'A night out buying old furniture?' If his eyebrows raised any further, they were in danger of popping off the top of his head.

'Well, no...' she said, trying to stop the feeling of deflation. 'The day would be spent buying old furniture. The night could be spent doing whatever we wanted to do.' She said the last five words slowly, for emphasis.

'I'm not sure a day walking between the musty smells and woodworm would get me in the mood,' he said. 'I was kind of hoping we could just hole up here. You know, one of those blissful weekends we used to have where we spent at least ninety per cent of our time in bed and only ventured out for food, or drink?'

Remembering what Jess had said about Ant being a clean freak, she softened, but just a little. 'I know, but things are different now. We've had that conversation, Ant,' she said. 'How about we drive up together. You relax in the hotel and I'll do the market myself, meet you in the hotel afterwards? We can get room service if you want?'

It was less than ideal, but she was trying to compromise, even though she was pulled that he didn't want to help her look for the furniture she needed. It seemed very much like the only thing he was really interested in was getting her into bed, and keeping her there.

'It's not the same. And, sure, what would I do with myself for an afternoon in Belfast? I'd be bored stupid,' he said, and Libby heard a hint of spoiled brattishness in his voice.

'Ant,' she said, after she had taken a deep breath, 'you know I have my deadline for the shop – and that it's going to be intense. You've known that all along. This market is only held every few months. I need to go to it. I need to be free at the weekends for the next while at the very least. I don't have time to spend a weekend doing nothing.'

'It's not doing nothing,' he said. 'It's doing me!' He flashed her his best smile – the smile that normally made her feel funny inside. Now, it just made her cross.

She put her fork down. It was safe to say her appetite had all but disappeared.

'Doing you,' she said calmly, 'no matter how much fun – is not going to get the shop open.'

'But I helped. I sent you some heavy lifters? Surely that has given you a day or two in credit? A day you could devote to us?'

'Didn't I break our not during the week rule and drive down here tonight – just to see you?'

'It's not the same.'

'I'm sorry,' she said, but if she was honest, she wasn't really sorry at all.

'I get that this means a lot to you. An awful lot – but it feels as if I don't mean anything to you at all at the moment,' he said.

'You're being silly,' she said, wrong-footed by his sudden neediness. It wasn't his form – not at all. They weren't a needy couple. If anything, their relationship still had a sort of casual feel to it, which had suited them both just fine. Or so Libby had thought.

'Ant,' she said, 'since we started talking about this shop, we knew it was going to take most of my time. That was always a given. You can't keep making me feel bad about it.'

Her tone was probably a little harsher than she intended, but Libby was trying – really trying – not to be disappointed in him. Disappointed that it seemed as if all his big talk of the last few months, all his encouragement that she was doing the right thing, was not what she actually thought it to be. It had existed only when the idea of how it would eat into their time together was abstract – simply a notion. Once reality had hit, Ant had very quickly become nothing more than a child, annoyed that his access to his favourite toy was being rationed.

'I'm not trying to make you feel bad about it,' he replied.

'So you will come with me, to Belfast, on Saturday and we'll have a nice time?'

He shook his head. 'If I'm not going to get you to myself, I might as well stay here and get some work done. You know vintage isn't my style – and musty old markets even less so. Why not ask Jess? Get some bonding time in? Seems the only person you see less than me is her.'

So now he was not only having a go at her for how little time she spent with him – but also with Jess? The afterglow of their lovemaking was now well and truly gone.

'Look,' Libby said, 'I didn't come here to fight or justify myself. We've been having a lovely evening. God, not that long ago, we were having the best evening! Maybe just think about Belfast for a bit?' she asked him, and he nodded, but they limped through another half hour of stilted conversation before the sun started to drop in the garden and Libby felt a shiver run through her that was from more than the cold. 'I'd better be getting back,' she said, faux smile on her face.

'I suppose you have an early start in the morning?'

'I do. The glazer is coming to look at the windows, see what can be salvaged. He'll be there first thing.'

Ant nodded but didn't say anything.

Awkwardly, Libby kissed him on the cheek, lifted her keys and told him they would talk later in the week. 'Think about the weekend,' she said. 'It could be fun. Different, but still fun.'

'I'll think about it,' he said as she climbed into the front seat of her car, switched on the engine and was temporarily deafened by the loudness of the radio. Turning it down, she nodded in Ant's direction and drove off – not quite sure what to think any more.

10

LOVE STORY

Libby Quinn had been blissfully single – well, perhaps not blissfully, but single all the same – when on a night out with Jess, she bumped into the proverbial (and actual) tall, dark and handsome stranger at the bar. From the moment he looked down at her, his eyes hungry, he made her feel delicate, dainty and utterly edible. She was powerless to resist him. And by the time Ant whisked her back to his house in a taxi later that night, unable to keep his hands off her, she didn't want to.

This was the electricity charge people spoke of. The air around them fizzed and crackled and Libby had never felt anything like it before and she gave in to it.

They fell into a pattern – a relationship based on great sex, a good laugh at times and minimum commitment, which suited Libby completely. She wanted to concentrate on getting her new life up and running and she had neither the physical nor emotional energy for anything more.

Libby had wondered if she should feel more for Ant – knowing that on paper he was the perfect match. Handsome. Self-sufficient. With a house by the sea, a good and secure job, the ability to make her weak at the knees. But she didn't feel more for him – she cared for him, she liked having him in her life, but she didn't love him. He didn't love her either – not in the way people thought she should be loved. She liked how he made her feel like the sexiest woman alive and for a long time that was enough. It was more than enough. They had a comfortable arrangement where each got what they needed from the other and had fun in the process. That was exactly why it worked – and it suited them both. Not that Libby had ever, ever in her life imagined she would find herself in a friends-with-benefits kind of a relationship.

So this new, possessive side of Ant surprised her a little and she couldn't really understand where it was coming from or why things had to change. Why did he have to make her feel guilty about work? She never ever made him feel guilty if he had to travel for his job, or work extra hours, or if he had to cancel one of their 'sacred' weekends at the last minute.

And until now, he had been equally as relaxed with her.

Was it that he sensed things were changing? That she was growing stronger and taking back control of her life – all her planning now becoming a reality. Was it possible that what had worked for so long simply would not keep working for much longer? Could he sense that too?

She stopped at the garage to fill her car up with petrol when her phone pinged. It was a message from Ant. He hadn't even taken five minutes of his time to consider her proposal and decide against it. It read:

Look, just ask Jess to go with you. This weekend isn't for me. No hard feelings

Dejected, confused and a little pissed off, Libby paid for her fuel and then drove her car towards the riverfront and Jess's apartment. She needed to curl up on her best friend's sofa and share her worries with her.

When Jess answered the door, she was already in her pyjamas – and her blonde hair was pulled into a messy ponytail at the top of her head.

'I was just putting on a cup of tea,' Jess said, hugging her friend. 'Do you want one?'

Libby nodded and followed Jess through to her pristine, glossy white kitchen. Libby was always impressed with how shiny and clean her friend's kitchen was – especially as Jess loved cooking. Even though she lived alone, she always cooked from scratch. Both she and Ant shared a love of the culinary, while Libby was more of a Marks & Sparks ready meal kind of a girl.

'You don't mind me calling over?' she asked as Jess shook the kettle before topping it up with water and switching it on.

'Of course not – it's nice to have a bit of company. I was just going to watch *90 Day Fiancé* and paint my toenails or something equally thrilling.' Jess dropped teabags into two mugs and took milk from the fridge while the kettle bubbled and hissed. 'Is everything okay? I thought you were seeing Ant tonight.'

'Erm... I was. But it didn't go the best, to be honest.'

'Oh?' Jess asked as she handed over a mug of perfectly made tea to her friend.

Libby walked through to the living room and sat down while she explained to Jess what had happened over dinner, and her deeper concerns about her changing dynamic with Ant.

Libby took a breath, one thought having landed in her head while she had been offloading. 'I think... I think maybe Ant and I are coming to the end of our relationship,' she told Jess, who, for the shortest time, seemed shocked into silence.

'Do you not just think, maybe, that he needs time to adjust to your new reality? And you too? This a big period of change. With some work, do you think things could settle down, improve?'

'You know what, Jess – I'm not sure it's worth the effort,' Libby said, and it was only as she said the words that she realised she meant it. Ant had never been a long-term prospect. She guessed she'd always known that, even if she'd never admitted it to herself completely before, but now that she had opened that box in her head, she didn't think she'd be able to close it again.

She couldn't help but see the confusion on her friend's face.

'But, I thought things were going well. You were having fun?' Jess said.

'We were – God, we still do, when we want to. But, you know, Jess, he was never going to be the big love of my life. Does that sound awful? I know – maybe it does. But if it's going to take time and effort for him to adjust, when I don't think either of us really sees a long-term future in our relationship, I'm not sure it's worth the heartache?'

Jess sat her mug on the floor and turned to look Libby head-on. 'I know things have always been on the casual side with you two. But, still, I have to ask you, honestly, why is he not the one? I always assumed you were just being closed off because, you know, you were grieving and one day you would open up and, I don't know, walk in here and tell me you were madly in love.'

Libby shrugged. 'Maybe I thought that would happen too, but I don't think it will and it's not just because I'm annoyed at him for not coming away with me, or not doing more to help with the shop. I can't pinpoint exactly what it is. But that feeling that we couldn't possibly live without each other for the rest of our lives? It just isn't there. We have fun – but on a very superficial level. But I think that's it.'

Jess's expression changed. She rubbed at her temples and stiffened. 'Let me get this right. He's not the one because all you do is have fun?' There was a definite hint of disbelief, possibly even annoyance, in her voice.

'I know,' Libby said, feeling herself cringe. 'But, you know, I don't think he'd disagree with anything I've said. We've been together for long enough that you'd think we'd be talking about taking things to the next level, maybe, moving in, I don't know, marriage, kids...'

'You've never even *talked* about a next step?' Jess asked, incredulously.

'Jess, don't you think I'd have told you if we had? And, you know, we've never ever discussed the "L" word and I don't think either of us are sitting pining to have the conversation either. We just rubbed along because it was fun, and now it's not as fun any more and all the other problems are starting to become more pointed.'

'Relationships aren't meant to be fun all the time though, Libby. We both know that. You have to work at these things.'

There was something in Jess's tone – a judgement or something, she couldn't quite put her finger on it – that made Libby uncomfortable. Maybe it was because it almost sounded as if her best friend in the entire world was fighting Ant's case, instead of offering the unwavering support she had come to expect from her.

'Jess, don't you think that if you're with the one – the proper one – the one that works on all levels – that you'd know it and you wouldn't question it? You'd want to tell them you loved them and have them say it back. It shouldn't be the case that you don't care if they do or don't.'

Jess sat back, took a breath. Libby could almost see the cogs working in her mind – trying to understand how she could be in a relationship of sorts with a man who ticked all the boxes but didn't fit all the same.

'I suppose,' Jess said softly. 'But here's the thing, I know what you're like, Libby Quinn. I've known you since we were four years old and when you get involved in a project you give it one hundred per cent – which is admirable. The thing is, nothing should take up one hundred per cent of our life – no project, no job, no hobby, no man. Don't put all your eggs in the one basket – don't move on to the next gung-ho adventure without realising the last one still has a little to offer. It doesn't have to be a case of either/or. Ant is a good guy – don't make a mistake. That's all I'm saying.'

'I suppose,' Libby conceded, to keep the peace, if nothing else, even though she knew deep down how she felt and that it was unlikely to change. Maybe Jess had been the wrong person to speak to after all. She felt this conversation run away from her. Just as it had run away from her when she had been with Ant earlier. She decided to try and move things on. 'Look, how do you feel about coming with me to the vintage market at the weekend instead? We can hire a van. I'll even let you choose the music we listen to. We can stay overnight – really kick off our heels? Or our flats?' she said, looking down at her flip-flops and Jess's slipper socks.

'Oh, God, that sounds great,' Jess said, in a tone that didn't quite match her words. 'But I can't this weekend. I have that mental health conference at the university in Coleraine. It's all booked and I'm representing the practice. I'm sorry, you know I would if I could.'

'Don't worry about it,' Libby said, but she couldn't help but feel disappointed and, if she was honest, worried that her friend might have been lying to her.

11

THE HELP

Libby was very good at distracting herself with work. Especially when it was work she was enjoying – but by Thursday she had started to feel overwhelmed by the dust, the noise and the mounting bills.

'It has to get worse before it gets better,' her dad had told her. 'You'll be surprised how quickly it will start to come together.'

'I hope so,' Libby said, pulling her hair – which seemed to have a permanent coating of dust, no matter how much she washed it – back in a ponytail.

'It will,' he said. 'Remember, I've done a lot of these projects and without fail I've had this conversation with every single person who has hired me. But you have to look at how far you've come.'

Libby looked down at the counter top, where her notes and plans were all laid out. She could see it coming together on paper. She'd even had the chance to check out the online catalogue for the auction Craig had told her about and had found some brilliant pieces she had already decided she absolutely had to have,

including two ercol desks and an industrial-style table which
would work brilliantly to display books in the centre of the shop.

She could see that progress was being made around her too.
There was no doubt her dad had sway in the building community. Terry The Spark was working flat out, along with a spotty
apprentice called Gerry. Libby wondered whether Gerry would
someday adopt the moniker of Gerry The Spark – she liked to
think he would. She loved the symmetry of Terry and Gerry.

Billy the plumber was working round the clock, replacing
some frankly disgusting pipework and planning how best to
plumb in what she would need for the coffee bar.

On top of that, she had a stream of joiners, glazers and plas-
terers calling in and out. Craig was in almost constant contact and
her father was very much enjoying his role as a pseudo project
manager.

On some days, she felt as if she was relegated to the role of
tea-girl, but if it kept things moving along at the shop to provide
tea and biscuits on demand, she'd suck it up and keep doing it.

Her newly enforced role also kept Harry happy, as Libby
traipsed up and down the street several times a day to buy milk or
coffee, or another packet of Rich Tea, from his shop. He perked
up as soon as he saw her walk in – and even though she knew
that she was never going to get out of there without hearing at
least one of his rants, she liked that he had taken no time at all to
accept her as part of the Ivy Lane community. That Thursday the
subject of his ire was the number of domestic waste bins people
were required to have these days.

'I put the wrong bin out this morning because I was still
sleepy and, of course, they didn't lift it, so now I have to sit with
all that rubbish rotting for the next two weeks – and with this
lovely weather and all. There's some out-of-date chicken in there

and, I can tell you, it wasn't smelling too fragrant when it went in. Imagine it after two weeks in this heat?'

Libby wrinkled her nose in disgust but decided she would rather not think about it in too much detail if she could help it.

'I suppose you could always take it to the municipal dump?' she suggested, lifting a bag of sugar and wondering how her workmen didn't all have type 2 diabetes from the quantity of the stuff they got through.

'Just the chicken? Seems a bit extreme,' Harry said, and for just a second she didn't know if he was serious or not. It was only when he flashed her his pearly false teeth and winked at her that she laughed – his belly-shaking chuckle kicking in just after. 'Your face, Libby! You are a card! Tell me this, are you single? What age are you? Because my grandson is twenty-five and he could do worse than have a lovely wee cuddy like you on his arm.'

'Ah, he's a bit young for me, Harry,' Libby said, not actually telling him whether or not she was single. 'I'm the wrong side of thirty for him.'

'You could be one of those cougars?' Harry asked, with a wink.

'Ah, God no. I don't have the energy for that,' Libby laughed, 'but I'm sure if your boy has even half the charm of his grandad, it won't be long until he snaps up a lovely woman of his own.'

'I hope so,' Harry said. 'I'm not getting any younger and it would be nice to hold a great-grandchild before I pop my clogs.'

'Harry, you'll outlive us all, so none of that talk,' Libby chided, handing over the money for her purchases.

'Can I come down and have a nosy around the shop sometime?' Harry asked – for once looking a little less than his usual bold and brash self.

'Of course,' Libby said. 'I mean, there's not an awful lot to look at just now – it's a bit of a building site – but you are welcome

down any time. The door's usually open – just pop in. I don't tend
to travel far from my spot at the counter most days.'

Harry nodded, handing her the change. 'Good. Good. I'll call
down then. I remember when it was the drapers – although that
seems like forever ago now. People don't make clothes in the way
they used to. That shop used to be busy all the time. My Mary
was forever in and out of it – fabric and buttons and wool. It will
be nice to see life back in the old place.'

'Well, I hope I can get it half as busy as it was before then.
Definitely call in. And bring your lovely wife with you if you
want?' Libby called as she walked out of the shop and back down
the street – grinning like a lunatic – happy with her day.

The grin – perhaps a little calmer – stayed on her face until
her phone rang just after four and a very apologetic, but young
and inexperienced-sounding, car hire assistant told her that there
would be a problem with her rental of a van to take to the vintage
market that Saturday and they were very sorry, but due to over-
booking, they would be unable to honour her booking.

'But I called on Monday? Paid a deposit. Surely you're able to
sort this out?'

'I'm very sorry, Ms Quinn,' the baby-voiced assistant said.
'I've been told to call you and say we're very sorry and we'll
offer you ten per cent off your next booking as a goodwill
gesture.'

'How about, as a goodwill gesture, you just have the van I
booked ready for me on Saturday morning? It's very important
that I have it. It's for work – and I need to be able transport furniture back with me – there's no way it will fit in my car. Not even
one piece of it. So, you see, the only goodwill I even want to
contemplate is you doing what I paid you to do.'

'I'm terribly sorry,' the baby-voiced assistant said. 'There
really is nothing we can do about it. We have tried to source

another van from one of our other depots, but it seems this weekend is booked out.'

Libby sighed and reminded herself to keep her cool. It wasn't the assistant's fault that the system had messed up. There was no point in losing her cool over the phone. 'Fine,' she said, sourly. 'Well, I suppose there's nothing that can be done.'

'We really are terribly sorry. If we can be of assistance to you at any time in the future, please do get in touch.'

Libby thought it highly unlikely she would ever look for assistance from that company again, but she stopped short of saying so, simply ending the call instead.

She was just about to launch into the mother of all swearing outbursts and possibly throw something, when she heard a female voice say: 'Is this a bad time? It's just I was finishing up and thought I'd call in for a nosy?'

Biting back the very bad f and b words that were itching to come out of her mouth, Libby squinted a little to make out that it was Jo standing in the door frame – a look of fear on her face, as if she knew she had just stumbled into a breakdown in the making.

'Erm, come in. Of course, come in,' Libby said.

'I've brought some flowers from Harry's shop. He said you might like them,' she said, handing over a plastic-wrapped bundle of red and yellow carnations which had probably seen better days. There was clearly something about Libby that made Harry feel compelled to foist his on-the-turn goods off on her. She had the good grace to smile at the gesture, though, and took the flowers, filling a drinking glass with water from the five-litre bottle she used to make tea and coffee and standing them up on the thickened glass top of the counter. At least it was a burst of colour about the place.

Jo was walking through the shell of the shop, oohing and aahing: 'You feel it, don't you?' she said, turning to smile at Libby.

'The history in the place? You feel the souls of the people who've been here before, not in a haunty way, just in a sense that this place could tell a hundred different stories.' She took her dark-rimmed, tres chic, glasses off and rubbed them on her T-shirt before putting them back on and looking back around. 'I have a thing for old buildings. For things that can be reinvented,' Jo said. 'Maybe because I like being reinvented myself. It's nice to think people and places can get a second chance, or a third chance, or whatever.'

Libby nodded, made the appropriate affirmative noises.

'Listen to me rambling,' Jo said and walked back to the counter. 'Noah is always telling me that the customers don't need my life story – but, sure, isn't that what it's all about? Talking to people? Having a laugh? No point in doing anything if you're not enjoying it?'

The way she looked at Libby made her feel as if she could see right into her thoughts and it unnerved her. The question over whether or not she should continue with Ant, when she wasn't enjoying it as much as before, was still in her thoughts.

'You must love this. I mean – who wouldn't. It must be a dream project.'

Libby nodded and smiled again. It was a dream project – she had no problem telling anyone who wanted to hear just how much of a dream project it was. 'I'm very lucky,' she said. 'I just hope it all works out. I need it to.' Libby fought the tears that were pricking at her eyes. This was stupid, being brought to tears over a stupid van and a stupid vintage market trip which was causing her nothing but trouble.

'It's stressful too, I imagine,' Jo said, as she looked pointedly at Libby. 'Is everything okay? I'm sensing maybe not?'

Libby sniffed, annoyed at herself for getting upset. 'I know it sounds trivial, but I'd a van hired to drive to the vintage market and auction on Saturday in Belfast and the company have double-booked. The auction only happens a couple of times a year, and they have some great pieces, but I think I'm going to have to let them go. I know that sounds like a stupid thing to get upset over, but I really want an authentic feel to the place.'

Libby thought of the conversations she'd had with Grandad Ernie about how old things still had value and could bring their story with them, and she was gone. A fat teardrop rolled down her dusty cheek and plopped unceremoniously on the counter.

'Oh, pet,' Jo said, as she whipped around the counter and pulled Libby into a tight hug. 'Do you know what my mum always says? There's no point in getting upset over something that can be fixed. And I happen to know exactly how to fix this.'

Libby watched with curiosity as Jo took her phone from her handbag and scrolled through her screen before tapping on a number and holding it to her ear.

'Noah, what are you doing on Saturday? Yes, I know it's a busy day – but we can hold the fort without you, the place won't burn down. I have something that you could do that would really help our new neighbour. You know, Bookshop Libby? She needs a van to take to a market or auction or something in Belfast and the hire company has let her down. I was thinking, sure, don't you have a big van you could drive for her? It would get you out of my hair for a bit too, and you've no need to worry about Paddy. I'll mind him. I'll even take him for a walk.'

Libby was caught somewhere between feeling hopeful at the thought of getting to the vintage market after all and feeling uncomfortable at imposing on Noah in this way. This was a big ask. For him to take the day off work, to drive her to Belfast. They barely knew each other and the thought of almost two hours in a car either way (longer, if the interminable roadworks were still in place) was awkward, to say the least. She imagined it would be quite rude to put her earphones in and listen to her latest Audiobook.

Libby tried to gesture to Jo that it didn't matter – but it seemed that the diminutive redhead, who believed in second chances for people and places, was not easily dissuaded when she thought she was doing someone a good deed.

She waved Libby away in a 'Don't worry, it's fine' manner before she turned her back and continued her conversation, in slightly more hushed tones. 'You can consider it your good deed for the week and I'll definitely owe you. Yes. If that's what you want. Yes. I know you always want one of those,' Jo whispered, laughing.

Oh God, Libby cringed, unable to escape the feeling that Jo was offering Noah all sorts of sexual favours if he would drive the poor sad sack of a neighbour to Belfast. She wanted the ground to open up and swallow her.

She tried to hide her embarrassment when, moments later, Jo ended the call and turned to her with a smile.

'All sorted. Your friendly local landlord will take you in his van. I used my powers of persuasion.' Jo laughed.

'Thank you,' Libby said. 'But, really, neither of you should go to any trouble. It's a busy day for you. I can't ask you to do that.'

'You're not asking,' Jo said, with the kind of quiet determination which made Libby think that she could perhaps be quite scary when she needed to be. 'We're offering. And we're happy to do so. It won't do Noah any harm at all to get out from behind that bar for a day. You're doing us a favour really. He never takes time off unless forced.'

When Libby climbed into bed that night and tried to shut her brain enough to sleep, she wondered what kind of mood a man who had been forced to take a day off and who had to be bribed (probably with sexual favours) to take her to Belfast would be in during their long journey.

She also wondered how she'd break it to Jess that she was as sure as she could be now that Noah and Jo were very much a couple.

12

ON THE ROAD

To his credit, Noah was not at all surly when he picked Libby up outside the shop on Saturday morning. He'd offered to drive round to her parents' house to pick her up – but she had declined, still feeling guilty enough that he'd had to be persuaded to do this trip in the first place. She didn't want to put him to any more trouble than strictly necessary.

She insisted on paying for a fill of diesel for the van, for any coffees or drinks they may need and for lunch, as well as buying breakfast before their 8 a.m. start – a couple of Ulster fries and a pot of slightly over-stewed tea from the local greasy spoon, which they ate in relative silence – both of them still a little bleary-eyed.

Noah declined Libby's offer to work a few hours in the pub to pay him back in some way, which, to be honest, she was glad of because her previous, very limited, experience behind a bar had not been successful. She still cringed when she thought of the disaster she'd made of pouring a pint of Guinness.

As they set off, Noah was the one to break the ice. 'I had a look at that catalogue online. There are some great pieces; I might get a wee something myself for the flat, you know.'

Libby nodded. 'Where is it you live?'

He glanced over, a little bemused. 'We live in the flat upstairs above the pub. Directly opposite you, as it happens. I can see right into your front windows from the living room.'

If Libby thought she'd hidden the look of mild horror on her face, she was wrong.

'You've no need to worry, Libby. I'm not a peeping Tom or anything. I hope you're not one either.'

Flustered, Libby started to protest her innocence until Noah burst out laughing.

'I'm only teasing you,' he said. 'Jo says my dodgy sense of humour will get me in trouble one of these days.'

'Jo's a nice girl,' Libby said.

'She's the best,' Noah said with a smile. 'She's my best friend, you know. I'm lucky to have her.'

A little pang of regret or sorrow hit Libby. Neither she nor Ant would ever say the other was their best friend.

She had taken a few days to think about their situation, just as Jess had urged her, but, if anything, it had only made it clearer in her mind that her relationship with Ant had run its natural course. The lack of a 'good luck' message, or even a 'how are you?' text from him that morning had solidified those feelings further.

To try and push down the emotions rising up in her, she just nodded and reached into her handbag to take out the bag of brandy balls boiled sweets (best before date unknown) which Harry had pressed into her hand that morning. She popped one in her mouth and offered one to Noah.

'Harry said we had to have sucky sweets for a long journey in the car,' she told Noah with a smile. 'He said it would stop the car sickness. He then gave me chapter and verse on which sweets had saved his car when his sons were younger and not at all great travellers. Brandy balls, barley sugar and Everton mints are the best ones apparently.'

Noah took a sweet and smiled. 'Barley sugars remind me of being sick as a child. My mum used to force them and Lucozade into us if we were ill, as if they had the same healing powers as an intravenous antibiotic drip.'

He popped his sweet in his mouth and Libby laughed. 'God, Lucozade was the cure-all, wasn't it? And you only ever got it when you were sick.'

Noah nodded. 'And now people drink it just for the craic!' He laughed and Libby laughed too.

'Harry's a character though, isn't he?' Libby said. She'd already grown fond of Harry and his harmless rants.

'He's the best,' Noah said. 'Part of the furniture. He's been a part of Ivy Lane for as long as I can remember.'

'You've been there long, then?'

'Not with the pub. I only took that over a few years ago. But, yeah, I grew up close by. My grandparents used to live on the Lane. They minded me after school, so I spent a lot of time there. I've a great fondness for the place. I suppose that's why I took the chance at the pub when I got it. Made me feel a little closer to them.'

Feeling a lump in her throat – one that had absolutely nothing to do with boiled sweets – Libby nodded. 'I know what you mean,' she said, when she could speak without fear of it coming out in a strangled sob – then she kept her eyes firmly on the passing fields and hedgerows. 'My grandad always dreamed of opening a bookshop one day, but he never had the confidence, or maybe the means, to do it. The shop is kind of my tribute to him. He gave me a great love for reading.'

'He sounds like a good man.'

'He is. Well, he was. He passed away two years ago,' she said, still focused on the fields they passed.

'I'm sorry,' Noah said quietly.

'Thanks,' she replied and they fell into what was, this time at least, a companionable silence. After a while, Noah reached over and put the radio on and both of them spent most of the remaining journey deep in thought about the people in their lives they had loved and lost.

* * *

Once they arrived at the vintage market, the mood in the car changed. Noah seemed to have switched into peak mansplaining mode, which, on another day, might have annoyed Libby. This time, however, she felt amused at how excited he got explaining the auction process to her, and showing her what the other sellers had on offer.

He delighted in telling her she should never offer the ticket price on an item, and that she should never, under any circumstances, look too interested, because the vendors would take full advantage of her vulnerability. 'You want to do this for as little money as possible,' he said, 'because whatever you think this project of yours is going to cost, you might as well add at least twenty per cent on as a contingency – one that will be eaten up quickly. There will be something you've not thought of, trust me. So keep your cool.'

Libby reminded herself he was trying to be helpful and not necessarily a condescending arse. She also reminded herself that her twenty per cent contingency had already been eaten in to and she'd take whatever advice she could get to stop it disappearing altogether.

She was impressed when he produced a notebook and pen

and eyed up what was available with the appearance of someone who knew exactly what he was doing and what he was looking at. He took notes and measurements and thoroughly inspected the pieces for any signs of wear and tear. He was exceptionally thorough.

He gave her a thumbs up when he spotted an ercol desk that had not been listed on the auction catalogue and which was going for an absolute steal. While normally a vintage ercol would sell for anywhere between four and six hundred pounds. This one was a bargainous three hundred and fifty pounds.

'I think you should take it,' he said. 'The auction price won't go as low as that.'

She could see other people starting to sniff around, so she nodded to Noah. 'Yes, I think I should take it too.'

'Do you want me to do the talking?' Noah asked, as they approached a rather elderly and aloof-looking gentleman, complete with neckerchief and tweed jacket. His nose hair was as bushy as the hair on his head.

'Have I lost the power of my own voice?' she answered, with a cheeky smile and a confidence in her ability to haggle that was very much not based on past experience. During a holiday to Morocco, she'd been the only one in her party to pay more than the seller in the souk was looking for.

'I'm not trying to offend you,' Noah said. 'It's just I know men like this,' he whispered. 'We'd all like to think the world isn't a sexist place and that women are treated as equals, but it's not true. Men like him – old-school – converse better with other men. I'm not saying I agree with it, but if you want what you want...' He left the question hanging there, and Libby chewed her lip and tried to weigh up whether to sacrifice both her sense of pride and her feminist principles for the sake of a perfect-condition ercol desk at a bargain price.

'Okay,' she said. 'Thank you.'

She watched as Noah was majestic in his negotiations. It seemed he could charm the birds from the trees, the knickers from a nun and an ercol desk from a sexist gentleman with a further ten per cent discount. She could have thrown her arms around him and kissed him. A thought which caught her by surprise.

'Get a grip,' she whispered to herself. This was just the result of an adrenaline surge. She didn't really want to kiss Noah. That was Jo's job. And Jess would kill her. And for all the good it did her, she still had a boyfriend. And, on top of all that, she absolutely and categorically did not fancy him. At all.

That she'd had the momentary lack of judgement to even consider it alarmed Libby so much she was determined that the next purchase would be entirely down to her and her alone. She suggested to Noah that they split for a while and meet again before the auction started.

He nodded and said he wanted to check out some records and music memorabilia that was on sale. Libby breathed out a sigh of relief as she watched him nonchalantly walk across the hall towards the smaller stands.

Libby stayed with the furniture and was drawn to an exceptionally stylish woman dressed in a pair of black capri pants and a red wrap-around blouse. Her glossy dark hair was styled in victory rolls, held back with a red scarf, and her make-up was very much the fifties bombshell look – winged eyeliner and red lipstick. With a pair of leopard-print pumps completing her look, this seller embodied vintage and Libby was sure she would share her dream of creating a vintage-inspired writing space in her shop. She also wanted to ask her how she got her eyeliner so perfect.

Having a look around the items on offer, Libby's heart quickened a little to see an upcycled desk. It had an air of *Mad Men* meets shabby chic about it that made her want it desperately for the shop. She immediately imagined an author, smiling, holding an award in their hand at a swish ceremony, recounting how they had written the most inspired passages of their magnum opus sat at a quaint desk in the creative environment of the bookshop on Ivy Lane.

'You like it?' a female voice said, shaking Libby from her daydream.

'I do. Very much. I love it.' Libby cringed a little. She had absolutely zero chill and she was already breaking one of Noah's rules – she was not supposed to come across as overly keen.

The seller smiled. 'I love it too. I'll be sorry to see it go, to be honest. It's a really splendid piece too – not just some old tat attacked with chalk paint. You're buying quality when you buy from me. Are you buying for yourself?' she asked, raising one perfectly shaped eyebrow.

'Well, yes and no. I'm buying for a shop I'm opening.'

'I don't do trade,' the woman bristled. 'I mean my pieces are priced for sale, not to be put in another shop and sold on. I'm not in a position to drop the price any.'

'Oh, I don't want to sell it,' Libby said. 'It's a bookshop I'm opening and I'm creating a few writing nooks so that authors can work there.'

'Oh, well that sounds exquisite,' the seller said, outstretching her hand. 'I'm Stella – let's see if we can find you what you need. Have you thought of lamps or lighting? I have some great pieces – could really set the scene. And chairs...'

Libby shook Stella's hand and introduced herself. She was delighted when Stella gestured for her to follow her to the back of the warehouse to see a number of 'unique pieces'.

'I don't put these out with the other things,' Stella said with a smile. 'They're only for special people. It's hard to get quality pieces, but I can sense you're the kind of person who likes quality. I mean you could get repro stuff fairly easily, but I find it's often not worth the money you spend on it. Buy cheap, buy twice, that's what I say. You want to make your shop the best it can be, I can tell that about you. Not afraid to pay for quality.'

Libby gave a half-hearted nod. Yes, she wasn't necessarily afraid to pay for quality – but she just didn't always have the money to pay for quality. She was starting to feel a little in over her head.

'Well, I do have a budget,' she said meekly.

Stella laughed, shooed the very notion away with a, 'Sure, we all have budgets. But, in my opinion, they are made to be broken for the right pieces. The worst thing you can do is see something you love, forsake it because of a few quid, and then live to regret it the rest of your days. Trust me, when you do that, every time you look at the space you hoped to fill, you'll feel that pang that you missed out on the one thing that could have made it just perfect.'

Libby felt a thin film of sweat break on her forehead. She was a people-pleaser – found it hard to say no to people anyway, never mind people who told her that she would regret saying no to them for the rest of her life.

'Ah, here – look,' Stella said, 'I knew I had these. Now, they've not been upcycled – just refurbed. A new coat of varnish, the leather refitted. But they are great pieces – comfortable.' She was standing in front of two swivel captain's chairs – exactly the kind Libby could imagine in the shop.

Libby reached out and touched them even though there was a little voice deep down that told her that no good could come of this. Genuine antique captain's chairs were not within her budget – no matter how much she desired them. In fact, when she spotted the price tag, they were absolutely so far outside the budget, they could only wave from far away – where the fresh varnishy smell could not be smelled nor the soft leather stroked.

'And I have these lamps as well,' Stella said, gesturing to a collection of desk lamps that almost made Libby weep at their beauty. Beaten copper, exposed bulbs – the kind of lamps that would look perfect with the exposed brickwork and deep green paint she had planned.

'And how much do they cost?' Libby asked, looking around to see if Noah was close by – ready to swoop in with his negotiating skills.

Stella moved her head around a little, pursed her lips, looked at the lamps, the chairs and no doubt considered the desk she also had her eye on.

'Best price?' she asked.

'If you could?' Libby asked, hoping that Stella would see a like-minded businesswoman in her and would offer her a deal she couldn't resist in the name of the business sisterhood.

'You would be cutting my profits to almost nothing,' she said, 'but I like the sound of what you're doing – love that you're into vintage. If you took the desk, two of the chairs, and say two lamps?'

'Three lamps,' Libby said.

'Well,' Stella smiled brightly, '£1,600 and it's all yours.'

Libby was pretty sure her face was so frozen in shock that there was a danger that it would stay that way forever. At least, she thought, she was smiling. It was in a slightly maniacal way, but it was a smile all the same.

'Is there any wiggle room?' Libby eventually asked, hoping for maybe somewhere between £600 and £800 worth of wiggle room.

'It really is my best price,' Stella said. 'And I do have interest in these pieces, so, you know, I would be doing myself out of a profit if I let you have them for any cheaper. I suppose you have to ask yourself if you want to miss out.'

'Oh, I don't want to miss out,' Libby said and was just opening her mouth to say that she didn't have much choice, when Stella jumped into the void of noise left by Libby's intake of breath.

'Great, brilliant. Let me go and get the invoice book. You'll be taking these with you today? Paying in cash? Great,' Stella said, leaving Libby standing, open-mouthed, on the verge of cardiac arrest and angry with herself that she had ever, ever doubted Noah and his negotiating skills.

'Libby! There you are!' Noah's voice boomed. 'I was looking for you. The auction's about to start.'

So now, not only had she got herself into a bit of a mess, she would have the pleasure of Noah witnessing the final, heart-breaking transaction, in which she would hand over twice the money she had been hoping to spend. She'd have to make savings elsewhere. She wondered, did she really need food, or heat for the new flat?

'Your girlfriend has been making some very astute purchases.' Stella smiled as she approached with her invoice book, and pen at the ready.

Libby opened her mouth to correct her about the nature of her relationship with Noah, but before she could so much as inhale, Noah had his arm around her shoulders and was kissing the top of her head. 'Have you, honey? The thing is, I was just talking to Keith – over there by the door – and he has some old shelving units, you know the exact kind we were looking for, that he's willing to give us for a steal. He just agreed to hold them until I came over to see how the budget was holding out.'

'Erm... well, the thing is... honey, Stella has some great pieces – pricey, you know, but good.' She looked up at him, eyes pleading, hoping he would understand that she did indeed need his help.

'I'll show you,' Stella said. 'I'm sure you will agree your girlfriend has amazing taste.'

'Oh, I already know she has amazing taste,' Noah said, pulling Libby closer, squeezing her tightly towards him. 'Sure, she chose me.'

Libby played along, even if internally she was cringing.

Noah released his grip and followed Stella to look at the desk, chairs and lamps.

'All genuine,' Stella said. 'I know your girlfriend doesn't mind going the extra mile for quality.'

'Well,' Noah said, a perfectly pleasant smile on his face, 'it does kind of depend on just how much of an extra mile it is. You know, we can all get carried away sometimes. Especially with pieces as beautiful as these. They really are exquisite.'

Stella beamed.

'So, how much are we talking?' Noah said, smile still fixed.

'£1,600 is my absolute best price,' Stella said, and if Libby wasn't mistaken, there was a slight wobble to her voice.

Noah sucked in a breath through his teeth and crossed his arms while looking the pieces up and down. 'Seems a bit steep,' he said.

'Not overpriced for pieces of this quality. I mean, they are sturdy, authentic – not to mention they've been treated and upcycled. They are good to go for years to come – it would be hard to buy better,' Stella replied, her voice a little brittle now.

Libby was torn between admiring Noah for haggling and feeling fear well up in her that she was about to lose these pieces altogether.

'I'm not denying their quality – but, you know, I've done my research and I've seen similar pieces priced more competitively. I'm not looking to rip you off – you know, just pay a fair price.'

Stella looked uncomfortable. Libby stood, her face blazing.

'I think it's a fair price,' Stella said, crossing her arms. The two were facing each other in a vintage furniture stand-off. Libby could not take her eyes off them.

'I'd say half of that would still be a fair price,' Noah replied, still smiling but jaw set.

'There is no way I'd be able to accept anywhere near that,' Stella hissed, her smile now as false as the eyelashes she was wearing. Libby waited for her to tell Noah she had already offered her very best price and that he and she could take it or leave it – in which case she hoped Noah would accept the price and perhaps help her to make savings elsewhere by employing his best negotiation skills with the other vendors.

Noah remained silent.

Stella cracked. 'Look, £1,300. And you are robbing me. But I like your girlfriend.'

'So do I,' Noah grinned. 'But I was thinking more £1,000.'

'£1,200, they're yours.'

'£1,100?' Noah asked.

'£1,150 and it's a deal.'

'It's a deal then!' Noah said and Libby felt her heart flip-flop – and flip-flop all the more when Noah spun her round to him and planted the quickest of kisses square on her lips. 'We did it, honey,' he said with a wink – leaving Libby speechless and, to her surprise, a little breathless too.

When they walked away five minutes later – deal done and plans made to pick up the pieces when they were finished with their shopping – Libby felt her head spin. Was it the fear at almost having massively overspent? Was it the joy at getting the deal done? Was it the way her breath had caught when Noah's lips had brushed against hers? She feared it was the latter – especially as she felt acutely aware of her lips after. It was like they were bruised – even from that most fleeting of touches. She felt as if they were bee-stung, pouting, and had to fight the urge to gently prod at them with her fingertips just to make sure they weren't swollen.

Was it that he was that good a kisser that even something that was little more than a peck could make her weak at the knees? Or was it, she wondered, more like she was having an allergic reaction to him? That would also explain the knee weakness, the slight breathlessness and the feeling that her lips were forming into a permanent pout.

And, oh God, what about Jo? Jo, who had gone above and beyond to help her out. And Ant, who didn't yet know that they were breaking up. She knew the kiss meant nothing. Not really. Certainly not to Noah, but still, she felt wretched all the same.

Noah held her hand as they walked away, but as soon as they were a safe distance from Stella, Libby pulled her hand away and shoved it into her jeans pocket so he wouldn't be able to grab hold of it again.

'That was fun,' he laughed, 'but I did tell you to be careful. These people know a newbie when they see one. They'll bump the price up quick as anything.'

'I thought it was a fair price,' Libby lied. 'I'd done some research and it wasn't that far off the mark on prices I saw similar pieces going for.' She knew her lie was see-through, but she couldn't stop herself. She wanted to distance herself from him and the confusing feelings that had swamped her with that stupid pretend kiss.

Noah stopped and looked at her, raised his eyebrow, and smiled. A slow, shy smile. He was quite handsome, she realised.

Not perfect. Not groomed like Ant. A little rough around the edges. Hair just a fraction too long, but he wore it well. Dark, with the slightest wave to it. Tanned and toned arms. A plain white T-shirt, jeans and Vans. Cool but not trying too hard. His face had that slightly weather-beaten look to it. She wanted to know more about him, she realised, then pushed the thought away. This was absolutely not the time to be having any kind of lustful thoughts about her neighbour. No good would, or could, come of it. Ever.

'Really, Libby?' Noah asked and she could see that he saw right through her and suddenly it made her very nervous. Nervous enough to clam up and shut down whatever madness had overcome her.

'The shelving units,' she said, not breaking his gaze. 'Tell me about those.'

'Oh, that's the icing on the cake. Keith, who I'll introduce you to, has just closed his bookshop in Bangor. He has a job lot of shelves – that he just wants sold. He has a couple of interested parties, but, as it happens, I was able to talk him into offloading them to this bookseller I know – if she wants them, of course. And all for a knock-down price, some dinner and drinks in the pub next time he's in Derry and a book token or two.'

'When you say "knock-down price"?' Libby asked.

'Two hundred pounds. And when you see them, you'll snap the hand off him.' Noah looked so incredibly proud of himself, and so he should be. He had just saved Libby a small fortune.

She kept her hands in her pockets this time though. No hugs, or pretend kisses or over exuberance. She simply said. 'Let's go and look at them, then.'

She could hardly believe her luck when she saw them. A set of four oak shelving units, which she already knew would look amazing along the back wall of the shop. They would fit in well with the rest of her design scheme and there's no doubt she would be saving a fortune. It seemed almost criminal to offer the asking price.

'Your pal there was telling me your story,' Keith said. 'About your grandfather and this shop being a part of his dream. I can't think of a better home for these shelves in that case,' he said. 'We were heartbroken to have to close our bookshop. This will make it feel a little more bearable.'

It was Keith who Libby hugged, and when she escaped to the loo shortly after, and just before the auction started, she allowed herself a few moments to sob into a hankie. And this time it wasn't just for Grandad Ernie, it was at the confusion she felt welling up inside her.

Libby was grateful for the radio in the van on the drive home. It allowed her the chance to sit back and distract herself from whatever was going on in her head.

She tried to focus on what was real and solid about the day that had passed. The furniture and lamps secured in the back of the van that she would take to the disused garage at the back of her parents' garden for storage until the shop was ready for them. The shelves that Keith would arrange to be delivered in about ten days – giving her the chance to get the majority of the heavy work done in the shop.

She thought of the third desk – a second ercol, which she had won at auction, and she indulged in one of her favourite hobbies: imagining how the shop would look when it was all up and running. She closed her eyes, tried to picture it as a busy, cosy escape from the real world. The low hum of the radio commentator, combined with the vibration of the van driving along lulled her into a doze, from which she was rudely awakened by a gentle jab to the ribs.

'Wakey wakey, time to stop snoring and drooling and tell me exactly where your parents' house is?' Noah asked.

'Larkhill,' she mumbled, dragging her arm across her mouth before declaring she didn't drool or snore, to which, of course, Noah laughed.

'You even did the biggest snort when I nudged you there. How you didn't wake yourself up, I'll never know.'

She blushed, the thought of snoring in front of anyone, let along Noah, making her feel embarrassed. 'I was tired,' she said. 'And snuffly. Probably all the dust from the warehouse. Or a cold or something.'

Noah just laughed. Libby sniffed. She did feel a little congested. She hoped it was just a reaction to dust and not the sign of an oncoming cold. She simply did not have the time to get sick. She had the tech people scheduled to come on Monday to discuss her requirements – phone line, internet, WIFI, stock management and till.

Not to mention she had to finally settle on a name for the shop and start working on her promotional material, and get the signage in place for the shop.

She felt her head thump a little, so she rubbed her temples.

'I'm only teasing you, you know,' Noah said. 'You only snored a little bit. I barely noticed. I mean, compared to Paddy, you were practically silent.'

'Paddy snores?'

Noah laughed. 'Oh God, yes. I never realised that dogs snored before he came to live with me. I've been known to resort to earplugs.'

Libby couldn't help but laugh too. 'Does he not sleep in a different room?'

'Oh no. Poor thing was abandoned, you know, before he was rescued. He doesn't do well being on his own. That's why he's down in the pub so much. The rumour that he only comes down to sniff out a sneaky bowl of Irish stew is just that. He needs the company.'

The thought of Paddy being abandoned made Libby feel sad. So sad in fact that she wondered if she would cry. What the hell was wrong with her? Mood swings and tearfulness and a sore head. Maybe she was due her period. She tried to count back in her head. No. She wasn't due, not yet anyway. Not for another few days. But PMS could be a bitch all the same.

'Poor Paddy,' she croaked.

'Poor Paddy nothing,' Noah laughed. 'He's the most spoiled dog in Derry! Everyone fusses over him. He's fed well, gets his walks every day – round St. Columb's Park or over the Peace Bridge and back – he sleeps on top of a king-size bed. He does okay. He deserves it all, of course.'

Libby wondered if she could detect a small crack of emotion in Noah's voice. It endeared him to her in any case, but she immediately stiffened, thinking she could not, and would not, let him under her skin. There was no point. And she was just premenstrual and emotional and, chances were, when her hormones aligned again, she would go back to seeing him just as her nosy, occasionally helpful and sometimes supremely patronising, neighbour.

When the furniture was unloaded and Libby's father had oohed and aahed over her choices, while Noah had bigged her up as a very canny businesswoman, she travelled with him back to the pub, where she had left her car that morning. As Jo had promised him, he was home by five – in time for the early-evening crowd, with a quick bite before their night began.

Libby had the good grace to thank Noah – and to realise what an asset he had been to her. 'I really appreciate your help,' she said, as she climbed out of the passenger seat and glanced over at the shop – which already looked a little less forlorn. 'I owe you.'

'You do not,' Noah said. 'Sure, didn't you buy the breakfast? And those overpriced sandwiches at the market? An extra three quid before something is made from sourdough and they put the word "rustic" in front of it. You paid for the diesel and I got some great vintage vinyl, so let's just call it even?'

She nodded. 'Okay, if you say so.'

'I say so,' Noah said, just as the door to The Ivy Inn opened and Paddy lolloped out to greet him, jumping up and showering him in sloppy dog kisses.

Jo wasn't far behind. 'You're back!' she said, smiling broadly.

'We are indeed,' Noah said. 'And wait 'til you see what I got for an absolute bargain. An original Undertones LP, signed by Feargal Sharkey himself.'

Jo's eyes widened. 'Ah brilliant. Will we have a listen after work? Been a while since we pogoed around the place to "Teenage Kicks".'

'It's a date,' Noah said, and Libby started to feel very much surplus to requirements.

'Guys, I'll leave you to it. Thanks again, Noah, and thanks, Jo, for loaning him to me. Have a great evening!'

'Do you have to run off now?' Jo asked. 'Why don't you come in and grab a drink? I'll introduce you to some of the regulars if you like?'

'I'm driving, so no drink for me,' Libby said. 'Not until that flat is ready to be lived in – which is very much not the case at the moment. It makes the shop look like a palace in comparison.'

'You could drop your car home – jump in a taxi. We have a good band on tonight. I'm clocking off soon, so I could even keep you company,' Jo said.

The invitation sounded so very appealing, but no, she would refuse. She needed to try and sort her head out. She needed to see Ant and make a decision about their future once and for all. She needed to talk to him about how she felt.

'Nice as that sounds, I have plans.'

'Washing your hair?' Noah asked.

'Very funny,' she teased. 'I'm going to see my boyfriend.'

There was a momentary pause – before Noah spoke again. 'Ah, a boyfriend? Was he not available for vintage furniture shopping?'

Her cheeks grew warm again. 'Erm, no. He was working and couldn't get the time off.'

Noah glanced briefly in the direction of the pub. The pub he should have been working in himself that day. Libby was crimson at that stage.

Jo was next to speak. 'Why not bring him in tonight then? If you're seeing him, he'll become a part of the Lane as well?'

Libby didn't want to try and explain to Jo that she had plans to have a discussion of a more serious nature and the backdrop of the local pub, with live music blasting around them, wouldn't be the right environment.

'I'll ask him,' she lied. 'We might see you both then. Thanks for asking. And thanks again, Noah. For your help.'

'Don't mention it,' he said, before the door to the pub opened and one of their regulars walked out, calling his name. Noah smiled at Libby, turned and cheerily greeted his slightly-worse-for-wear customer with a friendly pat on the shoulder before guiding him back inside, saying he would order him a taxi and get him a strong coffee. Jo followed, chatting to Paddy as he wagged his tail in contentment.

Libby watched as they walked back inside – and probably looked at them both for a bit too long before she shook herself from her reverie and headed to her car. She had messaged Ant to say she would be over between six and seven, so she'd have to hurry if she wanted to get home, showered and changed. She looked down at her chipped nail varnish, the result of heavy lifting and heavy cleaning, and she knew she should touch it up as well.

Normally she would enjoy a bit of pre-Ant pampering, but she no longer felt the same pull towards him. Maybe it was simply because she dreaded what was to come. Given a choice, she'd have much rather just headed over to Jess's flat with a bottle of Prosecco.

Yet another wave of guilt washed over her. She'd really neglected her friend. She could see that now. She'd broken the girl code and put Ant and his needs and wants – not to mention her own desires – above spending time with her best friend.

She sighed. There was no point, she realised, in scratching that particular sore. Jess was at a conference. She had to talk to Ant. She had to 'woman up' and just get on with things.

Or she could just pack away her doubts like the big coward she was and let herself fall into her usual Saturday night behaviour with Ant. Wine, good food, and good sex. She could be a proper adult later.

She pointed the car towards home and drove off, leaving Noah, and her myriad confused feelings, on Ivy Lane for the night. Her head thumped a little more.

Libby arrived at Ant's seafront house shortly before seven, just as she said she would. She had showered and changed, slipping into something a little more flowy and feminine – a strappy maxi dress, flip-flops and a soft white cardigan to keep the evening chill from her shoulders. Her hair was wavy, hanging around her shoulders – pulled back from her face only with her sunglasses. She had put on only the most minimal of make-up – making the most of her face being sun-kissed and freckled.

Her time at home had allowed her to calm down – to deflate a little and gain some perspective on what had happened. The kiss meant nothing, she told herself. Even if it felt different at the time. It was the surprise of it that threw her, not anything else. She was playing a role. As was Noah. She was, for now, with Ant, and Noah was with Jo, and that was simply how it was.

The roads had been busy on the drive to Ant's – with day-trippers making their way home, sand-covered and a little sunburned perhaps. Others were just heading to the beach – ready for an evening stroll, hand in hand with their loved ones, or letting a beloved pet run ahead of them while they got their own sense of calm from the to and fro of the waves. It was Libby's favourite time of day – when the air was warm, the sun bright, the day starting to reach its lazy best. Chill-out time. Happy hour. Bury your head in the sand and a bottle of wine o'clock.

When she pulled into the gravel driveway, she was more than a little confused to see Jess's distinctive yellow Mini Cooper parked in her usual spot and the bi-fold doors already wide open, the sound of music and laughter drifting out into the garden.

Parking her Corsa behind Jess's Mini, Libby got out of her car and walked towards the laughter, as she tried to make sense of why Jess, of all people, would be here.

Jess, who was supposed to be halfway up the country at a mental health conference. Jess who didn't really seem to like spending time with Ant in the first place.

Libby had even sent her a WhatsApp message earlier, telling her she missed her and had been thinking about their last conversation. A message that remained unread, which Libby had assumed meant her friend was still busy at the conference and not able to check her phone.

Popping her head in through the French doors to the large open-plan living place, she saw Jess, head thrown back in laughter, sitting on a stool at Ant's kitchen island, while he chopped vegetables and held her rapt with one of his many stories. The tableau before her eyes was very much like an advertisement for an interiors magazine – the perfect couple, sitting in the perfect kitchen – large wine glasses in front of them, preparing dinner together, laughing – looking stunning. The sun caught the highlights of Jess's hair just perfectly as it sat in loose waves, giving her, in her white summer dress with her bronzed legs and arms, the appearance of a Grecian goddess.

Ant stood, barefoot, in baggy cargo pants, his shirt unbuttoned at the top so that a tuft of chest hair was just about visible.

His sleeves were rolled up, exposing his tanned arms. If Libby wasn't mistaken, his hair was damp – as if he wasn't long out of the shower. They looked so comfortable in each other's company that Libby almost felt as though she was intruding. Where she would normally just have walked straight in, called out for Ant and gone to the fridge to pour herself a glass of wine, she stood at the door and tried a subtle cough – which, given the sound of the music, the laughter and the chat, went unnoticed.

She knocked on the glass of the door, offered a slightly louder 'Hello?' and tried to make her voice sound as normal as possible.

'Baby!' Ant called, his voice bright – happy – a little tipsy perhaps.

'Ant... Jess,' Libby replied and, if she wasn't mistaken, Jess shifted a little uncomfortably in her seat before giving her a smile, saying hello.

'This is a bit of a surprise,' Libby said, walking to where Ant was standing with his arms outstretched to pull her into a gentle hug and kiss the top of her head.

'That I'm cooking dinner?' He laughed. 'Sure, I always cook dinner. We all know better than to let you loose in the kitchen.'

Jess laughed too. And while that was true and Libby would never, ever be gifted in the culinary stakes and certainly had nowhere near the love for cooking or the talent that both Ant and Jess possessed, she still felt a little pulled by their laughter.

'I meant it's a surprise to find Jess here,' she said, her voice not betraying her uneasiness.

'Jess is always welcome here,' Ant said. 'You know that. I've always known your best friend came as part of the overall Libby Quinn package.'

'I think, maybe, she means because I was supposed to be at a conference today,' Jess offered, and Libby noticed she at least had the good grace to blush about it.

'Well, yes... that. And other things, but mostly that,' Libby said.

'It was cancelled, yesterday. Last minute, you know. The key speaker has some sort of gastro bug. I knew you'd already made plans, so I didn't see the point in disrupting them at that stage. So I found myself at a loose end and decided to take a drive down to the beach – for a walk on the sand. I was just heading back to the car when I bumped into Ant. He invited me over for a cup of tea, and, well, we've just been chatting.'

'And making dinner?'

'We didn't realise how much time had passed, and then I realised you'd be here soon, so I thought I'd just invite Jess to stay for dinner. She had no other plans, so we threw caution to the wind and opened a bottle of wine,' Ant said. 'You don't mind, do you?'

'Of course I don't mind,' Libby said, but that wasn't exactly the case. The truth was, that while it was nice to know that Jess could turn to someone as she was feeling a little lonely, it felt a little strange that she had turned to Ant. Especially after the conversation they'd had earlier in the week. Jess knew the state of play of their relationship. 'It's just a bit unexpected,' Libby added. 'But it's a nice surprise.'

'It is, isn't it?' Ant said. 'Now, do you want to pour yourself a glass of wine before Jess and I empty this bottle? You snooze, you lose!'

Libby took a glass from the cupboard and poured a large measure and drank the first few mouthfuls a little too fast. A medicinal measure. Entirely allowed.

'How did the market go?' Jess asked. 'Did you get the stuff you wanted?'

'I did!' Libby replied, delighted to be able to talk about her purchases. 'And a few extras too. They had some amazing stuff there – really great pieces. I could have spent a fortune.' She decided not to tell them that she almost did spend a fortune.

'I don't get the vintage thing,' Ant said as he sipped from his wine. 'I mean, I get it has a certain appeal – but to me there's something a bit, well, musty and mouldy about it all. Don't you think?'

'Well, no,' Libby said. 'And in many cases, it's a much more superior quality than you would get now.'

'Not if you go to the right places,' Ant said. 'I mean, personally I think it's hard to beat smooth clean lines in a workplace. Something sleek – minimalist even. Lots of natural light and light tones for it to bounce off. It makes me feel lighter in myself – to be in that environment.'

Libby couldn't help but feel that with every new word Ant spoke, the crack that existed between them grew bigger and bigger until it became a chasm. Or maybe the blinkers had just started to come off.

She had told him many times how she loved the feel and look of a traditional bookshop, that the industry had lost that little bit of something as technology had moved on. She wanted the shop to feel like a treasure trove, an escape from the bright lights and big noises of the increasingly hectic world. She wanted to bring just a hint of that back – with modern technology to back it up, of course – and here he was describing vintage as 'musty and mouldy'.

'I think we'll have to agree to disagree,' she said, taking another long drink of her wine.

Ant looked at her closely, held her gaze for a moment perhaps longer than necessary, before he said, 'Yes, I suppose we will.'

Libby was aware that Jess had once again shifted uncomfortably in her seat. 'I think I'll just go and use the bathroom,' her friend said, as she slipped off her stool and straightened her dress.

Libby wondered, in the course of Jess and Ant's bonding afternoon, had her friend told Ant that she had been having doubts? Surely not. That would break all the rules and she had always known she could confide anything in Jess and it would go no further.

But there was something off with Ant – and she would hardly be able to get into a serious conversation with him about it now.

They stood in an uncomfortable silence for a bit before Ant spoke.

'Who did you go with anyway? To the market? You didn't say?'

'Noah. The landlord from the pub. He had a van and Jo offered his services,' Libby told him. It wasn't that she had been keeping the identity of her companion secret, she just genuinely didn't think it would be of any consequence to Ant who went with her.

'And who's Jo? A man or a woman?' Ant asked.

'Jo is a woman, not that I think it matters. I've told you about her. The barmaid who helped me out when I got locked out of the shop.'

'We're pretty sure Noah and Jo are an item,' Jess interjected.

He shrugged as if all this was news to him.

They fell into the same uncomfortable silence.

'Did you get much work done today?' Libby asked him. She wanted to know a little more about how he'd managed to bump into Jess. It wasn't like Ant to go for a stroll along the beach. He took what he had on his doorstep for granted, as so many people did.

'I got through lots this morning. Then lunchtime came, and the weather was nice. My head was turned, looking at figures all morning, so I decided to stretch my legs – and that's when I met

Jess. She seemed a little out of sorts, so I invited her in for a cuppa and we just got talking. She's good company, you know.'

'Cheers,' Jess laughed. 'That's nice to know.'

'Yeah, I've worked that one out myself over the years,' Libby said, ignoring Jess's light tone and not even trying to hide the sarcasm in her voice.

'Of course you have,' Ant replied, as if he hadn't even registered her tone. He thrust a wooden spoon, ladled with some sort of tomato-based sauce, under her nose. 'Taste this,' he said, and she did as she was told. 'It's good, isn't it?' he asked and she nodded.

'Jess has a secret recipe,' he explained. 'Well, it was a secret, but she shared it with me.'

He looked so completely delighted with himself, and so much more animated than he had appeared in months that Libby couldn't help but feel a pang of regret.

He was a good man. She wished she'd been able to make him happy. And she very much wished he had been able to do the same for her. But, the truth was, he hadn't.

He smiled and pulled her to him, kissing her on the lips. But there was no tingle. No bee-stung feeling. No anything. Sometimes a kiss really is just a kiss, she thought.

15

THE BOY IN THE STRIPED PYJAMAS

'Why don't you stay over, Jess?' Ant asked, as bottle number three of wine was tipped upside down in the ice bucket.

'I'll get a taxi home, don't be silly. Give you some space,' she said, placing her wine glass on the floor. 'In fact, I've probably taken up enough of your time and your hospitality.' She uncurled her legs from under her and stretched as she sat up.

'Don't be so silly,' Ant said. 'It's been lovely to have your company. You can have the spare room – and it's actually a nice spare room – not just somewhere I've thrown all the junk that I have nowhere else to put. It even has clean sheets on the bed. Go on, stay – there's no point in getting a taxi and going to that expense when you'll just have to come out in the morning to get your car back.'

Libby noticed Jess look at her. As if she needed her approval to say yes. Libby just shrugged her shoulders. It was unlikely she and Ant would have any kind of a discussion now anyway, and it was late.

'I don't know...' Jess said.

Libby had been just about to jump in with a quick 'honestly, I don't mind' when Ant cut her off at the pass.

'Please, Jess. You'd be doing me a favour really. There's only so much talk of bookshops a man can take.'

He laughed, a deep throaty laugh, and Libby watched as Jess smiled. She didn't smile herself. She felt wounded.

'Okay then. You don't mind, do you, Libby?' her friend asked.

'Of course not,' Libby lied. 'If you two have each other for company, I can sneak off to bed. I'm absolutely exhausted anyway.'

She hoped she kept the hurt from her voice. She hoped nothing about her demeanour belied the fact that Ant's words had cut to the bone.

On another day, she may have laughed it off.

On another day, she may have jabbed him playfully with her elbow and teased him about how much he talked about investment banking (mega yawn!).

On another day, she may have seen his words as just playful banter, but the truth was, she didn't see it that way. She saw it as someone who was supposed to care about her using one of the most important things in her life to make her feel bad.

And that hurt.

She stretched and stood up.

'You don't mind, do you?' she asked Ant, even though she knew by the way he was already reaching for more wine that he absolutely didn't mind. Not even one bit.

'Not at all. You get a good rest, Libby. You're at danger of working yourself to the bone.'

She nodded, not trusting herself to say any more, and left her best friend and her boyfriend to their evening.

As she walked up the stairs, she listened to the hum of conversation between Ant and Jess, who had moved on to talking about world politics. For the briefest of seconds, her mind wandered to what Noah might be doing at that moment – working hard, stealing a kiss with Jo perhaps. Getting ready to dance around the living room.

Her head hurt some more, but not as much as her heart.

She climbed the stairs, walked into Ant's room and changed into one of his T-shirts before brushing her teeth and laying down on the bed, where she looked out again into the inky night and allowed the sound of the waves to lull her to sleep.

She slept, deeply, through the night – not even waking to get a glass of water to quench her wine-induced thirst. When she woke, the house was quiet and all she could hear, bar the waves, was the quiet rumble of Ant's breathing as he lay beside her. She turned to face him – to watch him sleep. She wanted to look at his face. Drink in his features. Remember the fun they'd had. Because it had been its own kind of fun.

She reached over to stroke his stubbly face and slipped her hand under the sheets to feel the beating of his heart. When she discovered he wasn't bare-chested, as he normally was when they slept together, but was instead wearing a pair of pyjamas, she pulled back. Everything had changed already, it seemed.

She looked at the time on her phone and saw that it was after nine. She wanted to get to the shop as soon as she could, see properly what work had been done in her absence yesterday. That would be her focus. That would be her dream. She wasn't going to let herself get distracted by matters of the heart again. Not by Ant and not by anyone else either.

She dressed quickly and quietly and crept out of the room into the silent house. Jess, it seemed, was still asleep.

Downstairs, the detritus of the night before – now including scattered CDs and some whisky glasses – lay around the floor. Jess's sandals were kicked off beside the chair where she had been sitting. It was a nice scene. The sign that a good night had been had and that Jess and Ant had finally bonded. It was quite possible it was at her expense, but she would just have to deal with that.

She found an old envelope and scribbled a quick note to both Ant and Jess, saying she hoped they didn't feel too bleary-eyed and that she'd gone to work. She'd catch up with them later, she wrote before she lifted her bag and her keys and stepped out into the warm morning air.

June was making itself known with an early-summer heat-wave and Libby enjoyed the feeling of the rays on her face as she walked to her car.

Having arrived at the shop, she realised this place made her feel like nothing else mattered. It felt like home. Each and every time she walked in the door. Even though she could taste the dust as soon as she opened the door. Even though it smelled of wood, and plaster and dust. Even though the floor had all but been ripped up in preparation for tiling. Even though she hadn't been brave enough to look upstairs to see what, if any, progress had been made on her flat.

As Libby stood, in the quiet of a Sunday morning in the shell of her shop, she thought of Grandad Ernie and how he would read to her. Were there any words as comforting as 'Once upon a time', that feeling that new adventure was waiting and you couldn't dare guess what would happen next?

And just like that the bookshop name that had been alluding her all this time popped into her head and immediately felt perfect.

'I'll make you proud of me, Grandad,' she said to the cavernous space. 'I'll make this the place you dreamed of. The place where you could have written that book of children's stories you always wanted to.' She felt tears prick in her eyes – she tried to head them off at the pass. She resolved that they were happy tears and that the only thing that mattered now was avoiding any further distractions and keeping the project on the move. She had eight weeks left until the planned opening, and still so very much to do.

Libby allowed herself a little cry, dabbed at her eyes and decided to treat herself to a coffee to bring herself round a bit. As she walked up the street towards Harry's shop, she found herself hoping he would be working. There was something about Harry that had won her over. Perhaps it was because he reminded her of her grandad, with his broad smile and sense of humour. She also realised she'd come to look forward to finding out what issue would be the subject of his rants each day.

Harry was old-school and, it seemed, indefatigable. He seemed to run his shop single-handedly. There was talk of an assistant who worked part-time, but Libby had yet to meet them. Libby got the feeling that Harry's life revolved around his work and that if he retired he would find himself at a total loss at not being able to see all the comings and goings on Ivy Lane each day.

She was smiling by the time she reached the shop and found herself cheerily wishing Harry a very good morning as he launched into a rant about the number of supplements and advertising brochures included with the Sunday papers.

'Lifting these will give me a hernia,' he said. 'And most of it's nonsense that goes right in the recycling bin. There's few people from round here interested in property pages which only feature ridiculously priced houses in London. A million quid for a two-bed flat? Sure, they call it an apartment to make it sound posh, but a flat is a flat. Imagine what that kind of money could get you here? A palace, that's what!'

He wasn't wrong. Property prices in Northern Ireland were

incredible, far removed from the stratospheric prices in big cities. She wasn't sure she'd ever seen a listing come in at over a million pounds here, and even the most extravagant of homes would generally still get you change from half a million.

'I'll stick with my wee shop and my flat.' Libby laughed, emphasising the word 'flat' and Harry laughed.

He laughed loudly and Libby laughed along too.

'You do right, and, sure, why would you not be happy? This is a great street and a great community.'

'Do you live on the street yourself?'

Harry laughed. 'Not quite. Two streets over mind. My Mary said if we lived on Ivy Lane, I might as well set a bed up in the shop and sleep here and she'd never see me at all.'

Libby laughed, mostly because she knew that Harry's Mary probably wasn't far wrong. 'You do love your work, don't you? Would you never think of retiring? Or slowing down even?'

Harry shook his head. 'Sure, why would I do that when I'm fit and able to stand behind this counter? And I get to see my friends and neighbours, day in and day out, and hear all the gossip too. I couldn't stand having nothing to do with myself.'

'Ah, but you have to look after yourself too, Harry. None of us are getting any younger!' Libby took care not to imply it was simply that Harry was getting on in years.

'You're only as young as you feel,' Harry said. 'Anyway, Libby, you're one to talk. You've been in every day since you started work on that place. You'll end up exhausted yourself! All work and no play, you know?'

'Harry, it doesn't feel like work half the time,' Libby replied softly. 'And I really do want to open on schedule. Get at least a little of the summer tourist trade if I can.'

He nodded. 'Well, I wish you well. Between you and Noah

Simpson up in the pub, you'll have this street attracting more and more people. It'll be good for us all.'

Libby made her coffee and stood at the counter, for once not eager to get back down to the shop. 'Have you been running this place long, Harry?'

'A lifetime and then some,' Harry said. 'Since 1967, when I wasn't all that long married and we had our two boys both still in nappies. There were none of them disposable ones either – not in our day. Towelling nappies all the way. Mary used to love the sight of them all hanging, bright white on the line. She would help me out in the shop here sometimes – but her hands were full with those boys of ours. Rascals they were.' Harry chuckled. 'But, yes, a lifetime – and I'll be happy to keep going until they carry me out in a box!'

'Well, hopefully not for a long time yet,' Libby said, glancing at the clock on the wall, which told her she really should be getting back to the shop. She wanted to decide once and for all how many power outlets she would need. She might even venture up to the flat, just to see how bad it looked.

'That's my plan,' Harry said, cutting into her thoughts.

The bell over the door rang and another customer walked in. This was the perfect time for Libby to make her excuses and leave.

She said her goodbyes, only to be greeted by one of Harry's offers that simply could not be refused.

'Here, before you go – how do you feel about crisps?'

Libby couldn't say she had strong feelings either way, if the truth be told.

'It's just I've a few bags here just about out of date,' Harry continued. 'Well, maybe, thinking about it, they are actually out of date... but not by much. Why don't you take a few bags down to that shop of yours? Feed those big workmen walking in and out every day? Keep them sweet and they'll do an extra good job for you,' he said, tapping the side of his nose as if he was imparting the wisdom of the world to her.

'Thanks, Harry,' she said, smiling as he handed her several multipacks. 'Have a good day now.'

'You too, Bookshop Libby,' he said with his trademark dazzling smile.

Back at the shop, she set to work, planning her comms needs to the final detail. Then she climbed the stairs to the flat, threw open the windows, switched on her digital radio to Magic FM for optimum sing-a-long ability and set to work there. She filled a basin from the temporary tap Billy, the plumber, had fitted with sugar soap and water, put on her rubber gloves and set about scrubbing down the few walls that had not needed stripping back and re-skimming. She was able to lose herself in the repetitive action – get a thrill as she saw the layers of grime lift and a relatively clean surface emerge (one that would still need a healthy dose of a nice neutral colour).

She worked until her arms ached and she was covered in a not-so-fine layer of sweat. She wiped her brow with the back of her arm and decided she might just treat herself to a packet of Harry's dodgy crisps when she heard a knock on her door – followed by the shout of 'Hello! Libby, are you in there?' from a female voice.

Pulling off her rubber gloves and pushing her hair back from her now sweaty face, she clambered down the stairs and opened the door to find Jo standing, beaming face, make-up still perfectly done, with a covered plate in her hands.

'We thought you might be hungry – so I've brought you some lunch. Just a bit of everything from the carvery.'

The smell was mouth-watering – and Libby's tummy groaned

loudly in anticipation. This was definitely something more appetising than some out-of-date crisps.

'You shouldn't have,' she smiled. 'I mean, I'm glad you did – but you didn't need to.'

'Ah, nonsense. I know you've limited facilities over here and we couldn't have you getting too hungry and maybe collapsing on us now, could we?'

'I appreciate the gesture,' she said, taking the plate from Jo and smiling. 'Do you want to come in for a bit? I mean, it's a case of sitting on bare floorboards and the rooms now smell strongly of bleach, but you're more than welcome.'

Jo shook her head, before jerking it in the direction of The Ivy Inn. 'Naw, I'd better get back. It's busy over there today. Can't be giving Noah something to complain about. But enjoy your lunch – just drop the plate over when you get a chance.'

She waved a cheery goodbye and crossed the road – leaving Libby to take her dinner upstairs, where she opened a bottle of water, sat on the floor and started eating. It wasn't the most salubrious of surroundings – not by a long shot – but in that moment she felt happy and content in her own little bubble.

Looking out the window, she noticed Jo leave the pub with another covered plate and walk up the street towards Harry's shop. In that moment, she was wowed by the sense of community in her new street – and nothing else mattered.

16

WATERMELON

The plate of roast beef – melt-in-the-mouth tender – roast potatoes, carrots, cabbage Yorkshire pudding and a healthy serving of gravy would normally have been enough to send Libby into a food coma for the better part of the afternoon – but, as it happened, it was just what she needed to give her the energy to get through the rest of her afternoon scrubbing and cleaning.

When six o'clock came, she locked up both the shop and the flat and, after throwing her bag into her car, she carried the plate Jo had left with her back over to the pub. The lunch crowd had thinned out and what was left was a group of jovial drinkers enjoying the embers of the weekend with cold glasses of wine and frosted beer glasses in front of them. Noah was holding court behind the bar – and, to Libby's dismay, there was no obvious sign of Jo. It would've been so much easier if she was there and Libby didn't have to so much as break breath with Noah. He was simply a complication she didn't need just now.

She walked to the bar and sat the plate, along with her freshly washed knife and fork, on the counter top. She cursed the fact she had put her bag in her car as she could have tried to get away with writing a quick thank you note to Jo instead of waiting until Noah was done telling one of his long-winded stories to the delight of his listening fans.

He glanced over to Libby and raised his hand to gesture that he would be with her in just one minute, so she took a seat and stared longingly at the cold bottles of wine in the fridge that looked oh-so tempting after the day she had put in.

A long soak, a glass of wine, perhaps even an hour in the garden reading a book – she had the latest Marian Keyes novel and she was dying to get stuck in – was exactly what she needed and she longed for Noah to hurry up so she could thank them for dinner and be on her way.

She felt a physical swoop of relief when, seconds later, she saw Jo emerge from the office behind the bar and smile in her direction.

'I brought these back,' Libby said, gesturing to the plate and cutlery on the counter, as Jo walked over. 'Thank you so much. It was absolutely delicious. Can I settle up?'

'There's no need,' Jo said. 'Consider it a...'

'Welcome to the street?' Libby laughed. 'There have been so many welcomes to this street, I need to pay for something!'

'I was going to say a neighbourly gesture. We like to look after each other around here.'

'You do a very good job of it,' Libby said, as she recalled how she saw Jo taking a plate of food up to Harry.

'I'll let you into a secret,' Jo said, leaning over the bar. 'It's not me. It's Noah – he's very determined that we all do our bit. He's always wanting to give something back to the community. Sometimes I have to remind him this is a business not a charity. But I can understand why he feels the need to give back too, you know?'

Libby was about to ask Jo exactly why did Noah feel he owed

Ivy Lane so much, when Paddy wandered out from the back office and jumped up on Jo, demanding cuddles.

Jo ruffled his fur before smiling back at Libby. 'I think I'll have to take this one out for a walk. If you'll excuse me.'

'Of course,' Libby said. 'I just wanted to return your plate and thank you again.'

'I'll pass that on to Noah,' Jo said as Paddy started to whimper, desperate to get outside. Jo laughed and told the scruffy dog to calm down. 'You're supposed to be Noah's dog, you know!' she faux-scolded the dog. 'But it will be me picking up your poop again today, won't it?'

Paddy's tail wagged furiously. He didn't seem too bothered about who was going to lift his poop as long as he was getting outside to run about.

Stopping off at the pub had been a mistake. The loss of momentum caused Libby to feel just how very tired she really was. She said goodbye to Jo and Paddy, gave a quick wave to Noah and left, virtually collapsing into her car.

* * *

Libby's bottom had barely hit the bottom of the bath, her aching muscles just about started to ease in the warm soapy water and her wine glass had not yet even touched her lips, when her phone rang. She knew she should have left it in her bedroom – or, even better, she should have switched it off. But she hadn't. She had brought it into the bathroom and put it on the little stool beside the bath where her wine glass and book also rested.

Of course, she wasn't obliged to answer it. But she knew by the ringtone – 'Bootylicious' by Destiny's Child – that it was Jess calling and she imagined that after last night she would want to chat to her.

Libby pulled herself up to sitting and reached for her phone, sliding her finger across the screen to answer it. 'Jess,' she said, 'everything okay?'

There was a slight pause. 'Well, that's kind of what I wanted to ask you,' Jess said. 'I didn't see you this morning and you went to bed early last night.'

'It wasn't that early,' Libby said, stretching her legs in the water to soothe a knot in her calf muscle. 'And I needed to get to the shop this morning and you were both out for the count.'

There was a pause.

'Are you cross with me?' Jess asked.

Libby wondered if she was cross with Jess. She definitely felt something, but she couldn't name it. Or maybe she just didn't want to.

'Why would I be cross with you?' she asked.

'Did I steal your time with Ant? I know you said I wasn't being a third wheel, but maybe I was? We wondered if that was why you went to bed early.'

'We?' Libby said, feeling, once more, a little put out. 'You and Ant?'

Another pause. 'Yes. It's not that we were talking about you. Not really. Not much. It was just general chat and then you were gone before we got up and I haven't heard from you all day.'

'I left you both a note,' Libby said, 'and I've been busy all day. I'm just tired now. All the hard work must be catching up with me.'

'Well, if you're sure,' Jess said, but Libby noticed a hesitancy in her voice.

'I am,' Libby replied, even if she wasn't entirely sure. Yes, she trusted Jess implicitly. Probably more than she trusted anyone else. She wasn't worried that her friend and her boyfriend would get up to anything behind her back, but she did feel out of sorts all the same. Was it simply that, in seeing how well Jess and Ant could get along, how they could talk and laugh and how they enjoyed shared interests, just highlighted how superficial her own relationship with Ant was?

There was a third, prolonged, pause before Jess spoke again. 'I really didn't know until the last minute that the conference wasn't happening. I hope you believe that. I'd have gone with you if I'd known earlier.'

Libby bristled a little. This was a different issue and she realised she did feel let down by Jess. And she definitely felt as if Ant's support for her dream project had waned considerably as soon as it got down to the heavy lifting.

She realised she didn't have the emotional or physical energy for trying to unpick this particular issue just now though. 'Look, Jess, I'm tired. It's been a long weekend. Can we talk during the week? I'll send you a WhatsApp as soon as I know how the week is shaping up properly.'

'You're working too hard,' Jess said, her voice filled with concern. 'Ant and I both think so.'

It was that comment which changed Libby's mind and made her think that she did, perhaps, have the emotional energy for this conversation after all.

'You both do, do you?' Libby said and she could hear the harshness in her voice.

'I knew you were annoyed,' Jess said.

'Oh, for goodness' sake,' she muttered. 'If you want to know, then yes, I am annoyed. I'm annoyed you and Ant seem to have decided I'm working too hard when you both know I'm pushing a tight deadline. What did you expect would happen? It was always going to be tough-going. And you both talk about how hard I'm working, but you don't offer to help. Not really. You've been to the shop once. Ant barely made it in the front door before he cleared off. Neither of you wanted to come with me to Belfast. Even though I promised a night away and a bit of fun. And I understood that, because you were working. But then I find that you didn't go to the conference but instead spent the lion's share of it with Ant, of all people, who himself was supposed to be working. Even when I was there, you two seemed to be lost in your own little bubble, and, to add insult to injury, you decided to talk about me behind my back.'

There was silence, then a sniff. 'You asked me to stay. You both did. I would've got a taxi home. I hadn't planned to be there.'

'Was I really going to be that bitch? The person that told you to go on home to your lonely flat while I sat there and drank the rest of the bottle of wine you opened?'

'My lonely flat?' Jess said, her voice now stern. 'I'm very good at keeping my own company. God knows I need to be, since I'm so far down your list of priorities these days. I wouldn't be surprised if you saw your dentist more than you saw me.'

Libby felt her face redden. She knew she had neglected Jess over the last few months. Ever since she had been seeing Ant, if truth be told. Ever since Jess had seen the shop up for sale and the project had consumed her.

Jess was in her stride now though. 'But, look, I'm okay to be there when you're feeling sad,' she continued. 'Or stressed or whining about how terrible it is that you don't know whether or not you're in love. Or you want someone to go to Belfast with you. As a second choice, Libby, for God's sake. I wasn't even your first thought! Don't throw in a "but it would have been fun". This wasn't about me and you. It was just about you.'

Libby felt stung. Everything Jess said hit her hard. She couldn't argue against any of it. Shame rose in her.

'I know you've had a tough time,' Jess said, her words cutting through, 'but almost everything about the course of the last two years has been about you. How you feel. What you want. What you're getting, or not getting, from your relationship, or fling, or whatever the hell it is with Ant. And that bloody stupid bookshop!' Jess stopped talking then, as if she knew she had gone too far.

Libby just sat, frozen. Her shame gave way to something altogether more toxic. She was angry and bruised. She could not believe what her friend had said. It wouldn't have hurt more if she had punched her right in the gut.

That bloody stupid bookshop.

She didn't trust herself to speak. Instead, she stared, blinking, at her phone for a moment or two and then ended the call. Having placed the phone back on the footstool, she immersed herself, head and all, under the water, where she wondered what the hell had just happened, until she couldn't last one more second without a breath.

17

FIGHT CLUB

Libby Quinn did not fall out with people. In fact, she normally went very much out of her way to make sure that no one ever thought badly of her. She had been born a people-pleaser and she was pretty sure she would die a people-pleaser.

It was quite extraordinary – the lengths she would go to just to make sure she kept those around her happy, frequently tying herself up in all sorts of knots to be there for everyone. Even if it meant saying yes to things she absolutely wanted to say no to. Even if it meant smiling sweetly and turning the metaphorical cheek if someone was overtly mean to her. Even if it meant not correcting someone when they got her name wrong for the forty-seventh time in case it embarrassed them. For the full three years of her university career, she was called Elaine by the girl who lived across the hall from her and she never once corrected her.

Libby was the sort of person who would apologise to people when they walked into her. She had even been known to apologise to inanimate objects. If she thought she had annoyed someone, she would genuinely lose sleep over it.

So, if she absolutely did not fall out with people she barely knew, then falling out with people she considered as close as her own family was definitely not something she had much experience of.

Falling out with Jess knocked her for six. It gave her a constant dull feeling, which pulled her down and filled her with doubt and self-loathing.

First of all, she knew there had been real hurt in Jess's voice. And truth in her words. Maybe Libby was not as much of a people-pleaser as she thought.

The thought that Jess had made some valid points hit her in waves of differing strengths throughout the day. She had neglected her friend. And she had been focused on the shop, and all the preparation that had brought her to this point. But she needed to focus on the shop. It was important. Probably the most important thing she had ever done in her life. Surely Jess understood that. And she would have been there for Jess if she needed her. In a heartbeat. She'd have dropped everything and come running.

She lay on top of her bed and looked at the reminders of her teenage years and of simpler times. The posters were gone now, but she could still remember where they had hung. Westlife and Robbie Williams, grinning down with their pop-star pouts.

This place had been her sanctuary. If she closed her eyes, she could conjure an image of her teenage self, sitting on the floor, her back leaning against the wall, long bronzed legs stretched out in front of her. Jess sat opposite, legs crossed, singing along – badly – to whatever they were listening to as they drank from Coca Cola cans and laughed about their current crushes. Although, for Libby, quite often her crushes were the dark and brooding heroes of whatever book she was reading. How she would spend time imagining them holding her and kissing her the way they kissed the heroines that she read about. She lost hours fantasising about Heathcliff from *Wuthering Heights* – only to realise as she grew that he was a much more sinister character than her fourteen-year-old self had realised. Jess's crushes had been mainstream. They included actors, singers, and even footballers, during a particularly short-lived but obsessive football phase.

So many secrets had been shared in this room – so many hopes and dreams too. Not to mention all the promises that they would stay friends forever and ever and never ever fall out.

Who would have thought the fall out would come when they were both mature women, living their own lives? And that it would, technically, have a boy at the centre of it?

Libby had wanted to fix it, of course. So she sat up, phone in hand and composed at least a dozen text messages which she, ultimately, would never send to Jess. First, she apologised. Then, she ranted a bit – her hurt pouring from her fingers as she jabbed at her phone screen. Then, she tried a conciliatory approach. But none of it felt right – so she deleted them all and instead lay back staring at the ceiling, trying to work it out.

She thought, for a moment, of going downstairs and asking her parents if she was a thoroughly unlikeable person, but she knew she couldn't rely on their answers – on account of them being her parents and thinking the sun shone directly out of her arse. Then she wrote and rewrote a number of different text messages to Ant – some pretending as if nothing had happened with Jess – in her usual flirtatious tone. Some asking if he thought she was selfish? But she deleted those messages too. Least said, soonest mended, her grandad used to tell her – so she switched her phone off and allowed the tiredness of the day to wash over her – waking occasionally to let the wave of unease lull her back to sleep.

* * *

Libby woke late, without her phone switched on to beep her into consciousness, and stared at the wall at a shaft of light cutting through the curtains. It was another hot day – she could feel it already. Her bedroom was stuffy. The air dead. Her first thought was of Jess. Maybe she'd been overthinking things. Maybe they'd both just been tired and snippy, due to the heat of the day making them feel worse.

It would no doubt all get sorted that day, she told herself. Messages not written in the heat of the moment would be exchanged and by tea time the storm in a teacup would be a thing of the past. Something never to be spoken of again.

Except by tea time no messages had been exchanged, not one. Not from Jess or Ant. And Libby was certain she wasn't going to make the first move. Maybe, just like the weather, they all needed a little more time to calm down.

In the meantime, she was busy. Building work continuing apace. Minor crises being solved every day. Some horrible surprises (the pipework running through the yard at the back of the shop needed replacing, at Libby's expense) but some high points as well. When the tattered lino was ripped from the shop floor, everyone had been astounded to find a stunning parquet floor, which just needed a little TLC, had been hiding underneath. Libby could've wept with joy.

It was enough to distract her, but by Thursday she was feeling very much on edge.

The heatwave had become almost insufferable, especially as she and the tradesmen tried not to fall over each other as they worked. And not one message had travelled across the airwaves from Jess to her or vice versa. Her WhatsApp was barren of new messages from the woman who was supposed to be her best friend.

By the time the thermometer had climbed into the mid-twenties on Thursday, Libby's hurt was starting to fester.

Jess had left her in limbo and she had also hit her directly where she knew it would hurt. Criticising anything to do with her shop was the lowest of blows. Jess knew, more than anyone, how much it meant to her. Grandad Ernie had been a de facto grandparent to Jess as well. They'd all spent so much time together when they were younger.

Things had been cooling even more with Ant too. They'd exchanged cursory text messages. She didn't send him pictures of how things were going. If Jess was telling the truth, Ant didn't really care anyway.

She'd made no plans at all to see him that weekend. Yes, he'd asked if she would be working and she'd replied simply that she would. She didn't go into any other details. God forbid, her telling him that she finally had a shop name and was starting to work on their branding and marketing materials would prove to him she was as single-minded as her friend had said she was.

No. She would do it herself. Well, with the help of her parents and a team of tradesmen who she was actually starting to grow quite fond of. She resolved that she didn't need Jess or Ant to hold her hands.

But God it was hard. She might've been angry, she might've been hurt. But that didn't mean she didn't miss Jess. They'd never gone this long without communicating before and she felt as if a part of her was missing – a part that knew exactly how her mind worked and how to calm her down when she started to spiral.

And she was starting to spiral a bit. Despite the builders being great and her parents being lovely. Despite Harry letting her have a free ice lolly, and offering to buy her a half-pint in the pub some evening. Everything still felt off-kilter without her support network.

She wanted Jess to be in her life. She needed Jess to be there for her at this time more than any other. Just as Libby herself had been there for Jess when she wanted to pack in her medicine studies after throwing up the first time she cut into her cadaver.

The lack of a blinking light on her phone signalling a new notification taunted her. Libby turned the phone face-down on the counter and went back to trying to drown out the sound of Terry and Gerry The Sparks singing – or rather, screeching – along to 'Bohemian Rhapsody' on the radio as they worked.

A while later, a knock on the glass of the open door caught her attention and she looked up to see Noah standing in the doorway. 'You don't mind me calling over?' he asked.

'No, of course not,' she said, but really Noah was just another complication in her life she didn't need right now. Not that anything else had happened since Saturday. He'd behaved perfectly normally towards her.

'I just wanted to check you were okay with the shelving units arriving tomorrow? Keith has been on, just checking. He said he tried to call you but he didn't get an answer. I knew you were over here, so I figured I'd be as quick walking over and asking you myself.'

Libby cursed at the phone on the counter. 'I'd put my phone on silent, to try and concentrate some more on work,' she said, turning it over and seeing two missed calls from Keith – and no notifications from anyone else. 'But, yes, tomorrow, should be fine.' Libby looked around the shop. The walls were still bare. Wiring exposed. The plasterboard needing to go up before the shelves could be fixed to their intended spot, but she supposed she could store them in the stockroom, which now, at least, was rodent-free.

'Grand,' Noah said, walking in and taking a good look around the shop. 'It's really coming on, Libby. It's looking good.'

She laughed. 'Really? Do you not think it looks like a giant mess? Good is not a word I would use.'

Noah shook his head. 'Really? Because I see all the nuts and bolts going in. That exposed brickwork, is that where the coffee bar will be?'

She nodded.

'Thought so. Keith's shelves on that far wall? And here, look at this flooring. It's amazing. You've saved yourself a clean fortune there. This is the tough bit. Before you know it, it will all be coming together. When are you getting your comms fitted?'

'They've said two weeks to get it all planned and arranged with the phone company for it go live.'

'That's good,' Noah nodded. 'So I assume a lot of the heavy work will be done around then?'

'Well, that's the plan,' she said. 'If we can get the construction side sorted, on the inside at least. But the damp course will need time to dry out, and the front of the shop needs re-rendering. And that's without even mentioning the flat upstairs. At the moment, it's a shell with an old sink and little else.'

'You'll get there,' he said, gently. 'Have faith. I've seen more done in less time. You've made a great start. I heard a couple of people chatting about it in the pub last night. Asking me did I know what was happening over here. I'd get your sign up as soon as you can, if I were you.'

He had a point. Even if it would take weeks to get all her promotional materials printed up, the sooner she had a sign up outside, people would know what she was at.

'I have a name for it,' she said, realising she'd not run it past anyone yet. Not Jess or Ant, or even her parents. It was as if she was almost afraid to say it out loud for some reason. 'Do you want to know what it is?'

'Of course I do!' Noah said, and there was genuine interest in his voice.

'Once Upon A Book,' she told him, blushing to her roots for a reason she didn't quite know.

'Well, I think that's just perfect.'

'My grandad, well his favourite stories were those that began with a good old once upon a time, so...'

'Well, then it's doubly perfect,' Noah said.

Libby felt herself colour at the genuine approval in his voice.

'Now, don't forget, if there's anything we can do to help, you have to just shout. And we mean that.'

'That's so kind,' Libby replied. 'You've all done so much for me.'

'Ah, we're all just really nosy, has no one warned you?' Noah teased. 'It's not really about you at all. It's about everyone wanting to know everyone's business.'

'Oh, that's great to know because I'm fond of a bit of nosiness myself.' Libby laughed.

'But, seriously,' Noah replied, 'there's a little bit of magic or something here on Ivy Lane. This might sound really flaky, but Harry once told me he thinks the street attracts people who need it most of all. We've all got our stories. We all benefit from being there for each other – helping each other. We are all healing from something, you know? I know that sounds really cheesy, but I believe him. This place has always felt special to me. Even as a child when I visited my grandparents. Did I tell you they ran the bakery here for years? Granny had a reputation for slipping an extra loaf, or a few scones, in the bags of people who looked like they needed a little help. Being decent to people never hurts anyone. Now, I'm hardly likely to slip extra pints to people, but I will help this community in whatever way I can and I know everyone else who lives here or works here thinks the same way. Maybe that's a bit old-fashioned in these modern times, but I just think we should help each other out a bit more.'

He spoke with such sincerity that Libby couldn't help but be moved. And she couldn't help but feel that Harry was right and that Ivy Lane would help heal her own emotional pain over the loss of her grandad. To her embarrassment, she felt the tears she had probably been holding in all week prick at her eyes and she was powerless to stop them falling.

'I didn't mean to make you cry!' Noah said, a little panicked. There was something in the timbre of his voice that seemed to register with Terry and Gerry, who stopped their work and looked at her, and then at each other, trying to figure out what to do next.

'Let's get some fresh air,' Noah said, nodding to the door. 'We'll go for a short walk. I'm sure Paddy will forgive me just this once for cheating on him.'

Libby smiled through her tears. 'Thanks,' she said.

'It's all part of the service,' he replied.

As they walked, Libby was able to compose herself. 'I'm mortified,' she told him. 'Crying all over you. It's been a tough week, and then just all that talk about your grandparents, and even saying the shop name out loud made me think of my grandad again.'

'He was very special to you,' Noah said, and it wasn't a question.

'He was everything,' she replied.

18

Grandad was always there. Always. Libby couldn't remember a time when he wasn't in her life. Her earliest memories were of sitting on his knee, him with his pipe in his hand – the wiry strands of tobacco peeping out of the bowl, in the same way his nose hair peeped out of his nostrils. Both were kind of disgusting, she could admit in hindsight, but at the time, there was a comfort in the messiness of him. The way, no matter how much Brylcreem he slicked into his increasingly greying hair, there were a few strands that always stuck out at right angles just above his left ear. The way the brown chunky-knit cardigan had been repaired at the elbows – patched and stitched together. How, while he shaved every morning, by the time he sat on her bed at night to tell her a bedtime story, his face would be scratchy with salt-and-pepper sprinkles of bristly stubble. The smell of Old Spice and tobacco smoke. It was strange, cigarette smoke made her nauseous but tobacco smoked through a pipe had a headier quality – a depth that made her feel calm. Like she was sat on her grandad's knee in his favourite armchair while he read her a story and she rested her cheek on that tatty brown cardigan.

They lost hours, days, in so many different stories. Stories told with happy voices, and scary voices, deep voices and funny princess voices. Stories that made her laugh until her tummy hurt and stories that made her cry until the only thing that would make it better was a glass of milk and a biscuit from the jar on the worktop – the glass jar which was strictly off-limits at all other times to little hands.

There were stories that she felt so keenly that she knew, even as a child, that the characters she heard of became a part of her life. They'd become the imaginary friends she would turn to again and again over the years. And, at the centre of it all, there was this bear of a man who brought those stories to life.

If she was lucky, really lucky, he would tell her one of his own tall tales. Stories from his own childhood, adapted, changed, sprinkled with magic. A speaking dog here, a friendly alien there – stories which held her rapt. Stories she told him he should write down.

'I'd really love you to, Grandad,' she would say to him over and over again.

'I will someday, I promise,' he always replied. 'For you, sweet pea.'

But somehow life got busy, and the stories got put on the sidelines, until he was gone and he would never put them on paper. It was strange how that hurt her. The stories were still with her though. She could close her eyes, wherever she was, and almost smell the smoke from his tobacco, feel the soft wool of that tatty cardigan, the scratch of his face with his night-night kiss – and each word would drop in place in her mind. But she longed to see them written down, in his scrawl, as if he was scratching at the paper with his pen. Always black ink. Never a blue pen. But Libby knew, she knew that no matter how hard she wished, or how hard she prayed (and she was never a person who usually turned to prayer), she would never see his handwriting again. Or smell his scent. Or feel the scratch of his stubbly face. She hated that when he was brought home, laid out in the living room of their house for people to file past and offer their condolences and tell her what a brilliant man he was as if she wasn't the person who knew it more than anyone else, that his face was smooth – not a hint of his bristle. Made-up instead – natural-looking but so far from natural. As if someone had airbrushed the lines and crevices that she loved so much out of his face, making him look both like himself and not. He was dressed in a suit – his good suit. The one he had worn to her graduation and to a family wedding or two. He would have hated it – pulled at his collar, loosened his tie, taken his suit jacket off as soon as he possibly could. Libby didn't know why her father and her uncle had decided he should be laid out in it – possibly because it looked the part. It was what people would have expected. They wouldn't have expected him to lie there in his comfortable flannel shirt, that blasted cardigan and his glasses on his face. His glasses instead were folded at Libby's insistence and placed in his hands – as if he were ready to slip them on, lift up a book, let out a subtle cough and start reading. In fact, she couldn't resist slipping a copy of *Great Expectations* into the coffin with him – the same copy they had read together.

She was a grown-up when he died. Thirty-two. She knew she got longer with her grandfather than perhaps most people got with their grandparents – but standing by his coffin, dressed in black in a room kept cool, where conversations were in hushed tones – the real chat, laughter and occasional burst of singing of a traditional Irish wake a comfortable ten feet away, at least, from the reality of what was happening – she had never felt more like a child.

He was her hero. Her storyteller. Her protector. They shared the same spirit. The same dreams. 'I will write your stories down.

I promise. I'll do it for you,' she'd whispered as she'd kissed his marble cold head, knowing that he was gone but that she was not ready to let him go completely. She'd make him proud. Share his love of books and storytelling with the world. She'd open the shop they talked about. One day. A place to find new adventures and also to encourage other people to develop that same glorious magical love of storytelling – she promised him.

And that, she told Noah, as they walked up to the grounds of the university, strolled through the gardens and back to the shop again, was why she would do everything in her power to make sure the shop was a success.

19

LES LIAISONS DANGEREUSES

Noah had been a good listener, which had surprised Libby. He'd let her cry and never once looked uncomfortable in the presence of her tears.

'God, I've a headache now,' she told him, as she thanked him for listening and handing her a tissue when she needed it.

'The amount of women who have said that to me,' Noah deadpanned, and she laughed.

She had started to relax around him, which was a good thing considering she had just offloaded her deepest secrets in his direction.

'Do you often give women headaches? To be honest, after spending all that time listening to you drone on in Belfast, I could tell you did.'

'Ha ha, very funny,' Noah said. 'Stick to selling books and leave the stand-up to the real comedians!'

Libby shrugged, rubbing her temples.

'You know, you are probably dehydrated – and I just happen to know of this lovely pub that provides liquid refreshment. And food too, come to think of it.'

Libby looked around. The tradesmen were all content in their tasks for the day and her dad, who had called in that morning, had said everything was on schedule. She shouldn't really take the rest of the afternoon off, but she felt so drained, she knew it might just do her some good.

'That is tempting,' she said.

'Let me tempt you some more. Now, what would a woman like you drink? It's a bit too warm for red wine. I don't see you as a beer drinker. But on a hot day like this, I'd recommend a cool cider in the beer garden, lots of ice?'

'Sounds perfect,' she said, already thinking of the condensation forming and trickling down the outside of the glass and that first, refreshing sip. 'I'll let the boys know where I'm going and give them keys to lock up and I'll be over.'

Noah feigned shock – put his hand to his chest, raised his eyebrows. 'Bookshop Libby leaving the shop before 6 p.m.? What madness is this?'

'A necessary one,' she said. 'Give me ten minutes and have that cider waiting,' she said with a smile. 'Oh, and maybe a toastie, ham and cheese?'

'All these demands,' he said with a wink. 'And Jo will be delighted to see you too. She's off shift soon – I'd say she'd be easily persuaded to join you if you wanted company?'

Libby felt something – something uncomfortable – twist in the pit of her stomach. This was crazy, she thought. She liked Jo. Jo was as nice as nice could be. She'd confessed her love of books earlier in the week and the pair had talked for a full hour about whether *Pride and Prejudice* or *Sense and Sensibility* was Jane Austen's finest work. She should be happy to know Jo was going to be off and she might have some company. She *was* happy. But there was a little, teeny, tiny part of her that was also just a bit jealous that Jo had the one thing she'd never have. Noah's devotion.

She shook herself. This was stupid. She didn't need Noah Simpson's attention. She just wanted his friendship and a feeling of belonging. So far Ivy Lane was delivering that in spades.

She called to Terry and Gerry that she was finishing up for the day, to which they responded by turning their radio up even louder. While she packed up her bag, she also glanced at her phone. When she saw there were no notifications, she didn't let it bother her. She was fine. She didn't need them.

As promised, when she crossed over to the pub a few minutes later, there was a bottle of cider on the bar and a glass loaded with ice beside it. Noah nodded towards it and shouted that he'd have her food with her shortly. She reached into her bag for her purse to pay, to which he shook his head.

'You have to let me pay sometime!' she called.

'Of course,' he said as he walked over. 'Don't think I won't. Actually, I might start a tab for you right now. And add my counselling consultancy fees this afternoon too? Two hundred pounds an hour sound about right?'

'You'd be lucky,' she laughed, 'but I get it – free coffee when I open? And a book of your choice – one with pictures if that's easier for you? And the next round is on me?'

He laughed and she heard a voice from beside her say: 'I'll hold you to that!'

She turned to see Jo, who was ushering an overheated and panting Paddy behind the counter and into the office. She filled his water bowl and then took out a bottle of beer for herself.

'Noah told me you were coming over – so I saved us a prime loca-
tion in the beer garden. I'm afraid that Paddy won't be joining us.
He needs some shade and a sleep. He was not made for this
weather.'

'I'll make sure to keep an eye on him,' Noah said.

'Anyway, to the beer garden. Our table is one with a good view
of all the goings-on – but maybe you're not as nosy as me?'

'I have my moments,' Libby said as she followed Jo through to
the patioed area to the side of the bar, which was already filling
up with cheerful drinkers making the most of the heatwave.

She hadn't long sat down when one of the waiting staff
appeared with her toastie, which she ate in record time having
not realised just how hungry she was.

'I was never sure a beer garden was a great idea – not in
Ireland, not with our weather – but for those few days of the year
when the weather behaves, it's worth it, I think,' Jo said. 'And this
year we've been particularly blessed with the weather. I could get
used to it. It makes everything seem a little better and brighter,
doesn't it?'

Libby smiled. 'Ordinarily I'd agree with you – but I'd like to
be a bit less sweaty working on the shop.' She laughed.

'Ah, don't talk – I'm as fragrant as a sewer after the day I've
just put in. Thankfully these seats are downwind of anyone who
would mind,' Jo said as she lifted the bottle of beer she had on
the table and raised it to clink against Libby's. 'Well, cheers,
lovely. We'll take this as an official welcome to the Ivy Lane
family – now that you seem to realise we're not all weirdos out to
assimilate you into our cult – or at least, if we are, it's a nice cult to
be a part of.'

Libby blushed – had her reticence, her shyness, been so obvious? Had she seemed offhand until now? She supposed she was
naturally reserved. Was that her character? She wasn't one who

made friends easily – acquaintances, yes, but not friends. Real friends.

Was it embarrassing that in her thirties she was excited that she was meeting new people – people she had a good feeling about? People who felt maybe like friends that she should always have had in her life?

God, she hadn't had more than a sip of her drink and she wondered if she was already a little drunk? She felt a bit giddy – or maybe it was just a nice high after a few days of feeling so low. Offloading to Noah must have done her more good than she thought.

Buoyed by her good mood, and the heat of the sun, she downed two ciders – probably a little too quickly. As a result, despite having eaten the toastie, she very quickly found herself feeling squiffy, telling Jo she felt squiffy and then taking a fit of the giggles at just how funny a word squiffy was.

'I definitely don't get squiffy enough.' She laughed. 'Don't you think we reach a stage of life where everything becomes serious? That we forget to laugh and just have fun? Or is it that things just aren't fun any more? Or is it me? Did I just stop having fun – or stop being fun? Do you think I'm fun?'

Jo sat back and looked at her and Libby blushed, suddenly self-conscious again. Had she slipped from squiffy to needy in the space of a couple of sentences?

'Ignore me,' she muttered. 'Too much sun and not enough food, and this cider is obviously stronger than I anticipated.'

'Libby, you don't have to doubt yourself all the time, you know. I'll tell you this – sometimes we all go through phases when stuff happens and we kind of lose sight of who we are or what we want. Or maybe we just don't really know what we want, so we make some mistakes. We've all done it. I've made my share. And Noah, God knows he's made a few clangers in his time, but, you know what, it's all swings and roundabouts. What's serious one minute will be fun again the next. If you let it. And mistakes are okay, as long as we learn something from them.'

'I get it,' Libby said as she narrowed one eye and took in all of Jo and how beautiful she was, although she doubted the other woman realised how attractive she was. Confident but not overly so. Her beauty was in her smile and in the way she put people at ease. A wave of fondness washed over Libby. 'I get you and Noah. How that works. You make a great couple.'

Jo's eyes widened and she choked on the mouthful of beer she had just taken. 'Couple?' she spluttered. 'Oh God, we're not a couple. Not in any romantic sense. Oh the very thought!' she grimaced. 'Noah is my brother! If you want to be picky about it, he's my foster brother. He came to stay with us when he was fourteen, and, well, he never really left.'

It was Libby's turn to widen her eyes. 'But I thought... I mean, dancing around the flat together. Shared responsibility for Paddy? Just how you speak to each other?'

'Nothing more than a brother-and-sister relationship, and friendship of course. I was twelve when he came to live with us, all angry and moody. I thought he was the coolest person on the planet. He thought I was an annoyance. He'd bat me away, hide in his room. But I won him round in the end – and he became my best friend. My true brother. I love him with every part of my heart, but there is no way I would ever or could ever think of him in a romantic way.' Jo shuddered, then laughed. 'Actually there was one time, I think I was twenty, so Noah was twenty-two, we wondered if there was something more between us. We were a bit pissed and had a snog in the back of a taxi that immediately felt every kind of wrong. We were never meant to work in that way.'

Libby could hardly believe what she had heard. She had been so sure they were a couple, but now, after Jo had explained it, she realised it was perfectly believable they were like brother and sister. Something pulled at her heartstrings though. Fourteen-year-old Noah, who found himself in foster care. Noah who always spoke about community and family and his grandparents. Who seemed almost indefatigable in his positivity. She was shocked to believe something so catastrophic had happened in his past.

She was just about to ask Jo a bit more about Noah's background when the man himself, accompanied by a re-energised Paddy, approached them and sat down. Paddy immediately jumped up on Jo for a cuddle before making his way around to Libby, laying his head on her lap and looking up at her with his deep brown eyes.

'You definitely have a fan there,' Noah said. 'We might have to stop inviting you over. Can't have Paddy switching loyalties!'

Libby laughed and ruffled the fur around Paddy's collar, who, once satisfied, padded back over to his master and lay down at his feet. 'I don't think you've anything to worry about,' she said.

'Oh, Noah, you'll never believe this,' Jo said, and Libby felt herself cringe. She knew what was coming next. 'Libby here thought you and I were a couple!'

'Oh God, no, perish the thought.' Noah grimaced and Jo swiped at him with the drinks menu she had been using as a makeshift fan.

'You'd never get that lucky,' Jo teased and Libby watched as they descended once again into their usual banter – jokes and fake insults flying back and forth between them. It seemed so obvious now, she wasn't sure how she hadn't seen it. But then, she hadn't been looking. She reminded herself that, honestly, Noah Simpson was not of any romantic interest to her and that she'd only been checking out his relationship status for Jess. Jess, who she hadn't spoken to in four whole days. Her mood dipped and she stared into the bottom of her glass.

Jo excused herself to go to the bathroom and after a minute of fairly awkward silence, Noah spoke. 'So, you thought Jo and I were an item?' he asked, a slight hint of amusement in his voice.

Libby shrugged her shoulders. 'You seemed... I don't know... close.'

'We are. As I've said, she's my best friend. But nothing more.' He pulled a face, and laughed. 'She must have told you about the worst snog in the world ever? It was like snogging my granny. Just plain wrong. Actually, you're the only coupled-up one among us three. And you've still not managed to drag your boyfriend in here yet.'

Libby's mood dropped further. 'No. Well... it's complicated,' she said.

'It's none of my business,' Noah said. 'But if you want to talk, Jo and I make for good listeners. Even Paddy here is a good man for sounding off to. And he never judges. Nor do Jo or I, for that matter.'

'Ant works hard. He's very busy at the moment,' she said, knowing, of course, that was only the tiniest part of the problems they were facing.

Noah nodded. 'You really don't need to explain anything to me, Bookshop Libby,' he said, his voice soft and his gaze warm. 'But sometimes you have to look at where you stand in a person's life. I'm an all-or-nothing person when it comes to relationships and nothing in the world comes before my friends or family, never mind any prospective partner.'

Libby nodded, unable to speak. So much came before her in Ant's life, and, if she was honest to herself, Ant was quite far down her list of priorities too. But two bottles of cider in, she didn't want to think about serious things. She was delighted to see Jo walk over to them with another round of drinks.

'One for the road?' Jo asked with a smile. 'You'll not be driving anyway, so you might as well make the most of this lovely weather and our dazzling company and have one more.'

Libby nodded and Jo doled out the drinks, including a bottle of beer for Noah. She'd definitely go home after this. No question about it. It was too risky to sit here while her emotions were spinning, and, more than that, it was definitely too risky to stay here when everything she heard or learned about Noah was making her see him in a whole new light.

She could feel the headache that had been nagging at her all week come back. And the cider didn't taste as sweet as it had before. Her little Ant-free bubble had been burst and she couldn't shake the thought of him, or of Jess, from her mind.

And all the while, every time Libby looked at Noah, at his warm smile, the dark hairs on his arms against his tanned skin, the strength evident in his hands, she felt herself pulled towards him. This handsome man, with some sort of tragedy in his past, who loved his community, and rescued his dog, and who was looking at her with a very quizzical expression on his face.

'Are you okay there, Libby?'

She jolted to attention. 'Yes. Of course, yes.'

'You seemed to zone out there for a bit,' he said. 'And you look a little pale.'

Did she? She didn't know. But, yes, she was distracted. And her head was actually verging on really sore now, and her throat felt scratchy. Probably hay fever, she thought. That would teach her for sitting out in the beer garden. She swallowed the last of her drink.

'Actually, I just think I need to go home now,' she said. 'I do feel a little out of sorts.'

'Noah will call you a taxi,' Jo said, her expression soft and warm. 'I think an early night and a good sleep will do you the power of good.'

Libby nodded. An early night sounded blissful. As did a long sleep. She could escape all her worries when she was dreaming.

20

Libby was feeling slightly nauseated by the time the taxi reached home. The sweaty driver, who reeked of cigarette smoke, had insisted that she keep the windows up through the entire journey, despite the blistering heat, and that he didn't need to put the air con on, as, according to him, it wasn't that warm.

Libby sat feeling progressively worse, while she felt sweat roll down her back and between her boobs, making her feel like a horrible, smelly, sticky mess.

Her legs were even a little shaky as she walked up the front path and put her key in the front door. She felt more than a little light-headed as she made her way to the kitchen and filled a pint glass with tap water and added some ice. She stood for a moment, letting water from the cold tap run over her wrists in an effort to help her cool down quickly. She lifted the pint glass, now slick with condensation, held it first to her forehead and then to the back of her neck, before downing half of it without so much as taking a breath. Still feeling wobbly, she made her way to the kitchen table and sat down, stretched her arms out in front of her and lay her head on them.

She drifted off within seconds, waking a short time later to the gentle nudge of her mother. 'Libby, pet. Are you okay?'

She lifted her head – which felt heavy and thick with the need to have a proper sleep – and blinked at her mother.

'Are you sick? Your eyes are all red and you're an awful colour,' her mother said, and placed her cool hand on Libby's forehead just as she used to do when she was a child. She looked concerned. 'You're a bit warm.'

Libby found she didn't have the energy to tell her mother it was probably because she had spent the best part of half an hour in the sauna-like environment of the smelliest taxi in the world.

'Pet, why don't you go on up to bed. I'll bring you some iced water and some paracetamol. I knew this would happen. I was only saying to your dad I was worried you've been working too hard. Not just now, but with all the prep, and you're not looking after yourself.'

'I'm not sick, Mum,' Libby muttered, a wave of nausea leaving her feeling a little unsure herself. 'But I think I will go to bed.'

'I'll bring a basin up too – just in case,' her mother clucked. 'And maybe the fan from the living room in case you feel too hot.'

Slowly, as if her limbs were stuck to the very furniture around her, Libby extracted herself from her seat at the table and used every last ounce of energy she could find to traipse up the stairs. Just as she reached the landing, the creeping nausea that had been nagging at her from the moment she got in the taxi turned into a tidal wave. She made it to the bathroom just in time before she was sick.

A glimpse of herself in the hall mirror on the way back to her bedroom did not paint a pretty picture. Her hair was damp with sweat and plastered to the side of her face. A grey pallor gave her a less than attractive look and her eyes were red-rimmed. She hauled herself into her room and on top of her bed, where she fell asleep before her mother came into her room.

When she woke in the wee hours, her head and her stomach were sore. What had been a scratchy throat now felt as if it was on fire. Her room was uncomfortably hot and when she got up to go and open a window, she felt unsteady on her feet.

Libby gripped onto the windowsill and pushed open the window, gulping in what little fresh air there was in the dead of night, before making her way back to bed and, without so much as lifting the covers, falling back down on it. It was only then she noticed the fan, but she had no strength to try and stand up again to switch it on.

She looked to the pint of water on her bedside table, the ice long melted, and wondered if there was any way possible she could get it to her mouth and drink it, without using any physical energy at all? How she wished she was a Jedi – able to summon the power of The Force to levitate it in her direction. Unable to do so, she simply fell back asleep, hoping that a few more hours would make all the difference and allow her to get on with everything on her to-do list for that day.

When she drifted back into consciousness, it was to the sound of her mother's voice. 'Libby, are you okay? I need to go to work, but I don't like leaving you like this.'

Painfully, she forced her eyes open – the sun was bright, her head still ached. In fact, her whole body ached. A familiar and very much unwelcome stabbing pain jabbed at her throat, and she struggled to swallow. To add to this abject misery, Libby was also no longer too warm. Instead she was freezing. She shivered as a film of cool sweat clung to her body and tried to haul her duvet across her, with limited success. She was, as her grandad would have said, 'As weak as water.'

'Close the window, please, Mum. It's freezing,' she muttered.

'Libby, it's the hottest day of the year so far!' her mum said, her voice thick with concern. Libby felt the gentle touch of her mother's hand on her forehead. 'Oh, sweetheart, you're burning up!'

'It's my throat,' she croaked. 'Again.'

It was only in her adult years that Libby started to suffer with tonsillitis. And it was guaranteed to hit whenever she was tired or stressed.

'I'll get you some ibuprofen,' her mother said. 'It will help a little.'

Libby tried to sit up. She really did, but her neck felt as if it was weighed down on the bed.

'You need to get some more sleep. You're exhausted. You slept through your alarm and everything. Your dad came in and switched it off and you didn't so much as stir. That was three hours ago.'

Libby groaned. She should be at the shop. Keith was delivering the shelves. And the new boilers were being fitted to update the long-defunct heating systems in both the flat and the shop. She'd had to scrap the idea of underfloor heating because of the parquet floor, so she desperately wanted to discuss the best way to install discreet heating that wouldn't impinge too much on her floor space.

'I need to go to the shop,' she croaked. The words sliced at her throat like razor blades.

'No you don't. You're not fit to walk the length of yourself.'

'But...'

'Now, listen to me, young lady. There's no but about it – you're going nowhere today. Your dad will oversee things today. He knows what your plans are, and what he doesn't know he can improvise. He's an old hand at this and there's nothing that can come up that he won't be able to deal with.'

'But he has to go to work...'

'Sure, he is at work! He's working at the shop,' her mum reassured her.

'But the shelves,' Libby said, though her eyes were growing heavy again. She was exhausted by a simple conversation.

'They're grand. They're in your stockroom. Terry The Spark helped and that fella from across the road? The fella that owns the pub? He saw the van arrive and popped over.'

'Noah?' Libby asked.

'That's it. I couldn't remember there, but I knew it was a biblical name. You didn't tell me one of the Simpsons was running that pub now.' There was a tone of concern in her mother's voice. 'Dear me, but they had their battles in life.' She made the sign of the cross as if offering up a prayer for the Simpsons and their battles. No doubt they were linked to Noah going into care at fourteen.

Libby would ask later, when she didn't want to cry out in pain. 'Ibuprofen, Mum,' she croaked to remind her mother.

'Oh God, yes. One minute. You stay there,' her mother said before bustling her way out of the room.

Libby grimaced, but it was hardly likely she'd be moving anywhere anytime soon, even if she wanted to.

Sick and a little emotional – Libby felt tears prick in her eyes as she allowed them to close against the strong sunlight. She had just enough energy to swallow the two small white pills her mum handed her, but that took all her strength. So much so that she couldn't shout 'No!' when she heard her mum on the phone to Jess, of all people.

'I'm not happy about her, Jess. Not at all. I know you're very busy, but if you got a chance, at lunchtime or something, could you call round and check on her? She looks like death warmed up. I know it's probably just tonsillitis again, and a good antibiotic will sort her out, but you read so many horror stories, don't you? I'd prefer she was looked at. Just to be sure. Just to rule out anything more serious. Aw thanks, pet. You're a great girl. Great. Look, I have to nip out for a bit. I've an appointment myself. But the key will be in the usual place – go on up. And there's soup on the stove if you don't get a chance for lunch before you pop over. Okay, pet. Thank you. I'm glad she has a friend like you.'

Libby cringed, an act that made every part of her, even her very eyelids, hurt. But she didn't have the strength to argue. She just lay there as she felt her mother stroke her hair gently until she could no longer fight the need for more sleep.

* * *

A soft voice cut through Libby's fevered sleep and she fought to open her eyes.

'Libby? Lib? It's Jess. Are you awake? Your mum asked me to check in on you?'

Libby felt the mattress dip as her friend sat down. Straining to open her eyes, she rolled from her side onto her back.

'There was no need,' she croaked. 'I'm sure it's my tonsils again.'

Jess reached over and placed the digital thermometer in Libby's ear, waited until it beeped and then informed her she had a fever. It wasn't exactly news to either of them. It was strange to see her friend in full professional mood. She watched as Jess reached towards her and felt around her neck, seeing if her glands were raised and then asked her to sit up so that she could listen to her heart and lungs with her stethoscope.

'Can I have a look at your throat?' Jess asked, taking a tongue depressor from her bag and switching on her torch.

Libby nodded and opened wide. She couldn't help but see

Jess wince as she looked into her mouth at her no doubt rather manky tonsils.

'Yep. Your tonsils are coated. I think both you and your mum were right. And you will definitely need an antibiotic.'

Libby nodded. She didn't know what else to say or do. There was so much that she wanted to discuss with Jess, but she felt so absolutely awful, she didn't know if she had either the physical or the emotional strength to do so.

By her friend's cool efficiency, it didn't seem as if she was much in the mood for talking either.

'I'll take a swab for the lab,' Jess said, 'just to be sure. But I wouldn't hold off on starting those antibiotics. It looks nasty in there. Apart from that, you know the drill. Paracetamol for pain and fever. Lots of fluids and, most of all, lots of rest.'

Whether it was because she was sick, or just because she was sick of things not being right with Jess, Libby felt wretched, and there was no warmth in her friend's expression when she spoke. It made her want to cry. Everything felt off-kilter. It was bad enough she was sick and it would have a knock-on effect on the shop, but having Jess cross with her was unbearable.

'Jess, don't be like that.'

'Like what?' Jess said. 'I'm here, aren't I? Checking up on you.'

'You know what I mean. You're being different. Cold.'

'I'm doing my job,' Jess said. 'What do you expect? Your mum asked me to come and check on you and here I am. In my lunch break too. So if we can just get on with things, I might actually get the chance to grab something to eat.'

'We both know there is more going on here,' Libby said, taking a sip of water, which hurt like bejeezus when she swallowed. 'I've not heard from you since the weekend. We never go that long without speaking. I'm sorry if I've neglected you. I didn't mean to.'

Jess looked at her for a moment and then reached into her bag and pulled out her prescription pad. 'I'll nip out and pick this up for you. I think you should start them as soon as possible.'

'Jess, please,' Libby said, her voice cracking. 'We need to talk about this.'

'Now's not the time,' Jess said. 'You're sick and I need to get back to work. We both said some things that were pretty horrible, and you're right, we do need to talk about this. But not now.'

Libby wiped away a tear that had crept out of her eye and was sliding down her face. 'I hate us being like this,' she said.

Jess just nodded. 'I'd better get to the chemists.'

With that, she stood up and left, and Libby fell back onto her pillows, where she cried herself back to sleep.

Libby hadn't woken when Jess returned with a box of really large pills and some antiseptic throat spray. She'd found them later, along with a note saying to make sure to take them an hour before food. At least, she thought, Jess had written that she would be in touch. That was something, no matter how small.

Her throat felt as though she had been eating broken glass and her head still felt heavy and sore. She could feel the sheen of sweat that had pooled then cooled between her breasts, behind her knees, at the back of her neck and anywhere else it could cling on to.

She lifted her head gingerly, swallowed one of the tablets Jess had left along with some water, wincing as she did so, and then she fell back on her pillows – the exertion of that simple act being too much. Through tired eyes, she looked to the clock on her dressing table and saw the time illuminated as 4.37. She'd been asleep for about three hours – but she felt no better for it. Three hours when she should have been getting a lot done in the shop. This was absolutely the worst time in the world that she could have been sick. She felt her stress levels rise.

For the first time that day, she reached for her phone. The brightness of the screen hurt her eyes, but she needed to try and stay on top of things.

She could see a number of messages had been left.

The first was from her dad, telling her everything was under control.

There were two from her mum, telling her to stay in bed and to take it easy.

There was one from Ant – saying he would call her later. That he knew she was sick. Jess had told him. It was formal in nature. No little kisses at the end of it or flirty undertones.

There were a few voicemails from suppliers. Emails marked urgent that she couldn't quite focus on.

Libby felt thoroughly sorry for herself – so sorry in fact that even her mum arriving home with some ice cream for her throat didn't lift her spirits.

'As soon as you feel a little stronger, we'll get you in the shower and I'll change these bedsheets,' her mum said, happy to have been able to adopt the role of chief carer for her child again.

Libby knew she must smell. Every now and again, she caught a whiff of something unpleasant. It wasn't hard to imagine the stuffiness of the room and her sweat-soaked body created a pungent aroma. Her mother fussed around the room, opening the curtains just enough to allow some fresh air from the open window in but not too much so that the brightness burned her daughter's retinas. Libby watched as she proceeded to light a scented candle. God, she really must smell quite extraordinary – and not in a good way.

'Now there, pet. Sip some water for me. Jess said you're to keep your fluids up,' her mum said, as she thrusted a glass of iced water, resplendent with a bendy straw, under Libby's nose.

It was nice to have someone care for her, Libby thought. It was nice to feel loved and safe. Much to her chagrin, this was enough to send Libby off into another flurry of tears.

'Libby, darling. What is it? You'll start to feel better soon, you know. These are strong antibiotics. Give it twenty-four hours and you'll be on the road to recovery. I know you feel rotten, but there's no need to cry.'

Her mother sat on the bed beside her and pulled her into a hug. She even kissed the top of Libby's greasy head, which proved the selfless nature of maternal love.

'Oh, Mum,' Libby sobbed. 'Things are a bit of a mess.'

'Ah now, pet. What's happened? I'm sure it's not that bad.'

'I'm sick. I'm going to be sick for a few days at the very least, and the shop needs so much work. And the flat – I've not even started on the flat and I can't see me finding the time. You and Dad have been so good to me, letting me stay here. But we all need our own space, and I don't want to take advantage.'

Her mum made soothing noises and held her just a little bit closer. 'You always have a home here, Libby. The flat will get sorted, probably sooner than you think. There's nothing there that isn't insurmountable. The shop will be fine. It's in safe hands with your dad in your absence. The important thing is, you rest and get better properly. Once the shop opens, you won't get that chance. It's not a mess, darling. It's just another hurdle.'

'But Jess,' Libby sobbed. 'We've fallen out, and, Mum, I'm sure she hates me. We never fall out, but she thinks I've been a rubbish friend. And maybe I have. I don't know any more. We said such absolutely horrid things to each other, Mum.'

'I'm sure she doesn't hate you. How could she? You two are like sisters, and, you know, sometimes sisters fight and say horrible things to each other. You should have seen me and your auntie Joan. We'd batter each other until your granny stepped in to stop us. Jess came to see you today, didn't she? Brought you medicine. There's nothing on earth that could split you two up.'

'Ant,' Libby muttered.

'What?'

'Ant. He could come between us.'

Her mother pulled back and looked at Libby. 'Oh no. She hasn't been having a fling with him behind your back? Oh God. I wouldn't have thought that of her.'

Libby shook her head, a movement which caused her so much pain she almost cried out. 'No. Nothing like that. I don't think. No. But they have made friends, and they have – well, it's like they've ganged up on me. I know that sounds really childish. Jess says I've been a neglectful friend – putting Ant before her. And now the shop, which she says I put ahead of both her and Ant.'

'And what does Ant say?'

Libby blushed. She wasn't sure her mother was quite aware of the full casual nature of her relationship with Ant.

'Not a lot, as it happens. But he's become more distant since work started at the shop. And last week he met Jess on the beach and, it seems they spent a good deal of time talking about me. She was there when I went to see him last Saturday and they were getting on like a house on fire. They chatted about more things in those few hours than I think Ant and I have ever discussed. I might as well have not been in the room.' Libby's head throbbed and pulsed. Her throat felt dry and swollen.

Her mum pulled her into a hug again. 'They met on the beach?'

'It was just a coincidence, they said. I do believe that. I think. But, Mum, it's just showed me how messy things are. Ant and I – we don't really have much in common, if I'm honest. We get along, but it's not love. As for Jess, she's lonely and I let her down.

I know I did. Seeing her so animated with Ant, well, I suppose it made me realise it's been a while since I've seen her that way. Happy and confident. She's not been herself and I've been too wrapped up in my own life to notice.'

'Libby Quinn, I can see why Jess might feel a little put out – but she's a grown-up. You're not responsible for fixing the problems in her life and you've always been a good friend to her. But neither you, nor anyone else, is perfect. People don't always get things right, but it doesn't make them bad people. And surely Jess understands just how much you have invested in the shop, and not just financially. As for Ant? Well, I don't know a lot about relationships. I was very blessed that I met your dad when we were so young. He was the only man for me, and we've been lucky over the years. That's not to say it's always been easy. Relationships require a lot of work, and even more patience. That said, I could work at things and be patient with him because deep in my heart I have always known he is the love of my life. You deserve that big love too, darling. And more. So much more. So if Ant isn't the love of your life, if he doesn't share your enthusiasm for your hopes and dreams, then it's okay to walk away. And, actually, for the pair of you, it's the right thing to do.'

Libby couldn't help but cry. Again. Because she knew her mother was right, and just hearing someone else say it – and tell her it was okay – had made it all very real.

22

THE UGLY DUCKLING

Libby had been snoring. She knew that as soon as she woke, the echo of her own loud grunting having hauled her from her sleep.

She lay in her darkened room and swallowed, and was delighted to find that her throat felt marginally better. It was the day after she'd started on her antibiotics and they had clearly started to kick in.

That's not to say she felt well. She still felt absolutely wretched, but the pain had at least lessened.

Her mother had helped her out of bed that morning and had cleaned her room while Libby had stood under the hot pins of water pulsing through the shower and made a half-hearted attempt at washing her hair, and her body. Even the exertion of lifting her hands above her head had been enough to fell her.

She was no sooner dressed in fresh pyjamas than she'd crawled into the fresh linen her mother had put on her bed and lay down.

'You can't go to sleep with wet hair,' her mother had immediately yelled, startling Libby from her already almost comatose state. 'Here,' her mum had said, 'let me.'

Libby had sat, powerless but grateful, while her mother had gently brushed and blow-dried her hair, just as she had done so many times when she was a little girl.

'Jess phoned,' her mum had said. 'To see how you were.'

'What did you tell her?' Libby had asked, worried that her mother might have challenged Jess over the falling out.

'I told her you were still really unwell, and in bed. And she was welcome to come round and see you.'

'Did she say she would?' Libby had asked, hopeful.

'She said she'd be in touch,' her mother had said, her voice soft. 'And if she doesn't, I'll be calling her back and giving her a piece of my mind.'

Once her hair was dried, Libby had fallen back into a deep sleep. She didn't even have the energy to worry about the shop. Her dad had told her everything was fine, and in her weakened state, she was content not to push for more details.

She'd no idea what time it was when she woke. The blackout blinds were more than efficient. She became aware of a knock on her bedroom door. There was something about it that was familiar – so familiar that she wondered had she heard it just seconds before. Had it been that, along with her snoring, that had woken her?

Her father's voice came through the door. 'Libby, love. Can I come in?'

She croaked a yes and rubbed her eyes to try and shake the sleep from them.

The door creaked open and her father walked in, straight to the window, where he lifted the blinds just a crack. It was enough to make Libby recoil, like a vampire afraid of perishing in the sun.

'I'll not open them too far,' her father said. 'But I've a surprise for you.' He then went on to mutter the six most terrifying words she was ever likely to hear in her life. 'I've brought Noah to see you.'

Libby tried to say no. She tried to hide under her duvet – but before she could open her mouth or hide herself from view, her father had walked back over to the door and ushered in an uncomfortable-looking Noah.

'I asked your dad how you were and before I could say anything else he'd invited me for tea and it seems he doesn't like to take no for an answer.'

'You've worked hard today. It's the least we can do to feed you a decent meal,' Libby's father said, clearly not taking on board the fact that Noah ran a gastro pub and had full access to a plethora of decent meals whenever he wanted. 'I'll go and open us a couple of beers and you can tell Libby about how good the shop is looking,' he said, before turning to Libby. 'Ach, Libby, you'd be delighted to see the place today. I actually think you've a good chance of pulling this off. Oh, and the glazers called and said they'd be ready to refit the windows next Friday. Sure, once that's done, you're laughing. And pest control have sealed up all entry points – they think some of the mice were coming in through your attic. But you're now a rodent-free zone. And this boy here wasn't one bit afraid to get his hands dirty either – lifting and moving. A real grafter, Noah. That's what you are. A grafter and a good man!'

At that, Jim Quinn nodded towards the stairs and told Noah he would see him soon. Beer in hand.

Libby just sat, pale-faced and pyjama-clad, in her bed, wishing she had an invisibility cloak.

The only, very slight, consolation to Libby was that Noah looked almost as mortified by the whole situation as she was.

'Your dad's a lovely man,' he said, shuffling awkwardly from foot to foot. 'He said you were sick, but I didn't realise you were as bad as this. I'd have stayed away. Maybe even painted a black cross on the door of the shop in case you left any traces of the plague there.'

'Ha ha, very funny,' Libby croaked, her throat aching at the effort of speaking, but she was surprised to find that he had at least put a smile on her face.

'You're looking well,' Noah said, pulling a horrified face, and she laughed a little more.

'Oh, don't make me laugh, it hurts,' she groaned.

'Well, looking at the state of you is hurting my eyes, if you must know,' he said with a wink, but his voice was so soft, she had no doubt he was teasing. 'But I'm going to be honest – I didn't have you down for a chintzy Laura Ashley kind of a girl? Where are the posters of hot young pop stars that you snogged when you were a teen? I was hoping to get a peek at an even geekier you than you are now.'

'Afraid you missed your chance,' she said. 'The worst of my teenage misdemeanours were hidden away a long time ago – my parents were keen to get their guest suite. I haven't always lived here, you know – I only came back when I started saving and planning to take on the shop.'

'Well, you are a remarkable woman,' he said with a smile. 'But I really had been hoping to be able to tease you mercilessly about the awkward years, Bookshop Libby. Jo bet me you'd be a Westlife kind of a girl, but I thought maybe more Oasis.'

'You owe Jo some money, I'm afraid,' Libby said with a smile. 'You should know that "cool" has never been a word used about me. Ever.'

'I should've known,' Noah said with a smile. 'How're you doing anyway? Is it fatal? Do I need to be organising a floral tribute? You're still a new girl, so we will probably only manage the letter L in carnations and not 'Bookshop Libby' in roses or the like.'

'Pee-the-beds will do me.' Libby laughed.

'Pee-the-beds?'

'Dandelions. That's what we called them growing up. There's something in them – that has a diuretic property. Or so I was told.'

'Every day's a school day,' Noah laughed, 'but, seriously, are you okay?'

Libby shrugged. 'I've been better. But I'll most likely live. This isn't my first fight with my tonsils. A few days and I'll be on the mend. Tired, but on the mend.'

'So, you'll have to slow down then!' Noah said, in a stern voice.

'Hmmm,' Libby replied, in as non-committal a voice as she could manage. 'Anyway, you're very good, helping at the shop. And humouring my dad like this. He's delighted to be bringing a friend home for tea.' She laughed.

'He's a sound man, Libby. I like hanging out with him.'

'Just how much have you been helping him?' Libby asked. 'You've your own business to run.'

'My business runs itself,' he said, which was a lie. 'Jo helped out, and one of the bar staff worked a double shift.'

'Well, let me pay you for that,' Libby said. 'I don't want you out of pocket on my account.' She would be mortified if he thought she was taking advantage of his kindness. Some kind of payment would at least assuage her guilt a little.

'Libby, would you ever stop? I told you. It's no big shakes. It's how we work on Ivy Lane. We help each other when we need to. That's what keeps us all going.'

'It is big shakes though, to help like that. It's very kind of you.'

'I actually enjoyed it. Good company and hard work. Besides, we can't have you falling behind on your big dream,' Noah said.

The way in which he spoke made her realise that he really got it. He totally understood how important this was to her. She felt herself well up, and immediately chided herself for being so pathetic that all she seemed to do when she was sick was cry.

'Oh God, don't be crying,' Noah said, his voice soft. 'I'm a man, I can't cope with that kind of a thing.' His expression was one of concern. She realised, again, just how handsome this man was. This man who seemed to understand her need to make a success of the bookshop more than her friends.

She felt something flip in her stomach that she was pretty sure was not an adverse reaction to her antibiotics. Oh no. He had to stop being so nice to her. She didn't have time for complications. She didn't want to feel things for him – and yet...

But she was sick. It was just that she was feeling unwell. She didn't really have any kind of feelings for him other than a casual fondness.

Neither of them spoke.

Thankfully, a call from downstairs that dinner was ready broke the gaze between them.

'You'd better go. They don't like waiting for dinner,' Libby said.

'Are you going to eat too?' Noah asked.

Libby shook her head before she lied and told him she wasn't hungry and actually just needed to sleep. It was much too risky for her to spend more time with him.

'Okay,' he said. 'Get some sleep, Libby. We need you back on the street soon.' With that, he left.

* * *

Libby woke in the dark and the house was silent. Either Noah had left or he had been poisoned by one of her mother's attempts at a fancy dinner and his corpse was lying downstairs waiting for rigor mortis to set in. Either way, Libby didn't feel well enough to investigate.

She shivered even though she knew the room was too warm. Glancing at her phone, she saw that it had gone midnight – and that there were two messages blinking at her. One from Ant and one from Jess. Ant sent his 'best'. It had the feel of a work email more than a message from a lover. Jess said she'd call round the next day. Libby noticed the messages had been sent just minutes apart. She wondered, for a second, while she had the energy to care, if they were together when they sent them, before dismissing that thought as ridiculous. Although there was no denying Jess seemed to have a better dynamic with Ant than she ever had.

She staggered to the bathroom, looked at the horror show she had become in the mirror and wondered how Noah hadn't run screaming from her room, before she wandered back into bed, pulled the covers up around her and tried to drift back off to sleep to escape all the many confusing and conflicting thoughts that were dancing around her head.

When morning arrived, she decided that she felt better and pushed all thoughts of resting properly from her mind. Libby dragged herself from her bed again – and stood under the hot streams of water from the shower, trying to convince herself that she felt a little more human. However, she took a full twenty minutes to dry herself – during which time she sat on the toilet seat and wondered if she was swaying or the room was spinning or if it was a combination of both.

Dragging her aching limbs back into her bedroom, she looked in her wardrobe for something to wear which weighed as little as humanly possible. She sat on her bed, then lay on her bed – hair wet and limp – naked and shivering even though the room was hot, but too tired to dressed.

It took almost half an hour before Libby finally hauled on a light cotton summer dress over her most comfortable (therefore oldest) underwear. She pulled her damp hair into a ponytail without brushing it and slipped her feet into a pair of battered Converse she normally reserved for wearing around the house when she was doing her cleaning.

The exertion was enough to cause her to break out in a sweat, but she was determined not to give into it. It didn't matter that her mum had told her she had to rest. It didn't matter that both her dad and Noah were on top of things at the shop. She needed to feel useful. By the time she reached the kitchen, and needed another sit-down, her head was fuzzy and her limbs like concrete. But she had to get to work – so she hauled herself to her feet and reached for her bag and keys, only to find they felt much too heavy.

She became vaguely aware of a voice fading in and out beside her.

'Libby, what on earth are you doing?' she heard and turned her head to see her mum's face swim in front of hers.

'Work,' she muttered. 'The shop.'

Her mother eyed her up and down, then Libby could hear the sound of her mother's gentle laughter. 'Oh, pet, you're going nowhere.'

She felt herself being led out of the kitchen and towards the bottom of the stairs.

'But the shop...'

'Didn't that big handsome friend of yours say he would help? And your dad has already left. I'm going to nip in later and see if I can help too.'

Libby tried to argue, but she was finding it hard to think of the right words to say, so reluctantly she let her mother guide her back upstairs and into bed.

When sleep finally loosened its grip mid-afternoon, she lifted her phone to find even more messages.

Ant wanted to know if he could call round. But only if she was sure she wasn't infectious because he had a busy week ahead. 'I hope you understand,' he said. At least he had put a solitary 'x' at the end of this message. Jess had also messaged, to check if she had been taking her medicine and saying she would be round after tea, and to let her know if she could bring anything with her. Libby took this as a positive sign that there was hope for their friendship after all. If they could both move past all the things they had said.

The next message was a picture from Noah, of him and her dad standing in front of the draper's counter in the shop – their thumbs raised and cheesy smiles on their faces. She could see that the exposed brickwork behind them had been repointed. It made her smile. Noah wrote:

I hope this makes you feel better. We've got it covered. And I've changed my mind. You owe me at least 500 shifts in the pub 😉

All she could bring herself to do was to message him back a thank you and say she poured a rubbish pint but she was sure she wouldn't damage his business too much.

Then she looked at Ant's message again – wondered where his offer to help in her hour of need was, wondered why the thing that mattered to him most about how she was feeling was whether or not she was contagious.

She'd never seen him as particularly selfish before, but clearly she had either been blind to this quality in him or he had decided that he too wanted to distance himself from whatever their relationship had been. She could hardly blame him. She had started to wonder what had ever truly brought them together in the first place. Aside from chemistry, they had little else to bond them. Everything in the last week had just highlighted that.

Again, an image of him and Jess chatting – properly chatting – and laughing together, in a very easy way, came to mind. There were no awkward silences, only made less awkward by distracting each other from the chasms that existed between them by falling back on their physical chemistry. In a strange way, she could see how Jess and Ant were better suited than she ever was with Ant. And if he hadn't been behaving like a spoilt brat ever since work had begun on the shop, and if it just wasn't so completely weird, pairing the two of them up could be the answer to her problems.

But Jess, who had always been a little softer at heart than Libby was, deserved perfection. No game-playing. No business-like text messages. Jess, despite her academic success and popularity with her patients, struggled to make close friendships and let people in. She needed a man who loved her so completely that she would have no choice but to love him back.

In that second, Libby missed her friend so very much and knew that she wouldn't ever feel settled until they had talked everything out and made up.

She unlocked her phone again and sent a message to Ant to tell him that she would be in touch when she was out of quarantine. She very purposely did not add any x's to the end of her message. As acts of passive aggression went, it was on the small scale, but it felt like a victory of sorts all the same.

Then she sent Jess a message telling her she was looking forward to seeing her and the only thing she needed her to bring was herself.

She was delighted when Jess replied within minutes to say she was on her way over.

* * *

Jess arrived within the half-hour. Libby heard her greet her mother and say she would go straight up. She also heard her mother tell Jess that the two of us would need to sort out our differences before she knocked our heads together. And that we were 'a bit long in the tooth' to be having fall outs.

Jess arrived up the stairs just a few seconds later, waving a white hanky as she walked in the room – a plastic bag of goodies in her other hand. 'I'm under strict instructions that we have to work this out,' Jess said. 'And, Libby, I do want to work this out. I'm so sorry for the things I said. I didn't mean them. Not really.'

Libby looked at her friend, her face sincere. 'Yes, you did,' she told her, but with no hint of bitterness or accusation there.

'I don't think the bookshop is stupid,' Jess said meekly, sitting down on the edge of the bed. 'And I don't think you're selfish.'

Libby paused. 'I have been though. I've been so caught up in my own life, I've put everyone else second.'

'But that's allowed sometimes,' Jess said. 'It's just... I miss you. You know? And you're right, I am lonely. My flat is lonely. My life is one big groundhog day of getting up, going to work, coming home and cooking dinner for one and watching Netflix until bedtime. Let me tell you, that Netflix and chill with just yourself for company is absolutely zero craic.' Jess smiled, but it was small and didn't quite reach her eyes.

'I'm sorry, I've been crap. My head has been all over the place since Grandad died. I feel as if I'm stuck in some strange world where everything looks the same as before but it's all changed. It all feels different. Duller. Numb, I suppose. Empty, and it's only now I feel as if I'm waking up and I'm scared and confused, but excited too. Does that make sense?'

Jess nodded. 'Grief does strange things to us,' she said. 'Maybe

I should've realised you were struggling more before now. I am a bloody doctor after all. All I could feel was my own hurt.'

'I've pushed you away,' Libby said.

They both stopped talking and looked at each other, seeing the mix of hurt and love in each other's eyes.

'I don't like it when we fall out,' Jess sniffed.

'Me neither.'

'And that was a spectacular falling out,' Jess said. 'Have we ever gone that long without speaking before?'

Libby shook her head. 'Never.'

Jess reached for her hand and squeezed it. After a minute, she spoke again. 'Libby, there's something else we need to talk about too.'

Libby knew exactly what her friend was going to say before she even opened her mouth. 'I know. My reaction when I found you with Ant.'

Jess nodded. 'It hurt me, Libby. It was as if you could actually believe that I would go behind your back. You looked at me so strangely. It was just a coincidence,' she said. 'That meeting on the beach. At first, I didn't even recognise him. I'd my earbuds in and my head down. I felt his hand on my shoulder and he very nearly got a slap on the face.'

Libby could just imagine Jess, who had insisted they both attend self-defence classes in their twenties, striking out at Ant.

'I know you were disappointed neither of us went to Belfast with you. And I know arriving to see that I was at his house must have been a bit of a surprise, but really, you've nothing to worry about. We'd just got talking and, to be honest, I didn't even realise how much time had passed. It was great to have the company, you know. To talk to someone without it ending up with them listing their symptoms or asking for medical advice. But it wasn't that we had lied to you or had anything to hide. We were just chatting.'

Her friend's gaze fell to her knees, and Libby watched as she picked a bit of invisible fluff off her linen trousers. She couldn't help but feel that Jess was holding something back, but she had to trust her. She did trust her. She'd trust Jess with her life.

'That's not what affected my mood,' Libby replied. 'Seeing you there. Yes, it was strange and, yes, I was hurt about Belfast. But... seeing the two of you together made me realise more clearly than before that there's no future for Ant and I together.'

Jess looked stricken. 'But we didn't do anything!'

Libby gave a sad smile. 'I'm not saying you did. But, Jess, you two? You just gelled. There was something in the way you were together that has never been there between Ant and I. And I want that, I suppose. Someone to chat to and laugh with and who I have shared interests with.'

'He's a decent man, Libby,' Jess said and her face coloured. 'I can see why you've held on to him so long.'

Libby wondered, did she see a spark of something else in her friend's eyes when she spoke of Ant?

'He is a decent man,' she agreed. 'But he's not the decent man for me. I don't see a future for us and I don't think that will come as a surprise, or a disappointment, to him. We had a good time, but it was never going to be forever.'

Jess responded by pulling her friend into a big, tight hug and telling her that everything would work out. Libby allowed herself to believe that with her best friend at her side once again, it might just.

* * *

Libby was wiped out by the time Jess left. She didn't think all their issues had been resolved, but she did feel they had made significant progress. Their rift would not be fatal to their friendship after all.

She was tired and craved a sleep, but she realised that she could no longer put off the conversation she had been dreading.

Scrolling through her phone, she hit Ant's number, coughed to clear the worst of the huskiness from her voice, and waited for him to answer. The nausea in the pit of her stomach seemed to be rising.

After three rings, she heard his deep Donegal-accented voice. 'Libby,' he said (not babe, or hon, like he may have done at other times), 'I thought you were still at death's door. Are you back in the land of the living?'

'Not quite, I think I'm maybe in some sort of purgatory – you know. Halfway between here and there,' she coughed.

There was a silence. Awkward.

'I suppose you won't be up for getting together? We need to talk,' he said.

'We do,' she said, hearing an unexpected wobble in her voice. 'But I'm not well enough to go out.'

'Are you well enough for a visitor?'

Libby thought about how tired she felt. She weighed it up with how much she wanted to get this conversation over and done with. It could wait just that little bit longer until she was feeling more rested.

'I don't think I am,' she said. 'Jess just left and I need to sleep. But can you do tomorrow? Could you come here?'

There was a pause. 'Tomorrow evening, after work?' he asked. 'We'll talk then.'

'Okay. I'll look forward to it,' Libby said before hanging up. Although she was baffled as to why she'd used those words. Who really ever looks forward to breaking up with someone?

23

THE SECRET

Monday morning – and when Libby woke, she found she could swallow without leaving herself feeling like she had been through the wars. The room didn't spin as much when she got up and there was a colour other than 'deathly pallor' about her. She showered without needing to do it in stages and found she had the energy to dress in a T-shirt and a pair of linen trousers afterwards. She was even able to brush through her hair and spritz on some sea salt spray to add a little wave to her look. Though, admittedly, she was exhausted when she was done and had to lie on top of her bed for a good thirty minutes before she had the energy to move again.

She padded downstairs to where her parents were sat at the kitchen table finishing their breakfast. On seeing her, Libby's mother jumped to her feet. 'Libby Quinn! You should be in bed! You're sick.'

'I'm feeling a bit better, Mum,' she said, 'and I just needed out of my room for a little bit before cabin fever set in.'

She made herself a cup of tea and sat down, trying not to think about Ant's impending visit.

'Is anyone at the shop today?' she asked her dad, who looked between her and her mother before speaking.

'We decided to give everyone the day off,' he said. 'They've all been working around the clock and this good weather isn't going to last forever. Your mum has even taken the day off to enjoy it and you know how little that happens. And besides, with a little help from your pal Noah, we got through much more yesterday than we'd hoped for.'

Libby felt her heart thud at the mention of his name. No, she was being silly. Her palpitations were not about Noah Simpson. They were at the thought of her lovely shop sitting empty – no work at all being done.

'He's a nice fella,' her dad said. 'You're lucky to have good neighbours. That one has his head screwed on. There's a man who knows what's really important.'

'Well, with his background, it's no wonder,' her mother said and Libby couldn't hold in her curiosity any more.

'His background? What about his background? You said before his family had their share of troubles.'

Her parents shared a glance. 'Do you not remember the Simpsons?' her mother asked. 'God, it was such an awful tragedy. Some families have so much to deal with. I remember thinking I'd never complain again.'

Libby furrowed her brow. 'No, I don't remember them, but I do know Noah went into foster care when he was fourteen or so.'

'Well, let me think, it would have been at least twenty years ago, or more. You'd only have been a child yourself. First, his poor mother died, God rest her. Cancer, I think it was. And then, his father and grandparents all killed in a car accident. Black ice. On the Letterkenny Road. It was devastating. I remember it so well. The coverage at the time. *The Derry Journal* ran a picture of him, a wee lost soul, at the funeral. He was fourteen, but he looked so much younger. A wee skinny thing. It would have taken tears from a stone. His other set of grandparents had died years before that, and his mum's sister was living in America at the time. There was no one to take him in, so foster care it was. I don't think anyone would've blamed him if he'd gone off the rails a bit, but no, he kept his nose clean and now look at him...'

Libby thought of Noah. Tall, toned, so strong and so passionate about helping people. He seemed so in control of his life, of his emotions. It broke her to think of him as a devastated young teenager having to start over after so much unspeakable tragedy.

But it did explain a lot. It explained why community and family were so important to him. It explained why he seemed to warm to waifs and strays, from Paddy the dog, to the stubborn young woman opening a bookshop just across the street from him.

He was like that with everybody, she realised. She was stupid to think it was anything to do with her personally. Not that she needed the complications of any more men in her life. Especially now. Especially when she had to concentrate on her shop. Especially when she was, technically, still seeing Ant, although she was under no illusion that both of them knew it was over.

The timing was so very wrong to even allow fleeting romantic feelings towards Noah into her mind. Because, yes, she *was* having romantic feelings towards Noah. She finally admitted it to herself. Admitted that he got under her skin, but not just in the way Ant had. This was more than an attraction based on chemistry. This was about the person he was. His sense of humour. His protective nature. His shared values. God, she was stupid not to have admitted it to herself before now.

But what was the point? Nothing could come of it. She could not do anything that would risk the happy equilibrium of Ivy

Lane and the success of Once Upon A Book. Taking a chance on the man across the road was too much of a risk.

And, she reminded herself yet again, she did still have a boyfriend. A boyfriend who was coming to see her today.

She brought her mug to her lips to sip and realised both her parents had been staring directly at her.

'Libby,' her dad said, 'are you sure you're feeling okay? We've been chatting away to you and you've been off in your own world altogether. We were about to ask you if you minded us kicking you out of your room today, just to see if it provoked a response.'

'God, yes. Well, not better, but I'm okay. Just a lot on my mind. Poor Noah,' she offered. 'That's a lot of tragedy.'

'It is. But he's a good man. He's made the best of things. And, I'll tell you this, that pub sells the best pint of Guinness in Derry,' her father said.

'You were drinking?' her mother asked, eyebrow raised. 'You were telling me how hard you were working. Not a moment to rest.'

'A man has to have his lunch,' her father replied. 'And Noah offered me a pint and a big bowl of Irish stew, it would've been rude of me to refuse, wouldn't it?'

'Aye, I'm sure your arm was twisted up your back,' her mother said, laughing.

Her dad just shrugged and laughed and Libby couldn't help but once again be reminded about what relationships should really be like. This soft, gentle ribbing. The accepting of each other's flaws. The joy in mundane things like talking about dinner, or what was on TV, or what they needed to get from the garden centre.

A feeling of immense love for her parents washed over her. She was incredibly lucky, and after hearing about Noah's sad past, she appreciated just how much.

When she had finished her breakfast, she realised she didn't feel quite as if she wanted to go directly back to sleep. In fact, she doubted she would be able to fully relax until after Ant had called. She figured she might even feel up to doing some work. Nothing physical, but she could do a little on her marketing. She wanted to get the shop social media feeds up and running, perhaps share some pictures of the refurbishment process. She quite probably needed to update her accounts too – not that examining her budget filled her full of joy. As long as there were no more hidden expenses, she was hopeful she would actually have money to stock the shop with books in the first place.

She cursed herself when she realised she'd left her laptop in the shop, not only because she needed it to do the work, but also because a building site was hardly the safest environment for a laptop.

'I think I might pop over to the shop,' she said. 'I want to pick some stuff up.'

'You will not be going near that shop!' her father said defiantly, and her mother nodded. 'Dear God, Libby, but you are only just finding the energy to get out of bed without the need to get immediately back in. You'll need another few days at the very least.'

Libby reached out and rubbed her daddy's hand. 'No need to worry, Dad,' she soothed. 'I really only want to pick up my laptop, and I left the catalogues for the coffee machine there too. I need to get the order in, and book some training on how to use the thing if it's all to be up and running on time. And I probably need to start advertising for another staff member. But I need my laptop to do all that.'

'We can go and get it for you,' her mum said.

But Libby really wanted to go herself. As much as she trusted her dad and Noah, she wanted to just double-check everything was going as well as they'd told her. If she was really honest, despite her decision just minutes before that having any romantic feelings for Noah was a bad idea, she also hoped she might just bump into him there too.

'I've cabin fever,' she said. 'I just need to get out for a bit. Not to mention, you don't need to spend your day off running errands for me. That's not the best way to enjoy a day off in the sun. I'll be back before you know it. Ant is calling over later.'

Her parents exchanged glances.

'If you insist on going,' her mum said, 'then we'll take you. Won't we, Jim? And that's an end to it. Sure, we can leave the garden centre to later.'

'Perfect,' her dad said, and both of them nodded.

The deal was done. She knew enough about how they operated to know there was no use in arguing with them.

'I'm excited to see it,' her mum said. 'And besides, I can cast a woman's eye over the place.'

'Erm, Mum, I have a woman's eye myself. Two of them in fact,' Libby said, trying to decide whether to laugh at her mother or be mortally offended.

'All right then, a mammy's eye, if you want to be fussy about it. Now, just let me get this wash out on the line before we go.'

'Do you want me to hang them out? You can get that other load in the machine. It's a great drying day after all,' her dad said, the pair of them slipping into their old familiar roles.

Libby watched as they set about their tasks, continuing their banter as if she wasn't even in the room or part of the conversation. It was comforting in its own way.

* * *

Libby felt every bit the teenager as she sat in the back of her dad's

Vauxhall Astra as they arrived in Ivy Lane. She had tried to persuade them to put the radio on as they drove, but her father had said no, it would be a distraction.

Her mother had, occasionally, turned around and wafted a bag of barley sugars under Libby's nose as if they were on some fancy day trip rather than the fifteen-minute drive across town to the bookshop. It surprised Libby just how many times a person could be offered, and refuse, a boiled sweet in such a short space of time.

'Have you got your keys?' her father had asked as he directed her into the back seat. She had told him she had, but still that didn't stop him asking her again to check and prove to him that she had by showing him. She tried to feel comforted by his concern rather than irked by his refusal to believe she was capable of leaving the house without his guidance. Just because, one time, when she was sixteen, he had driven all the way to Belfast Airport, only for her to announce she had forgotten her passport. (Thankfully, it was still in the days when people arrived at airports four hours too early and there was time for a quick dash home and back again, but not before she had been lectured on the price of petrol and the importance of forward planning.) After hearing what she had about Noah, she had vowed not to let her parents' quirks annoy her too much.

From the outside, the shop on the corner of Ivy Lane looked not too dissimilar to how it had done when she'd first seen it. The real transformation would come with the new doors and windows, and the re-rendering of the cracked and peeling façade. A bright new sign would add the finishing touch. But for now? Now it looked like a survivor of the Blitz.

'Here, Linda,' her dad called back to his wife. 'Come here so I can show you the floor. I can't believe they covered it with lino. It's brilliant.'

It was clear her dad was in his element and it made her smile. He looked animated in a way she hadn't seen since her grandfather had died, and proud too of how much had been done.

Libby followed them inside, while her dad waxed lyrical about the parquet floor, and she gasped. Okay, there were still a few wires here and there. And the lighting hadn't gone in yet. Or the radiators. But she could see the exposed brickwork that had been treated, the floor that had been uncovered and walls that had the beginnings of plaster on them.

'Libby, come and see this,' her father called, taking her hand and leading her behind the counter to the two doors which led off from the shop floor. One led to the stockroom, and the other to what would be the customer toilet and had hitherto been a cupboard, which offered nothing more than a dark space in which rodents could run free.

He opened the door and Libby gasped as he pulled a string and the room was flooded with light. Okay, it was still pretty much a shell. But it was a shell with an actual pristine white loo inside, which, as she discovered, actually flushed, and a working sink with shiny taps. Boxes of tiles sat waiting to be laid and it felt as if she was finally seeing what this place would become.

Libby Quinn had never thought the sight of a toilet could bring her to tears of joy, but here she was, crying anyway.

'Oh Libby,' her Mum exclaimed.

'That's nothing,' her dad said. 'Come and see this!' He opened the door to the stockroom and there was the frame of the small room that would become her kitchen. The plumbing was underway and she could see how it would look when done.

And she could see the shelves from Keith, lined against the wall, looking ready to be filled with books. She ran her hand along the wood and felt excitement surge inside her.

There was so much to do, but so much had been done in such a short space of time.

Libby saw tears form in her mum's eyes, which mirrored her own.

'It's coming together, isn't it?' she asked and her mum nodded, beaming with pride.

'It sure is. You've done a good job,' she said, to which her dad coughed politely. 'And you've done a good job too, love,' she said proudly.

'Sure, what would I do without you both?' Libby asked, pulling them into a family hug.

They were mid-hug when a male voice interrupted them.

'Ah, it's only yourselves,' she heard Noah's voice and her heart skipped a beat. She'd wanted to see him, of course, but what must she look like, with tears running down her face? 'Jim, Linda, Libby...' he said, walking in. 'Jo said she saw the door open and didn't know what was going on – just wanted to check nothing untoward was happening.'

'Only a big family moment here, Noah,' her mum said.

'So I see – and Libby – you're looking better. If still a little pale and emotional.'

'She is pale, isn't she, Noah?' her mum said. 'I told her she looked pale, but she insisted on coming to pick up some things. I think really she just wanted a nosy. It's been killing her not to be here the last few days.'

'Ah, do you not trust us to look after the place?' he said to Libby, feigning offence, and smiled at her parents. 'Your dad and I have been doing a great job.'

'Yes,' her mum said. 'I hear you've been working hard at the Guinness and the stews.'

'Working men need to eat,' Noah smiled. 'Although our chef has nothing on your cooking, Linda!'

Libby laughed. Noah absolutely knew how to wrap her mother around his little finger. She saw her mother blush.

'I suppose you've done an average job,' Libby teased. 'I mean, it'll do.'

'Well, I did try my best,' Noah said. 'I always strive for average.'

It felt good, really good, to be back in the bantering zone. Libby reminded herself this was a nice, safe zone to be in and not one which she needed to complicate at all.

Noah smiled at her, and the sun framed his face just perfectly. She saw the crinkle of the skin around his eyes, his strong jawline, and she realised he was so much more than handsome. He was perfect and she'd love to place her hand on his cheek and move closer and...

No. She had to absolutely and completely not move outside of the bantering zone. No matter how many butterflies were buzzing around in her stomach.

24

CAT ON A HOT TIN ROOF

Libby was retrieving her laptop and the paperwork she wanted from the drapery counter when there was a knock on the door frame and a booming 'hello' from outside.

All four sets of eyes in the shop turned to the door, where Harry, armed with a tin of fly spray, stood.

'Ah, it's just you, Bookshop Libby,' he said, lowering the can of spray and walking in. 'I saw the shutter up and I knew that wasn't your car outside. And Noah here had told me you were sick and that's why you hadn't been in, so I wanted to make sure there was nothing untoward going on in here. How on earth are you? Are you on the mend?' The look of concern on his face was genuine and Libby felt her heart swell.

'I'm a martyr to my tonsils, Harry. I think I'll have to bite the bullet and get them out one of these days, but, yes, I think I am on the mend.'

'She'll not be back properly for at least a few more days,' her mum chimed in. 'Who needs community watch with you two about?' she added, smiling at both Harry and Noah. 'Any burglars wouldn't stand a chance.'

Harry blushed. 'Well, I'm not sure my fly spray would have been much of a deterrent, but I figured a good spray of it right in the face would teach them a lesson.'

'You're a good man, Harry,' Noah said. 'But will you promise me if you ever plan to go gung-ho against would-be criminals in the future – give my door a rattle first? We watch out for each other round here, remember?'

'We do that,' Harry said, smiling – before he looked around the shop and his gaze stopped at Libby's parents. She realised she had yet to introduce them, so she sprang to action. 'Mum, Dad, this is Harry. He runs the corner shop. Harry – these are my parents, Linda and Jim.'

Harry brushed his hand on his trousers before extending his arm to shake hands. 'Well, Linda and Jim, I have to say to you this young lady has only been with us a couple of weeks, but you should be so proud of her. Great to see a young one work so hard. There's not enough of it about these days.'

Noah coughed, and Harry laughed. 'Present company excepted, of course.'

'Thanks, Harry,' Noah teased.

'You've done a good job raising this one,' Harry said, addressing her parents again. 'She's a very welcome addition to our Ivy Lane family.'

Linda blushed and Jim beamed with pride, while Libby felt a warm and fuzzy feeling which she didn't think was just a sign that her temperature was on the up again.

'Thank you for saying so,' her father said. 'We think so too. We're very proud of her – and we're glad that she's setting up in a place like this. Knowing what kind of people are around her makes it easier for us, you know.'

'Ah, we'll keep an eye on her all right. She'll be safe here.'

'I am standing right here, you know,' Libby said. 'But, yes, it is lovely to have you all, but, look, while we're all standing around chatting about how lovely Ivy Lane is, I'm starting to think I could murder a cup of tea. How about we walk down to your shop and get some milk and biscuits. I'm sure we'll find enough mugs around here to make do. It'll be a bit rough and ready, but it's the thought that counts.'

'That sounds just lovely,' Linda said, while Harry smiled.

'I've just the thing,' he said. 'Some apple tarts that are just out of date today – they'll be perfectly fine. I'll go and get them,' he said, turning to walk out. 'There's no need to come with me. You get the kettle on.'

'We could do better than that,' Noah said. 'No offence to your apple tarts, Harry, but why don't you all come over the road for a cup of tea and fresh scones before the lunchtime rush? You too, Harry. Keep the shop shut another wee bit.'

'I couldn't do that,' Harry said, shaking his head.

'You could, Harry. You work seven days a week – take a break,' Noah said. 'We'd enjoy your company.'

'We're only coming over if you let me pay,' Libby said. 'No arguments. You've done more than enough favours.'

'Of course you're paying,' he teased. 'What do you think I am, a charity?' He winked and her stomach flipped again. This was a bad idea. Spending any time with him was a bad idea.

* * *

Exhausted, Libby was delighted to get home just over an hour and a half later. Harry and her father had hit it off and had talked the ears off each other. Her mother had flirted almost mercilessly with Noah – while she had watched, mildly horrified but also impressed with how he had chatted so effortlessly with her mum, making her feel like she was the only person in the room.

The drive home had been difficult. It had felt like a fifteen-minute lecture on the merits of Noah Simpson. She didn't disagree with anything her parents said, but she didn't need to hear it. She was already sold.

Back home, she climbed into her bed for a nap. She needed to have her wits about her when she saw Ant. He deserved her to be honest and open. He deserved her full attention for one last time.

* * *

She jolted awake from her nap after hearing a knock on her bedroom door. She glanced at the clock on her bedside table. She had slept much longer than anticipated. Oh God, she thought. This was not the calm, collected appearance she wanted to project.

She called, 'Come in!' and pulled herself up to sitting, doing her best to smooth down her hair and wipe any suspect drool from her face.

The click of the door handle, the creak of the hinges and she took a deep breath, looking up to see Ant, his face solemn. He pulled a bouquet of clearly expensive flowers from behind his back. 'I thought you might like these,' he said, and she did. They were beautiful flowers. She had never been able to fault Ant on his generosity.

'They're lovely,' she said with a genuine but sad smile.

She looked at him. He was deliciously handsome. A real man's man – broad shoulders, tall, a thick head of dark hair, olive skin, dark eyes. He was movie-star handsome and he looked after himself. He was always groomed impeccably, and his commitment to exercise put Libby to shame. He was successful, wealthy, generous with gifts, and in the bedroom. He loved to cook and, what's more, he was good at it. He lacked an arrogance that he could so easily have had.

His pull was magnetic – and when they had been together, especially to begin with, he had made her feel like the most beautiful, alluring sex goddess on the planet. It had been intoxicating. He had been intoxicating. During the hours they were together she could forget all about her grief and her worries and just relish losing herself with this man and his ability to make her insides turn to molten lava with just one touch of his fingertip.

Such lust though – it didn't last. Something that intense couldn't just keep going indefinitely, not without more to back it up.

While Libby could still acknowledge his handsomeness, and all his many qualities, she couldn't help how she felt. The first hint that they were not suited had spiralled and she had a strong feeling he felt that too. There was an awkwardness to how he handed the flowers to her and to the chaste kiss on her forehead.

She realised she didn't need him like she once had – and she didn't suppose he had really ever needed her. He just enjoyed their time together, but had perhaps known all along that it would never go any further than that.

'You know you didn't have to bring me anything,' she told him and she caught his gaze – his dark eyes were staring straight at her.

'I suppose we need to have the big talk, don't we?' he said. He said it in such a matter-of-fact manner that part of her felt a bit sad that it had come to this. Any passion they had together had been replaced with apathy.

'We do,' Libby agreed.

'Or maybe we don't?' Ant said.

Libby raised her eyebrows. What did he mean? Was he backtracking? She had been sure they'd been on the same page. They *were* on the same page, weren't they?

'I think we do though,' she said, her voice steady.

'Libby,' he said as he reached out and took her hand. 'Do we really? I think we both know it's over? Can't we just agree it is and remain friends and not overanalyse it? We never really were ones for analysing what went on between us. We just enjoyed it. But all good things...'

Relief that he understood washed over her, but was quickly nudged to the side by a feeling of guilt that she had pulled away before he did. She'd always been so sure it would be the other way around.

'Do you blame me?' she asked.

'I'm not sure either of us is really to blame. But, no, I don't blame you. Why would I?'

'Because... well, this all started to go wrong when I got the keys to the shop. And Jess said you've both been talking. That you both felt I'd been a bit selfish and neglectful.' Her face blazed as she spoke.

She watched as Ant coloured slightly. He sighed and rubbed his chin – the scratch of his stubble audible. 'I think nothing went wrong so much as we both realised we're just not meant to be,' he began. 'I think for a while I was, maybe, confused. I'd gotten used to you being around – and then you weren't so much. And I acted like a complete arsehole because I was trying to make sense of it all. Because I do like you, Libby. I've always liked you. We just...'

'...Don't have that much in common,' Libby said.

'Exactly. We had fun and I'll never regret it, but, well – I'm getting older. Starting to think about what I want out of life. I suppose you chasing the dream of your shop is partly responsible for that. And the thing is,' he said, 'I think I want to stop acting like I'm in my twenties. I want to meet someone. I want to meet "the one".'

'And that's definitely not me,' Libby said sincerely.

'Sorry,' Ant said, and he did look sorry.

Libby smiled and brushed his hand. 'There is absolutely nothing to be sorry for,' she said. 'I agree with you. We are not "the one" for each other, and I agree you acted a little bit like an arsehole. But then neither of us are perfect.'

'I'm close to perfect though, aren't I?' he said with cheeky smile.

'Oh absolutely. You're neighbours with perfect. Perfect adjacent, some might say.' She squeezed his hand. 'You'll make some woman very happy.'

'Well, I hope so,' he said. 'It's time for me to grow up and settle down. I want someone to come home to every night, you know? To talk with and laugh with and travel with. Although, if you repeat any of this conversation to anyone, I will deny all knowledge. I've a reputation to protect!'

'Your reputation is safe with me,' Libby said.

He nodded. 'Thank you. Can I ask you, when did you know that it was over? Was there a moment or were you unhappy for a while?'

'First of all, Ant, I don't think I was really unhappy. But when did I know? The night I came back from Belfast to find Jess in your house.'

'You do know nothing happened between Jess and I?' he said, stricken.

'Yes. Of course. But I saw how you chatted. How you interacted. You were so relaxed together. It struck me that you were both quite similar really. Successful, generous, averse to Pot Noodles and ready meals. Maybe that's part of what drew me to you in the first place? That you reminded me a bit of Jess.

Although, I'll be honest, I have never, ever wanted to do the things with Jess that I've done with you. Don't ever entertain that little fantasy,' she smiled. 'But, yes, that night. I suppose, like you said, I realised I wanted more, I deserved more, and so do you.'

'Jess is cool,' he said quietly, and if Libby wasn't mistaken she saw the slightest hint of a blush creep up his neck. 'I'd never really spoken to her before.'

'We were usually occupied with other things,' Libby said, her face flushing.

'This is true,' Ant said. 'But she's a good person. And a good friend to you. You're lucky to have her. You know, that was the night I realised too. Or the night I finally admitted it to myself.' His voice was soft and he didn't meet Libby in the eye.

Libby didn't quite know what to say, but she knew with absolute clarity what he was thinking.

'You like her?' she asked.

'Would you hate me if I did?' Ant answered.

25

Libby shook her head, which hurt just a little. 'No. But that doesn't make it not weird.'

'I know,' Ant said. 'I don't know if she even would want to see me, but I can't deny that I like her. I know I don't really know her, of course, but... sometimes you get a feeling.'

Libby knew what he meant and blushed when she thought of Noah and how she felt about him.

'Look, if we're going to talk this one out, let's go into the garden. I could do with some fresh air, to be honest,' Libby said.

He nodded before she told him to go on down and she would follow him in five minutes. It would, she thought, give her enough time to run a brush through her hair, give her face a quick wash and brush her teeth. It would also give her time to try and gather her thoughts.

Because it would be weird. Even if she had seen how they were suited. She couldn't imagine it would be anything other than awkward if the two of them were to start dating. Would it have an ick factor she just wouldn't be able to shake? But if both of them felt something for each other even akin to the feelings she felt growing inside of her for Noah, should she really let her uncomfortable feelings get in the way of them seeing if they could make things work?

She looked at herself in the mirror and wondered why every little thing in her life had to be so complicated.

* * *

Ant was sitting on one of her parents' garden chairs, under the cover of the big oak tree at the bottom of the garden. It was one of Libby's favourite spots, where she used to sit and watch her grandad and dad working together, tending the flower beds and pruning the rose bushes.

'This is lovely,' Ant said, looking around.

'It is. My parents have always loved their garden,' Libby said. 'It's one of their shared projects over the years.'

He nodded. She and Ant had never had any shared projects.

They sat in awkward silence, listening to the buzz of a distant lawnmower and watching a gentle breeze ripple across the lawn.

One of them would have to be the first to speak, Libby realised, so she took a deep breath.

'So, you have feelings for Jess?' she asked.

'I think so. Or at least, I think I could have. When I saw her on the beach that day, I was just being polite when I said hello. It was a bit awkward really, at first. But we walked together for a bit and, well, we started talking. She's easy to talk to.'

Libby nodded. 'I know. She's a good person. A great person really. She's more of a sister to me than a friend.'

He shook his head, looked down. 'Crap timing, eh?' he said. 'If only I'd met her first. No offence or anything,' he backtracked, immediately mortified by what he'd said and who he had said it to.

'No offence taken,' she replied. 'Well, maybe a little bit of offence, but I understand. Sometimes I think Cupid is off his head on drink half the time and his aim sucks. I wish, for both of you, you'd met first as well. But we get what we're given.' She shrugged her shoulders.

'I suppose. I need to move on. Plenty more fish in the sea and all that,' he said with what was obviously fake enthusiasm. 'I need to know, though, has she ever mentioned me?'

'You know that asking your recently dumped girlfriend if her best friend has the hots for you is a bit insensitive?' Libby said. 'And weird.' She offered him a small smile.

He nodded. 'I do and that's me being an arsehole again. I just wondered, did I imagine it, or did she feel something too?'

Libby could hear the desperation in his voice. She thought of how Jess had spoken about him. How he was a 'decent' man and how she hadn't really noticed time passing when she was with him.

'She enjoyed your company,' Libby said. 'But she didn't say much more than that.'

He nodded, clearly disappointed that she wasn't telling him that Jess had the same feelings for him that he had for her.

'Look, I know Jess and I don't know how I didn't see it before, but if you want my opinion on it? I think you would, given the chance, be good together. Jess might not have expressed her feelings, but I am, or was, your girlfriend. I think that might have stopped her saying everything. But, as I said, she didn't say anything but I saw the look on her face when she talked about you,' Libby took a deep breath. 'That told me everything I needed to know.'

* * *

By Thursday, Libby felt well enough to go back to the shop. She'd achieved quite a bit of admin at home, but she felt the need to be right in the heart of things again. She wanted to smell the paint and plaster, see if the new heating system looked as good as it did in the pictures and finally start to see the outside of the shop start to resemble what she hoped it would eventually look like. The new windows were going in, and she'd managed to have the original wooden arches and panels replicated.

It was almost time to finalise her plans with Craig and start thinking about all the little touches that would make her shop stand out from others. The bistro tables for the coffee bar. A soft sofa or two for people to relax on while drinking their lattes. The copper light fittings she had dreamed of. The artificial plants to add some greenery. The artwork and decoration. All the fun touches that more than made up for the hours spent balancing the books, talking to suppliers over email or on the phone and planning her initial sales list. All the fun touches that would also distract her from the feeling of not-quite sadness she had after her break-up with Ant.

Not that she regretted the break-up. Not one bit. It had, without doubt, been the right thing to do. But he'd been a big part of her life for eight months and it felt odd knowing he wasn't any more.

She also couldn't get what he'd said about Jess out of her mind. One minute she'd find herself on the verge of calling Jess and telling her about it, and the next she told herself it wasn't her place to meddle and if it was meant to me, they would find their own way to make it work.

She had told Jess about the break-up on Tuesday. Jess had replied that she was sorry to hear that. They'd agreed they'd talk about it over a glass of wine when Libby was better. Jess, ever the

GP, of course reminded them both that no alcohol should be consumed while her friend was still taking her antibiotics.

Craig arrived just before four to discuss plans to finalise the layout of the shop.

'Libby Quinn, tell me this, how's the flat coming along?'

Libby pulled a face. It was coming along, just slowly. It had been stripped out and the new heating and wiring done. But apart from that it was still a shell in need of a kitchen and bathroom and, well, just about everything else.

'To be honest, it hasn't been my priority. I'm making sure everything down here is well and truly sorted first and then I'll use what's left over to finish upstairs,' she said, knowing already it was very unlikely to win any interior design awards. It would be basic, but she'd add her own touches to it over time. Thankfully, she still had most of her old furniture in storage and that was an expense she wouldn't have to go to.

'I might just have an offer for you that you can't refuse,' Craig said with a smile.

Libby liked those kind of offers.

'I may know where to get my hands on some nice bathroom fixtures and kitchen cupboards, et cetera. Job lot from a bust building site – good stuff, you know. Well made. It's going for half nothing. So, if you trust me to get something picked out for you, I'll get the lads on it tomorrow? You'll still need to get your appliances for the kitchen, and your shower or whatever, but it will save you a bit of time and money?'

Right then she didn't care if Craig was proposing a camping stove in the kitchen and a collection of buckets in the bathroom – if it was one less thing for her to worry about, she would embrace it with open arms.

'That would be amazing,' she told him and he smiled.

'Happy to help. I know what this place means to you. Noah told me all about it. About your grandad.'

Libby felt a lump rise in her throat, and she thanked Craig before offering him a hug. Maybe everything would come together, just as everyone kept telling her it would, in the end.

* * *

It was Friday evening before she saw Jess, by which stage Libby felt back in the land of the living completely. Yes, she was still pale from her enforced stay indoors, but she felt like a new woman – and a new woman in want of a nice of glass of wine now that she had finished her course of antibiotics.

It was gone six when she walked in through the heavy doors of the pub, pushed her sunglasses back off her face and looked around. Quite quickly, she saw Jess was seated in one of the booths by the window, smiling at her. In front of her sat two wine glasses and a bottle of white chilling in an ice bucket. Libby smiled, waved back and walked over towards her, doing her very best not to look as though she was actively scoping the place for signs of Noah.

She knew she should keep her distance if she wanted to focus on what was really important, but she couldn't quite bring herself to stay away.

Jess stood as Libby approached her – she looked fresh-faced and tanned, dressed in a knee-length linen dress and a soft white cardigan. She wore just a slick of lip gloss to complete her look.

Beside her, Libby, fresh from a day of admiring her new windows while poring over online catalogues from the book wholesalers she'd agreed to use, looked like a bit of a scruff in her cut-off trousers and vest top, with her favourite but distinctly well-loved Converse.

She was surprised to realise she didn't really care that she didn't looked as perfectly put together as her friend. It didn't really matter here. It certainly didn't matter to Noah, who had seen her at her actual worse – semi-conscious with tonsillitis, with hair that looked as though birds had been nesting in it.

Jess pulled her into a hug and she hugged her friend tightly back.

'It's so good to see you,' Jess said.

'You too,' Libby smiled, before she stepped back and slipped into the booth opposite her friend.

'It's been a long, and eventful week,' Jess said as she lifted the wine bottle from the ice bucket, shook the condensation from it and started to pour two large glasses.

Libby raised her glass to her friend and said, 'To no more antibiotics!'

Jess smiled. 'And perhaps to finally agreeing to see a throat specialist and have those bloody things taken out once and for all.'

'Yes, doctor,' Libby said with a smile, and they both sipped from their glasses.

They sat in a silence for a minute or two, both knowing they would have to talk about Libby's break-up with Ant.

'Are you okay? You know, about everything?' Jess asked, her eyes cast downwards.

'I am. I mean, it's a little strange, but I am.'

'Was it awful? The break-up?'

'No. Not at all. We both knew. It was okay. We talked things through, you know. We were adult about it. Sometimes things just aren't meant to be.'

Jess bit her bottom lip and looked into her wine glass. 'Did my name come up at all?'

Libby gulped. When push came to shove, she couldn't lie to her best friend. 'Do you want it to have come up?' she asked.

Jess looked up at her. 'I honestly don't know. Actually, no, don't tell me. I shouldn't have asked. Ignore me. No good can come of knowing.'

Libby nodded. Except she knew some good could perhaps come of it. It would just be goodness that was weird for her and, if it all went wrong, would she feel responsible in some way?

But Jess was a grown-up, and Ant had seemed very sincere. Both of them, at heart, were good people, who could possibly make each other happy.

'He did mention you,' she blurted. 'It was a bit awkward, you know. But, yes, he felt a connection. That wasn't news to me, Jess. I saw the pair of you together. What you do with that information is up to you, but, Jess, I want you to be happy. God knows you deserve it. If there's a chance that he could do that for you, then maybe you need to explore that. And I'll cope, because I'm a grown-up. Just spare me the intimate details.'

Once she'd actually said the words, she knew she'd done the right thing. The rest was out of her hands. She could only control what she could control – and that was all she'd try to do.

'And what about you, Libby? Are you happy? You deserve that too,' Jess asked, cutting through her thoughts.

'I think I will be. I am, I mean, but I think I could be even happier and that's okay. I'm finally where I want to be. Where I never thought I could actually be. About to make Grandad proud by opening this shop in his honour. So don't worry about me. I've got this.'

It was at just that moment she saw Noah walk out from the office behind the bar. Despite her best attempts to act cool, she found herself smiling. Jess turned her head to see what her friend was smiling at.

'There's that barman. He's the one who took you to Belfast?' Jess said, and Libby realised she hadn't confided in her friend about her growing feelings for Noah.

'Yes. Yes, he did. That's Noah.'

'And he's going out with that barmaid?'

'No. No, they're siblings. Well, foster brother and sister. Very close, you know, but definitely not going out together.'

Jess looked at her. 'Libby Quinn, is there something else you want to tell me?'

Libby saw that Noah was walking over towards them. No, there was nothing else she wanted to tell Jess – and certainly not now.

'Libby, have you seen Jo on your travels? She took Paddy out earlier and I was expecting her back by now.'

Libby shook her head while Jess mouthed 'Who's Paddy?' at her.

'Paddy's the dog,' she told Jess. 'I'm pretty sure you met him.'

Jess nodded. 'Right, okay, I remember.'

'I'm sure they're not far from here,' Libby said.

Noah glanced at the door and back at the growing queue of impatient drinkers and then back at Libby. 'I hope so. The hoards are getting restless.'

'Libby, you have some bar experience, don't you? Why don't you help for a few minutes?' Jess said, a sly smile on her face. Libby knew exactly what her friend was trying to do, but she wasn't sure it was a good idea. Besides, even if it was Jess suggesting she help, she had only just mended their friendship and the last thing she wanted to do was leave Jess sitting on her own.

'Well, some bar experience might be a bit of an exaggeration,' she said, thinking that she'd only helped out behind the bar at the golf club for half an hour one day and had almost cried when someone ordered a Guinness.

'Anything would be a help, to be honest,' Noah said, and she didn't think she'd ever seen him flustered before.

'Help the man out, would you?' Jess pleaded. 'I'll be happy sitting here on my own for a bit. I've some calls I need to catch up on from work.'

Libby knew her friend was lying. There was no way that Jess was making work calls in a bar, but she didn't want to call her out on it.

'Okay,' she relented. 'But no cocktails or pints of Guinness. You're on your own with those!'

'I'll give your friend back to you as soon as Jo arrives or the rush dies down. Whatever happens sooner. Or actually, just if I find her really annoying which is also a possibility,' Noah told Jess and Libby found herself playfully punching his arm and then desperately trying not think about the fact she had just felt the warmth of his skin on hers. Albeit only a very small amount of their skin had met, but it had been enough to make her feel giddy.

That slightly heady feeling didn't ease up as they stood together for the next half-hour and worked as a team. They manned the left of the bar and found their rhythm as they poured glasses of wine and opened bottles of beer. When Jo eventually returned, looking a little dishevelled and explaining that Paddy had insisted on dragging her the long way round the park – twice – Libby had almost been disappointed to be relieved of her duty and sent back to Jess, who was watching her with a broad smile on her face.

'Libby Quinn. You better tell me all about him, and now.'

'There's nothing to tell. He's my neighbour and he's very helpful. He's like this with everyone from the Lane. You should hear my dad talk about him – he'd have him beatified because he knows how to fit a Rawlplug properly and, of course, because he owns a pub.'

Jess put her hand up. 'Hang on a minute. Wind that back for me. The bit that he's your neighbour and nice to everyone on the Lane, I get that. But the bit about your dad? And Rawlplugs?'

'He's been helping Dad out while I've been sick. The two of them are like a double act.'

'He's been helping out? How much?'

Libby shrugged. 'Enough, I suppose. Dad invited him over for dinner the other night to thank him.'

At this, Jess almost choked on her wine. 'He's been at your house? For dinner? With your dad? Libby! This is something I feel I should've known.'

Libby blushed. 'But it didn't mean anything. You know. I was sick. I wasn't even there for dinner myself. I was up in my bed looking like something the cat dragged in. And everyone's been helping out, it's not just Noah.'

'But Noah's the only one you get giddy over?' Jess asked, and before she even thought about it, Libby replied.

'Yes.' Then immediately realised what she'd said. 'But it doesn't mean anything. The shop is my focus now, Jess. I'm not looking for any other kind of outside interest or commitment other than selling books and learning how to use a coffee machine that comes with a ninety-page instruction manual and a bespoke barista training course. Two full days it will take me to learn how to make coffee!'

'Hmmm,' Jess said, one eyebrow raised. 'I think the lady doth protest too much.'

'Well, I think the other lady should mindeth her own business,' Libby said with a smile. But inside she really did want Jess to stay out of it. She wanted everyone to stay out of it, because the timing was so completely wrong and the stakes were too high.

'Ladies, what are we talking about? Share the gossip,' a male voice boomed, making Libby jump, as Noah pushed his way into the booth. 'You don't mind me sitting down, do you? I need a few minutes. That was some rush. Thanks again, Libby. You're a life-saver. I mean, we totally need to train you on how to pour an ordinary pint, as well as a pint of Guinness, but you made a good start.'

'Cheers,' Libby said. 'Can we expect you to undergo training on book merchandising at any stage in the near future?'

'What's to learn? Stick some books in the window and sell them. Job done!'

'If only,' Libby said.

She glanced at Jess, who was wearing an expression which very much said that she would not, in any way, be minding her own business at any stage in the near future. Libby would have given her the evil eye in return, but the truth was, in that moment, she was much too lost in enjoying feeling the warmth of Noah's presence beside her, his thigh nudging against hers as they sat side by side in the booth. He smelled good. Had he always smelled good or was she just noticing now?

'I definitely think you should add to your skill set, Libby,' Jess said, cutting through her not altogether pure thoughts. 'You've always said you'd love to be able to pour a Guinness. Noah should definitely teach you.' Jess had one eyebrow raised and was barely suppressing a grin.

'Well, that's that sorted then, Bookshop Libby,' Noah said. 'Guinness lessons when you're next free.'

Libby didn't know whether to laugh or cry.

26

'I think, maybe, I think I need to make a phone call. If you just excuse me, I'll step outside for a bit,' Jess mumbled ten minutes later, lifted her bag and her wine glass, and edged her way out of the booth, leaving Noah and Libby sat side by side. She threw a look back to Libby which let her know, in no uncertain terms, that she didn't really want to make a phone call.

'So, how are you? Are you really feeling much better or just pushing through because you don't know how to stop?' Noah asked.

'I took almost a week off, Noah. I think I know how to stop.'

'You spent almost a week at home, but I know for a fact you were working for at least half of that. Just not the physical stuff.'

'It still had to be done. It still needs to be done,' she said. 'But if you want an answer to your original question. I'm okay. I'm really feeling better. Not one hundred per cent, but I'll get there.'

'Your dad told me about your break-up,' Noah said, not meeting her eyes. 'And how are you about that?'

'Well, I'll get there too. Actually, I'm pretty much there. It just wasn't right. He's a nice guy. He'll make some lucky woman very happy one day. He's just not my nice guy.'

She felt uncomfortable with this conversation. She hoped against hope that he wouldn't push for too much detail. That he wouldn't ask her what her idea of a nice guy was.

'Your dad says he was a bit of flashy sort. Big car, fancy house. Good job.'

'Yeah, well. That just about describes Ant. But he's generous and gorgeous too.'

Noah looked at her as if trying to make sense of what she had said and of why she'd made the decision to break-up with Ant in the first place.

'Woah there, Libby. You keep describing him like that and I'll be asking you for his number myself.' Noah laughed, then blushed. 'Not that I'm gay or anything. Not that there would be anything wrong with it if I was...' He looked so flustered that Libby couldn't help but laugh and nor could she help but feel herself warm even more to him. Any warmer and she would be in serious danger of combustion.

'He's pretty perfect on paper, but we just didn't gel. Not properly. It was going nowhere and, well, we both deserve more. I'm a romantic at heart, you know. Hard not to be when my first love was Mr Darcy.'

'Is that the guy Colin Firth played in the Bridget Jones movies?' Noah said, and for a moment he had her. For a moment she felt a sort of disappointment wash over her that this man did not know who one of the most iconic characters in literature was, then she saw a sly smile on his face. Relief washed over her. His perfect armour remained chink free.

'You're a gobshite, Noah Simpson,' she teased.

'Yeah, but a loveable one,' he replied, and that, she feared, was the problem. He was absolutely right.

She shook her head. 'Anyway, I am far from perfect girlfriend material myself at the moment. The only love affair I'm interested in is the one I'm having with my new shop. I don't have time for distractions.'

She was proud of her little speech, even though she didn't one hundred per cent believe what she was saying.

'I totally understand that – as someone who has been there – who is still sort of there. Having a passion project is great. It will fulfil you in ways you never thought possible. For me, stupid as it might sound, because this is a pub and pubs don't change the world, this place has given me a sense of achievement nothing else has. It feels like home and not just because I live in the flat upstairs. But a business can't hug you at night, or ask how you are, or massage your shoulders. So, you know, just keep an open mind.'

'How's that approach working for you? Do you keep an open mind?' Libby raised an eyebrow and he looked at her, directly at her. He didn't try to avert his gaze, or dodge the question with a witty response.

'It's working okay,' he said. 'You might not believe this, but I do find it hard to open up to people. To let them in. I've been okay with that until now, but recently...'

'Recently?' she asked.

'Recently, I'm starting to wonder if it might be worth taking a chance or two. With the right person, of course.'

All she could see in that moment were his green eyes, open, honest, piercing. She saw how he looked at her as if he could see her in a way no one else ever had. And it scared her and thrilled her in equal measures.

If only, Libby thought, the timing was different.

27

LONG TIME PASSING

Libby found herself doing everything that she could to avoid Noah. It wasn't that she didn't want to see him. She desperately wanted to, but the part of her that was scared of how she felt about him, and afraid it might derail her plans for the shop, forced her to keep her distance.

She always managed to find a reason why she had to go out somewhere whenever he called to the shop, and she told her father that he should refuse any offers of help on the grounds that they didn't want to take advantage of their neighbours' goodwill.

As a plan, it worked. But she hadn't realised just how much she would miss him. Because she did. Very much.

At least, she told herself, she was able to keep distracted from her longing with everything she had to do in the shop. Things had kicked up a gear and while it was exciting to see it start to come together, it was also exhausting.

Most nights, she'd fall asleep with her laptop still open, paperwork in front of her and her to-do list running through her mind on a loop.

No matter how much she seemed to get done, there always seemed to be something else to add to the bottom of the list. She thought she was prepared. She'd done her research, but there were things she had never considered. Not properly – like where she would source the baked goods for the coffee bar. Would she approach a local bakery, go for something like biscotti or pastries, or stick to the basics of scones with butter and jam, muffins and cake? How much should she order – not knowing how busy the coffee bar would be? Would a standard-sized dishwasher be big enough? What exactly would hit the mark with the non-book merchandise? Remembering she wanted to attract creatives, would a selection of pens, quirky literary-inspired gifts and book-marks be enough? Or should she expand to cards and wrapping paper, notebooks and e-book covers?

When it came to it, making these decisions was hard, even though Jess had resumed her role as supportive friend and they frequently talked over WhatsApp for hours at a time about what Libby should or shouldn't do.

Occasionally, she would distract herself further by asking Jess if she'd been in touch with Ant, or if he had called her. 'I'm still not sure it wouldn't be really weird,' Jess would tell her, but as time passed, and life got busier, Libby came to realise that it wouldn't be all that weird after all. Not in the long run anyway.

Jo popped in and out, sometimes bringing over plates of sand-wiches and the occasional lunch. 'We want to make sure you're eating and these workmen are getting fed too,' she would say, but Libby would always insist on paying something.

She didn't dare ask after Noah, even though she wanted to. And when Jo asked her if everything was okay she'd tell her she was just very busy. 'Come over for a drink sometime though,' Jo said. 'We miss you.'

Libby had nodded and said she would and had then spent the

best part of the next twenty-four hours trying to analyse the word 'we'. Had Jo meant Noah too? Surely she had. But did he really miss her? And did she want him to?

She managed to bump into Noah once in Harry's shop. He had smiled at her and said, 'Hello stranger! I didn't think you were allowed out of the shop at all these days.'

'A girl needs milk for tea and, erm, Maltesers occasionally,' she'd said, looking at the counter where she had laid her purchases.

'Don't work too hard,' Noah had replied. 'You don't want to get sick again. And we've still those Guinness lessons to get in sometime.' He'd smiled and her heart had fluttered.

'As soon as I have a free hour or two, I'll let you know,' she'd told him. 'Maybe next year sometime?' If she hadn't been mistaken she had seen a flash of something, disappointment perhaps, cross his face. When Noah had left, and Libby had started to make a coffee, Harry had leant against the counter and spoke. 'What's going on with you two?'

Libby had turned to look at Harry, fighting the rising heat in her cheeks. 'There's nothing going on, Harry. We're both just very busy.'

Harry had laughed, a deep rumbling belly laugh that boomed around the shop. 'Bookshop Libby, that's the biggest load of nonsense I've ever heard in my life. There's no way you look at me the way you look at him, and the same goes for him. I've been around a long time and I've seen a lot of things. There's a way you look at someone when you are truly avoiding them and then there's a look you give someone when you really, really like someone but are scared of something.'

'You're wrong, Harry,' Libby had said, convinced if she said it with enough conviction, she would start to believe it herself.

'Now, I'm very busy, so if I could just pay for my shopping, I'll be away out from your hair.'

'You do that,' Harry had said. 'But remember, you can't kid a kidder.'

She had given him a small smile, even though she wanted to tell him to butt out instead, and she went back to work, where, later that day, she would sign for her new coffee machine and her days of the watery brown water that passed for a coffee from Harry's shop would be numbered.

Then she'd spent an hour feeling guilty for having angry thoughts about Harry, who was a nice man and the very heart of the Ivy Lane community. She would go and see him later maybe. Take him some of the sample scones she was having delivered.

* * *

After four weeks of hard work, Libby was suffering from extreme work overload coupled with a healthy dose of cabin fever.

Jess told her she was feeling much the same and, in addition, that she was exhausted from the effort of trying to work out whether or not she should contact Ant. She lamented to Libby that Ant had sent her two WhatsApp messages in the last week, asking how she was and if she wanted to meet for coffee, but she'd been unsure of what to reply. Jess wanted to say yes, Libby knew, but she also knew Jess was scared of it not working out.

So, Libby knew that her best friend was very much in the land of the people needing to destress too.

A message from Jess pinged on Libby's phone.

Fancy going out? Like properly out? Town tonight?

She read it while listening to the clatter and thump of bookshelves being carried into the shop and assembled. With just three weeks to opening now, the shop was really taking shape. Craig was bringing to life his design and, in the matter of a few days, Libby's stock would arrive. She was feeling absolutely in the mood for letting off some steam.

But she had to contemplate the effort it would require to make herself presentable for any city-centre establishment on a Friday night. She was currently in dusty shorts, a once white T-shirt and her hair was pulled back from her face and neck in a bandana. There was also a foul and mysterious odour in the room, which she strongly suspected may be coming from her own body. The day had been warm, furniture she had started to shift around had been heavy and the hour she had spent mopping and hoovering in the flat – which was actually starting to resemble a habitable space – had left her sweaty. Her body ached and she longed to stand under a hot shower or slip under the suds into a deep bath and feel her muscles relax.

There was something tempting about dressing up and kicking back with her best friend. She'd forgotten the last time she wore full make-up, or heels for that matter. It had been a long time since she'd channelled any other look but Rosie the Riveter and she longed to feel fresh and feminine again. And, God, she longed to just have some fun. Along with Jess, she could show the world exactly what kind of modern, independent sassy lady she was. They could Carrie Bradshaw and Samantha Jones it with the best of them.

Libby called her friend. 'Okay, Silver Street at eight? We can take it from there?' she said, before Jess had a chance to say hello.

'Sounds like a plan,' Jess said. 'Dress to impress!'

'And under no circumstances are we to find ourselves anywhere near Ivy Lane, or near the beaches of Inishowen. Do you hear me? No matter how strong the alcohol content!'

'That's a deal. And I say we make a deal that no text messages are sent from either of our phones, especially after the consumption of alcohol.'

'That's a solid plan,' Libby laughed, 'count me in. You're a good friend, Jess. I hope you know that.'

'Of course I do. And yes, I am the best,' Jess said playfully, before they said their goodbyes and Libby set about planning just how she was going to transform herself.

By the time she was ready, she wasn't quite a siren, but she felt she looked pretty decent. She'd slipped into a fifties-style strappy swing dress in a pale blue, with a cherry pattern and a red bow at the bust. Teamed with a red headscarf, red ballet pumps and, of course, a streak of red lipstick, she felt confident enough to believe she had captured a casual retro vibe. Pulling her cream bolero cardigan from the drawer, she wrapped it around her shoulders, spritzed herself with some Jo Malone Black Cedarwood and Juniper perfume and padded downstairs, calling to her parents that she was going out with Jess.

'Going to the Ivy?' her mother asked – Libby able to sense the hopefulness in her voice. Her mother hadn't stopped extolling the virtues of Noah since they had met, despite the fact Libby had told her repeatedly that nothing was going to happen.

'No. We're going into town for a few. Nothing too wild. Just want to let our hair down a bit – now that the shop is on schedule,' Libby called back, sticking her head around the door.

'And the flat, love? How's that going?' her mother asked.

'Well... it's getting there. The kitchen and bathroom floors were done this morning. They really match the fittings Craig got sorted. It's looking well now, but, to be honest, I have to focus on the shop to bring that in on time. I'm on that stupid barista training course next week so that will take me away for a few days. But, sure, at least I have a bed here until it's sorted.'

The look on the face of both her parents startled her a little. They both blushed, looked to each other and down to the ground. Their moves were so in sync, it almost looked as if they had been choreographed.

'Of course you do, pet,' her mother spoke first.

'This will always be your home,' her father said. 'But I'm sure you'd love your own space again. No pressure or anything. Just saying, if you need help getting your furniture out of storage, or moving, or anything, you just have to ask.'

Libby smiled. It was so nice for her father to be so caring, but really, she didn't want to put him to any more trouble than he already had gone to. 'Dad, honestly. I'll get to it. You have both done more than enough already, I couldn't ask any more of you.'

Her mum cleared her throat. 'Well, the things is, Libby, you're not asking. We're offering. With all the love in the world. But, you know, we'd grown used to having the place to ourselves and I think we'd all probably benefit from having our space and our own privacy again.'

Her mother's face was the colour of beetroot, as was Libby's as soon as she realised exactly what her mother was saying.

An unbidden image of her parents walking around in the nip slipped into her mind – one she batted away as quickly as she did the following image of, God forbid, them having sex on the kitchen table. She had become a gooseberry in the lives of her own parents. She cringed internally, and maybe even a little externally at the thought. She'd been so blasé about getting the flat ready and so caught up in the shop that'd she'd never considered they might actually want her to move out.

'Oh God, okay. Right. Well, I'll get to it. As soon as the shower's fitted and the carpets are down, I can move. Everything else can be done around me.'

'Oh, there's no rush,' her mother said, her face still crimson.

But Libby knew there clearly was a rush.

* * *

'It doesn't necessarily mean they want the house to themselves for sexy time,' Jess said, as she tried to stifle another fit of giggles while she sipped her second strawberry daiquiri of the night.

Libby had told the barman to go heavy on the rum, so they tasted ever so slightly off, but the medicinal effects were already kicking in.

Shuddering at the mental image of her parents enjoying 'sexy time', Libby couldn't help but laugh at the amused expression on Jess's face.

Jess continued, 'I mean, maybe they just want to enjoy a nice game of chess on their own or play some croquet on the lawn without you watching over them?'

'Do you think,' Libby laughed, 'that maybe my parents are closet naturists? All this time I've been home saving and planning for the shop, do you think they've been itching to get their clothes off and wander about in the altogether?'

'And God, summer's nearly over, Libby! You've robbed them of prime naked time! I can't imagine it's too comfortable in the winter.'

'Not with the way my mother polices the central heating anyway,' she nodded.

When they moved on to their third drink of the night, without an extra dash of rum, Libby told Jess, in a more serious tone, that she really did have to sort herself out and get the flat in order. 'I'm really watching the budget now,' she said. 'I think I'll have to do the bulk of the decorating myself. I might start painting on Sunday. If you're handy with a paintbrush, I'll treat us to a nice dinner afterwards?'

Jess shifted awkwardly. 'I'm so sorry, Libby. I can't. I've a team-building day to go to in Donegal and it's definitely going ahead and I definitely can't get out of it.'

'Not to worry,' Libby said, as she bit back her disappointment. 'I'm a strong, independent woman and I can paint walls on my own.'

'You know, I'm sure you could find a neighbour or two to help?' Jess suggested with a raised eyebrow.

Libby put her hand up, signalling to her friend to stop talking. 'We are not allowed to mention neighbours or Donegal men. That is the rule. This is your cease and desist order!'

Jess saluted and barked a 'Yes, Sir!' response in a military style.

Three hours later, as they busted some moves on the dance floor to Destiny's Child singing about independent women (Jess had requested the DJ play it), Libby thought herself exceptionally lucky and definitely not in need of any man in her life. She'd be okay. She'd run her business. She'd live alone in her flat, which admittedly wouldn't have the best paint job on the walls, but which would be home. She'd be just fine.

She twirled around the dance floor, hands in the air, and she felt as happy as she ever had done. Libby was ecstatic she had worn flat shoes, which allowed her to throw some of her best dance moves into the mix and, by the time they were being asked if they had a home to go to by a burly and rather amused-looking bouncer, she was both really quite drunk and also aching all over from the most strenuous aerobic workout she'd had in years.

Jess hadn't been so sensible with her footwear and they were no sooner out of the bar onto the cool pavement than she had taken off her three-inch heels and was making almost orgasmic moaning sounds at the feeling of the relief the flat, cool ground was giving her insoles.

'Taxi,' she muttered, eyes still closed but finger pointing in the direction of the heaving taxi rank across the street.

'You only live ten minutes' walk away,' Libby said, thinking of Jess's riverside apartment. 'We'd be quicker walking.'

'So help me God, Libby. If you make me walk home on my poor pulverised feet, I will end you.'

Jess didn't often get cross, but with more than a few drinks in her, she unleashed her inner Dr Jekyll. So, wonky logic aside, Libby let her friend wrap her arms around her shoulder and limp gracelessly across the road to the taxi stand, where Jess promptly sat down on the pavement and would only shuffle along on her bum as the queue moved.

The smell of salt and vinegar over freshly cooked chips hung thick in the air, as did the aroma of at least fifty people with alcohol on their breath, who had all been sweating buckets in whatever pub or club they had just been in. Someone started a sing-song of 'Angels' by Robbie Williams and they were just reaching peak 'And throooouuugghhh it aalllll' when Libby felt a tap on her shoulder.

Through blurry eyes, she turned and saw that Jo was grinning at her, a bag of chips in one hand, which she tipsily waved in her direction.

'Libby!' she said with drunken enthusiasm. 'Do you want a chip? Were you out tonight? I had a night off, so I thought I'd make the most of it. Here, are you going back to Ivy Lane? Could I share a cab? I'm bunking in with Noah tonight – well, not in the same bed,' she grimaced, then laughed.

Libby tried to shake the image of Noah in bed out of her head and focused on what she was actually doing. 'Sorry,' she said. 'I'm taking this one back to her flat. I'll probably just kip there to make sure she is okay. Although maybe you could share anyway and just travel on on your own? We are going in vaguely the same direction.'

'That would be great,' Jo said, waving her bag of chips in front of Libby's face again. This time she couldn't resist and took one, biting into it, wishing she had a full bag herself to eat. 'My mates are going in completely different directions,' Jo added. She waved across at a group of people, who smiled and waved back, before diving back into their own chip bags.

'It's no problem,' Libby said with a smile.

'You're a good egg,' Jo added with a smile, before her face clouded a little. 'But here, are you okay? I've not seen you at the Inn very much these last few weeks. I know you're busy, but is there something more going on? You didn't fall out with Noah, did you? I asked him if anything was wrong, but he just told me to mind my own business.' She shrugged her shoulders and ate another chip before offering the bag back in Libby's direction. 'Noah never tells me to mind my own business. Well, rarely. But he's been moping around too and I've seen him staring wistfully over at the bookshop and he's started taking Paddy out for long walks, which he tends to do more when he has something on his mind.'

Libby pulled a particularly vinegar-coated chip and used the time it took her to eat it to think what to say in reply. Her brain was hazy with alcohol and she didn't want any stories getting back to Noah. She had to make sure not to say the wrong thing. Certainly not to tell Jo that her foster brother made her feel really giddy, but that she couldn't allow herself to be distracted because... because... Well, at 1.30 in the morning, with a blood-stream swirling with alcohol and the words of Robbie Williams swimming through her head, she found it hard to remember why.

Thankfully a voice from the pavement chimed in. 'Everything is just tickety-boo,' Jess slurred. 'Libby here, the best friend in the entire whole world, is just very busy with the shop. And the flat. And you know, her parents might just be naturists, so she has to move out quick smart.' Jess attempted to click her fingers at 'quick smart', but her fine motor control was gone to hell at that stage, so she ended up just staring at where her thumb and finger should have met. 'Here, Jo, are you any good with a paintbrush?'

Hung-over Libby was delighted with drunk Libby. Not only had drunk Libby made sure she'd taken off almost all of her make-up before falling into bed in Jess's spare room, she'd also made sure drunk Libby had taken two paracetamol tablets and, by the looks of it, consumed the better part of a pint of water. Hung-over Libby still felt very much on the ropey side but not as bad as it could have been.

Not as bad as Jess was.

Libby heard a low moan coming from her friend's room and soon after a crashing sound and a call of 'Ouch!' Seconds later, she heard Jess padding down the hall towards the kitchen, muttering something about her mouth being as dry as a furry boot.

Lifting her empty pint glass, Libby made her own way to the open-plan living area where Jess was trying to put coffee on while slugging on a can of Diet Coke as if her life depended on it.

'Morning,' Libby said, quietly, her voice hoarse.

'There's Diet Coke in the fridge,' she muttered. 'I'm

attempting to make coffee. And toast. Will we have toast? Carbs are medicinal you know, and I'm a doctor.'

Jess turned and looked at Libby, who could see her friend's make-up had not been removed except for whatever remnants she'd left on her pillow, and her eyes were red-rimmed with tiredness.

'I'm also sure I've some Dioralyte here somewhere. Although right now, a saline drip would be most use.' Jess and her medical knowledge were brilliant to have on your side during the very worst of hangovers. She was legend in their early twenties as she imparted all her newly learned cures on her friends who were enjoying their early twenties by drinking to excess at least three nights a week.

'It was good night though,' Libby said, touching the ice-cold can of Diet Coke against her pulse points to cool her down. It was another hot day and she was sure she was already sweating forty-per-cent-proof alcohol.

'It was. All of it. That I can remember anyway. Which reminds me, do you know where my shoes are?'

'You traded them with a woman three up in the taxi queue for her place. You told her your bladder was at "maximum capacity".'

'Shite,' Jess said. 'Those were good shoes too. From Faith. Absolutely crippled me – but pretty to look at.'

'You did tell me last night if you ever suggested wearing them again, I was to batter you over the head with them.'

'I did?'

Libby nodded. 'You were very vocal about that.'

Jess pinched the bridge of her nose, then laughed. 'Oh God, Libby. When was the last time we just went out and had silly fun like that? When did we get so serious?'

'Probably right after the last time we had a hangover like this one,' she moaned before asking Jess to make up some Dioralyte, known for its rehydrating properties, stat.

'Double doses,' Jess said. 'We've to get this bad boy out of the way by tomorrow. Team building is awful at the best of times, never mind on the second day of a nightmare hangover.'

'I need to get this hangover cleared by lunchtime,' Libby said. 'I can't take a full day off the shop – or the flat now that I have my marching orders from home. Hangover or no.'

'I suppose,' Jess said, grimacing. 'But at least it'll give you the chance to firm up plans with Jo a little for tomorrow.'

Plans? With Jo? For tomorrow? Something very vaguely recognisable gnawed at Libby's memory. Something after eating chips and before Jess handed over her shoes. Lovely Jo and a promise Libby had made to love her forever. Oh God.

'What did I do, Jess?' she asked, her stomach sick at the thought.

'Well, you asked her to help you paint the flat, and then – and you'll love this – you asked her if she thought Noah would use his van to help you shift some of your furniture out of storage because, and this is the bit I remember quite clearly, you really like him and just need to be near him.'

'Oh God,' Libby cringed, segments of the conversation coming back to her in horrific technicolour.

* * *

Libby's sense of horror at having her darkest feelings exposed only grew through the day. In fact, it consumed her so much that very little actual work got done in the shop or the flat. She spent a good hour sitting on the stripped-back floor of what would become her new living room just staring into space, willing her body to find an extra ounce of energy to get on with things.

At just after three, when the morning's carb loading seemed to wear off, she ventured up to Harry's shop to bulk buy cheese and onion Tayto crisps and Lucozade, along with a king-size Twix.

'Rough night last night?' Harry said, taking one look at Libby's paler-than-pale complexion.

'Well, it was a good night, if truth be told. Probably too much of a good night.'

Harry rocked back on his heels. 'You young ones. You know, in my day, women didn't go near a bar and there was no pint drinking either. A wee half did youse right.'

'Ah, Harry, now you're not that old, surely? And, sure, there's nothing wrong with a woman drinking a pint is there?'

'Well, first of all, I am that old. This sad article here was born during World War Two, you know,' he said and pointed at himself. 'I was born the night the Germans dropped the bombs on Messines Park. Such a commotion that night, my mother used to say. Only time the Germans hit Derry. When I was a young boy, she used to scold me for leaving my toy cars everywhere – said that the bomb in Messines didn't leave half the mess I did. She'd give me a good skelp around the ear too – back when it was acceptable to give wains a good skelp around the ear. They were good times, Libby. Hard times but good times.'

'Harder for the women who couldn't relax with a pint in their hands at the end of a long day,' Libby teased. 'You men aren't that easy to live with, you know!'

'Ach, sure I know it. A wee Babycham. That was Mary's drink back then. I'm not wanting to come across as one of the women haters, but there was a charm in it. Those drinks. The wee glasses that they served them in.'

Harry looked so wistful at the memory, Libby couldn't bring herself to launch into any more of a rant about the evils of the patriarchy or women's rights. Harry was a decent man – just from a different generation. One like her grandad's, and she imagined he would have been as courteous and respectful of women as her beloved grandad had been. For a second, she felt a wave of emotion threaten to floor her. Bloody grief, sneaking up on people when they least expect it! The hangover horrors weren't helping either. She'd have to get this Twix into her and her blood sugars up quick smart.

'But, Libby, I'm not meaning to offend you and your modern ways. It's a changed world, I know that. And not all of it bad. So don't you be getting cross with me and coming burning your brassiere outside or anything,' he said with a cheeky smile.

'As if I would,' Libby said, and laughed.

He totted up her shopping and handed the bag over to her. 'I didn't charge you for the Twix, pet,' he said. 'I figured your need was greater than mine.'

She felt herself well up more, and saw Harry's expression change to one of near horror at the sight. 'Don't be upsetting yourself, pet. It's only a Twix and it's almost out of date anyway.'

'You're very kind, Harry,' Libby sniffed. 'You've been very kind to me since I arrived here and you didn't need to be. You've made me feel very welcome.'

The old man blushed. 'You're one of us now. I can tell you're a decent sort. A welcome addition to our extended family here. Noah was right about you that first day you arrived. Said you brought a ray of sunshine with you. I told him, you know, that's what I always think about my Mary. The day she walked into my life, she brought a ray of sunshine.'

That was enough to tip Libby over the edge into a full-blown sob fest, which left Harry looking mortified and more than a little confused about how to handle her emotional breakdown. He walked out from behind the counter and pulled her into an awkward half hug and patted her back.

'There, there,' he soothed. 'No need to cry, my love. Sure, it's a nice thing he said. Noah knows a good 'un when he sees it.'

She walked away sniffing, and inhaling a Twix at the same time, thinking in her hung-over and emotionally fragile state, that 'good 'un' or not, she had thrown away what could be her chance to find love because of this stupid dream to open a stupid shop on this stupid street in this stupid summer.

Of course, a few hours later when she was back home in her room, the room she now felt there was an eviction notice hanging over, Libby's guilt switched gear to self-hate at thinking badly of the shop and the street and the summer.

It was a Saturday night and she was feeling sorry for herself. Scrolling through her phone, she tried to think of who she could call to sound off to.

She'd already spoken to Jess, who had informed her she was actually at death's door and going to sleep in the hope of feeling vaguely human again the following day.

The only name that jumped out at her, to her shock, was Noah. She realised that even though the thought of spending time with him scared her, the reality of not seeing him – and of actively avoiding him – scared her more. She knew he understood her – and her need to fit in. She thought of how he said Ivy Lane was the place he finally felt securely at home, and which had helped him heal after his own tragedy. She understood that. She felt it too.

But no. She wouldn't text him. Especially not now, when she was feeling emotional and needy. She'd see him soon enough, she thought, thanks to Jo and thanks to her own big mouth.

Libby wondered if Jo had told him what she had said in the taxi queue. Perhaps Jo had been as drunk as she was and would have a hazy memory of it too. Or no memory. It might, she realised, still be possible that Noah didn't know he had been volunteered to help, and that he certainly didn't know that Libby had feelings for him.

She sent a quick WhatsApp message to Jo, telling her that she had organised alternative help and that she hoped Jo wasn't experiencing the mammoth hangover she was, and then wrote:

I barely remember what I said last night, I was talking the biggest load of nonsense. I didn't mean half of it.

Jo did not reply.

Libby was cursing the fact she hadn't bought enough emulsion or wallpaper paste when there was a knock on the door of the flat just after three on Sunday.

She dropped her paint roller and traipsed down the stairs, wiping the sweat from her brow with her arm – still feeling the effects of her overindulgence on Friday night. She opened the door to find Jo and, to her horror, Noah, standing there, paint-brushes in hand. Jo was smiling broadly. Noah looked hugely uncomfortable.

So uncomfortable in fact that Libby knew beyond all doubt that Jo had indeed told Noah everything she had said. The awkwardness was coming off him in waves, and she was pretty sure she was projecting a similar vibe.

'The rush has just ended in the bar,' Jo said. 'We got here as quick as we could.'

'Did you not get my text? I'm fine. I have it under control. Honestly, you two go and enjoy a bit of downtime before the evening rush,' she said, struggling to even looking at Noah.

'Don't be so silly,' Jo said, bright and smiley. 'Many hands make light work. Besides, by the look of you, you could do with a little help.'

Libby looked to her paint-splattered arms and hands. The splodgy splashes of colour on her dungarees. 'I'm fine, honestly, and anyway – I'm not ready to move furniture in yet and I've to go out now and get more paint, so, really, you'd just be wasting your time.'

'Noah could take you to get paint?' Jo said with a sly smile, which earned her a death stare from both Libby and Noah. 'Actually, why don't we all go?'

Despite her own reaction, Libby felt irked by Noah's stare. This, she realised, was why it was a bad idea to allow herself near him, even for five minutes.

'I can drive myself,' Libby said. 'Honestly. And I can do this myself too. You two can go back to the pub. Give the other bar staff some time off, or do something yourself?'

Noah raised his head, looked at her and sighed. 'Libby, we both know that Jo here is quite persistent when she gets a notion in her head, so why don't we just get on with this? It won't take long and it will get her off our backs.'

Jo crossed her arms in front of her chest and smiled contentedly. 'He's right, you know. And don't worry, I'll be there to break the very obvious tension between you two.'

Libby blushed beetroot and shook her head. She couldn't think of a single thing to say other than, 'Let me just grab my bag and keys then.'

She turned to run up the stairs.

'Don't forget to give your face and hands a quick wash!' Jo called, and as soon as Libby walked into her newly installed bathroom and looked in the mirror Craig had fitted, she saw why. A large blob of white paint was streaked across her face. Her face was freckled with fine white dots, which only served to highlight the dark circles under her eyes, no doubt brought on by her hangover.

'Shit!' she swore as she did her best to scrub the paint away. 'Shit! Shit and double shit!'

* * *

Sitting beside Noah in his van, the silence was deafening. Any progress, any friendship they had built up over the last few weeks seemed gone. There was an awkwardness there. She didn't know what to say to him that wouldn't make things worse, and clearly he really didn't want to be there.

'I've always loved going to DIY stores. I know that's a bit sad, but I love it. I love choosing paint colours, and looking at the kitchen and bathroom displays. Not to mention the garden centre. I love that. Noah normally hates it when I suggest going,' Jo enthused. 'Don't you, Noah?'

'Yep,' Noah said. His voice wasn't exactly grumpy but he didn't seem excited either. He was firmly in neutral.

'Do you know exactly what you need to get?' Jo asked. 'Or are you still open to ideas?'

'At the moment I just need white emulsion and gloss. And wallpaper paste. I haven't decided on all the colours yet, but I did get a lovely paper for a feature wall.'

'I love a good feature wall,' Jo said. 'Don't I, Noah?'

'Yep,' Noah replied.

This was moving beyond awkward into excruciating.

'I can't believe it's all getting so close to your big opening,' Jo continued. 'You must be really excited? You've worked miracles in that shop. I always loved the look of it, but I'll be honest, I thought it was beyond saving, but you've done it.'

'Well,' Libby said, 'it's been a big job, but even when we open, it's not done yet. I'm so proud of what's been done, but I've always known that opening is only half the battle. Staying open is the other half. So many people have told me I'm taking a big risk. A bookshop in this day and age? Sure, who goes into an actual bookshop any more? But, you know, I have to try and I've sunk every last penny in it to give it the best chance.'

'Why?' Jo said. 'Not dissing your dream. I love the sound of a bookshop. I still love to shop in a place where I can hold an actual book in my hands and spend time looking at all the covers and all. But why is it so important to you?'

'My grandfather,' Libby said. 'It was his dream – and I suppose I'm trying to do it for him. In his memory.'

'Well, that's very admirable,' she said, softly. 'I'm sure you are doing him proud. Don't you think so, Noah? Don't you think it's a lovely thing to do? Take a risk like this to try and make someone else's lost dream a reality?'

'I do,' Noah said, staring straight ahead. 'I think it's incredible. The mark of a person.'

Libby felt her heart constrict at his words and all her emotions started to bubble dangerously close to the top. 'That's very nice of you to say,' Libby said. 'It's terrifying too. I can't stand the thought of it failing and me letting him down.'

'We'll do whatever we can to help ensure you won't fail,' Noah said, his eyes still facing forward, which was a good thing, because it allowed Libby to brush away a hasty tear without being noticed.

* * *

Somewhere between the trade-sized buckets of emulsion and the wallpaper displays, Libby noticed a text from Jess which read:

OMG, you will never believe what has happened! Call me!

Try as she might, she couldn't get a signal to call Jess, who, as far as she was aware, was in the middle of a team-building exercise in the middle of Donegal. She cursed at her phone and then slipped it back into her bag, vowing to call as soon as they were done, which didn't actually take all that long.

Libby could feel herself decompress at the thought of being back at the flat and on her own again soon. Jo, of course, had other ideas and insisted they all stop in a nearby café for coffee and cake.

* * *

After just a few minutes, and with his coffee untouched, Noah excused himself to go out to his van to make some phone calls. He had no sooner walked out of the door before Jo sidled up closer.

'What gives?' she asked.

'What gives with what?'

'You and Noah? There is a very weird vibe between the two of you. I didn't tell him, you know. That you like him. If that's what you're thinking. But, if you ask me, he knows. And, if you ask me, he feels something too. Noah Simpson is only ever off with people for one of two reasons. He either loves them, or hates them. And I know that he mostly certainly does not hate you.'

Libby looked at her cup, lifted her spoon and started stirring her coffee, even though she hadn't added any sugar. 'It's complicated.'

'Things are always complicated,' Jo said. 'Think of every big situation in your life. Have any of them ever not been complicated?'

Libby paused. Jo had a point. Nothing she'd ever wanted deeply had ever come easy.

'Look, okay. I do like him. It wasn't just the drink talking. But it doesn't matter whether I like him, or whether he likes me back. It's totally not the right time.'

'When is it ever the right time?' Jo asked, her eyebrow raised. 'I mean, if we waited for the right time to do everything, well, we'd never do anything.'

'I know that, I do. And I agree, for the most part, but sometimes it really is just the wrong time. I just split up with my boyfriend to concentrate on the business. Getting involved with someone when I have to put my heart and soul into making sure this business works wouldn't be fair on him. That's if he even wants me. I can't give him what he needs because I can't afford to get distracted.'

'You seem to think that the two can't exist together – hardworking you and romantic you,' Jo said, her face more serious now. 'That's a shame. In the right relationship, the two can feed each other. You've much more to gain than you have to lose.' She darted a look at the door, just as Noah walked back in.

Libby's heart leapt.

* * *

When she got into the van, Libby remembered the text from Jess. Pulling her phone out of her bag, she wondered would it be exceptionally rude to call Jess back there and then while in the company of others. It wasn't as if there was half a chance of getting any privacy in the confines of a van. She sent a message instead.

Can't talk just now. Couldn't get signal before. What's up? Tell me! A scandal at the team building?

The reply from Jess came just two minutes later.

OMG, I've been hanging on for your message. Still stuck at the team building of doom. Paintballing, for the love of God! Almost done. But we need to talk. Guess who I saw here? On his own paintballing nightmare? Ant! He asked me to go for coffee, but I won't if it would be too weird for you. Chat tonight?

Jess seemed so excited, Libby couldn't help but feel excited for her. Even if it was a bit weird. She'd get over it. And it was only coffee. It wasn't like it was a proposal of marriage. If any relationship bloomed between them, Libby guessed she'd have time to adjust.

She did feel something else though too. Jealousy. She couldn't fight it. It wasn't that she still wanted Ant, far from it. It was more that Jess seemed happy and full of hope for her love life while Libby felt so torn between heart and head.

She sent a quick text back to Jess, telling her she would call her as soon as she was able but that she should absolutely say yes to coffee.

The three of them sat in silence again for the rest of the journey through the city centre and on to Ivy Lane. But when they turned into the street, everything changed in an instant. They were greeted with the flashing blue lights of an ambulance and a small crowd gathered outside Harry's Shop.

'Stop the van!' Libby heard herself shout, but Noah had already pulled into the nearest parking space and had opened his door and was rushing out.

'Oh Harry, what have you done?' Jo whispered.

Libby followed hot on Noah's heels to the shop, with Jo just a step or two behind her. Mrs Doherty from two doors down was stood just inside the door – her hand to her face.

'Harry!' Libby called, as she looked past Mrs Doherty and saw two feet poking out from the behind the counter, while one paramedic stood talking into a radio, another disembodied voice from behind the counter asking for meds, shouting figures and medical terms.

'I came up to check in on him – he looked a bit peaky this morning – that's how I found him,' Mrs Doherty sobbed, while Jo put her arm around her shoulder and told her she would get her a cup of tea for the shock. 'I told him,' Mrs Doherty said, 'I told him he needed to slow down. That he wasn't getting any younger and, sure, there were any number of young ones who would do a few hours in the shop. Stubborn old goat,' she sobbed.

Noah walked forward towards the counter, but the female paramedic, who had been speaking into the radio, told him she needed him to stay back and give them space to work.

'What's happened to him?' Noah asked.

The paramedic looked at him sympathetically. 'It looks like a cardiac episode,' she said. 'We're doing everything we can. We have a second unit on the way.'

'He wasn't breathing,' Mrs Doherty sobbed. 'I did my best. I was calling for help, but there was no one about the street. I tried to do CPR... I don't know if I did it right.'

Noah just stood in the middle of the shop looking helpless and lost, while Libby found herself unable to move. Frozen to the spot just outside of the shop – memories of the day her grandad took seriously ill flooded back. That was a cardiac episode too. One he didn't come back from. She remembered crying as the doctors tried to explain what had happened and that they had done everything they could. But he was gone. And he wasn't coming back. It was the first time she had seen her father cry, rocking back and forth while her mother had tried to comfort him, desperately trying to hide her own shock and grief. 'He was fine this morning. Wasn't he, Libby? He was fine when you went on that walk together,' her mother had asked.

She'd wanted to tell her he had complained of being tired and she had wondered whether they should just have gone home early. Would that have stopped it? Had she been partly responsible?

Her breath grew shallow, standing there, outside the shop with Harry prone on the floor, his life appearing to hang in the balance. Was there anything she could have done? He had seemed fine when she'd spoken to him the day before, or had she been too distracted by her own hangover to really notice?

'Is there anyone we should contact?' the female paramedic asked, cutting into her thoughts. 'Family? Are you guys family?'

'No... no, we're his neighbours. He's like family... but no... He has no one, no one local anyway,' Noah stuttered.

'But his wife, Mary,' Libby said. 'We should let her know.'

Noah turned and looked at her, confusion all over his face. 'But Mary's dead, Libby. She died five years ago, he's on his own. His children live in England – I don't have a contact for them...' he said, turning back to the paramedic. 'We usually just watch out for him here on the street. He's one of us.'

Libby couldn't quite believe what she was hearing. That couldn't be the case. Oh God, poor Harry. 'But he always talks about her. He didn't say she was dead...' Libby said.

Jo sniffed and took her hand. 'Oh, pet, he would never tell anyone – not directly. Not a lie as such, but he liked to talk about her as if she was still here. They were so in love, he just couldn't stand the thought of being without her. That's why he spent so much time in the shop. He hated being at home alone. Oh Harry...' Jo said, her voice breaking.

Libby could barely take it in. Her heart was breaking, for Harry and Mary, for her grandad and for herself. It was she who was the lonely one now, she realised.

'We've got a pulse!' the female paramedic shouted, just as two more paramedics arrived and pushed their way into the shop.

'Folks, if you could all move back a bit, we need room to work,' one said, and slowly, in shock and reluctant to leave Harry alone with people who he'd never met before, they all moved out of the way of the paramedics. Libby was trying to make sense of it all, her fear overwhelming.

'I'll go with him to the hospital,' she heard Noah say. 'He shouldn't be alone. If they let me, I'll go in the ambulance.'

'I'll follow in my car,' Libby said.

'Good, good,' Noah said, but his eyes were never far from the door of the shop.

'I'll stay and get the shop locked up. Make sure Mrs Doherty is okay. What an awful shock for her.'

'She kept him going until the paramedics got here. She's a legend,' Noah said.

* * *

An hour later, they were sitting on blue plastic seats in the overly warm waiting room of the Emergency Department at Altnagelvin Hospital.

The place was busy, with everyone from young children with badly cut fingers to adults slightly the worse for wear who may have done themselves an injury while under the influence. A TV high on the wall was showing the BBC News channel; no sound, mind, just subtitles that were on a slight delay and didn't always make sense.

Noah stared into a half-empty cup of dark brown liquid that was allegedly tea, while Libby sat not knowing what to say at all. Harry, the last they heard, was still in Resus. Jo had at least been able to track down contact details for Harry's two sons and had called them to deliver the news that their father was unwell.

Libby's mind was in a whirl. Not only because of the echoes of what had happened to her grandfather but the revelation that Mary was dead and had been all this time. All these conversations she had shared with Harry when he had spoken about her in the present tense. She had assumed that come the end of the day at the shop he was going home to her, to a dinner on the table and the company of the love of his life for the evening.

Poor Harry. Was it any wonder that once he got to chatting he was reluctant to stop? She felt guilty for cutting her conversation short with him the day before; selfishly longing to get back to the flat to carb load and try to rid herself of her hangover. He had never been anything but good to her; making sure she was well fed with 'just a wee bit out of date' biscuits, crisps and even, on occasion, a block of cheese that he assured her had a good week in it at least, despite the mould.

Each time the door from the treatment area opened, she would look up, hoping against hope it would be a doctor to tell her Harry was going to be okay. She was aware that neither she nor Noah were family. Well, not in the biological sense anyway.

A tear slid down her cheek and, as she tried to wipe it away, she felt a hand reach out to hers and hold it.

'He'll be okay, you know,' Noah said, his voice soft and low. 'He's made of strong stuff. And we'll make sure he's well looked after.'

Libby nodded. She wanted to believe him so much. 'I can't believe that Mary is gone. That poor man going home alone each night.'

'Oh, he didn't. Not every night anyway. I meant it when I said that Ivy Lane people watch out for each other. A few of the neighbours have him round for tea a couple of nights a week. Mrs Doherty is a fierce one for dropping casseroles to him. You know, you might think you're special, Bookshop Libby, but I have it on authority, Mrs Doherty gets first picks of the out-of-date treats!'

Libby managed a weak watery smile back in his direction.

'Some of the lads take him to the pub a couple of nights a week. Not the Ivy, mind. He tells me that place is "for people with notions" even though he has yet to turn down a free dinner, or a free pint for that matter. No, they go to what he calls a "proper pub" with sticky carpets, a dartboard and the vague smell of smoke about the place despite the smoking ban being years old.' Noah squeezed her hand. 'We do look after each other,' he said. 'And we'll look after Harry. I'll have to get a rota done up. People who can help at the shop until he's back on his feet.'

Libby admired his optimism and wished she shared it, but she knew from bitter experience that no amount of wishing or hoping would make a difference if Harry's heart had simply decided it had had enough. Still, for now, until they knew otherwise, she would play along because it felt nice and was comforting.

'I'll help out. Just let me know how.'

'Ah, you've enough on your hands with that shop of yours to get up and running,' Noah said. 'I'm sure we can give you special dispensation.'

Libby shook her head and looked Noah directly in the eyes. 'No, I mean it. I'll do my bit. We watch out for each other. Us Ivy Lane ones. Isn't that how it works? If my shop takes a little longer to open, it takes a little longer to open. Some things are more important.' There was a look of admiration on his face, or affection, it was hard to tell, but she drank it in.

Even sitting tired, the strain of the last hour written all over his face, she saw a face that made her feel funny inside. A face that, if she took a chance, she knew she could love. A face, she realised, she wanted to take a chance on.

She was just about to open her mouth to tell him they really needed to talk, when the door to the treatment area opened and a rather sombre-looking doctor gestured in their direction to come through. She held on to Noah's hand even tighter as they stood up and walked towards the double doors.

31

THE GO-BETWEEN

The room was dark, save for a small swivel angled lamp above the bed. The only noise to be heard was from the corridor outside. Footsteps. The occasional beep of an alarm. A snippet of conversation between nurses. Life was going on, while in this hospital room it was frozen in time.

It was some time in the very early hours of the morning. Noah was sleeping in a chair, his body angled just like the lamp above Harry's bed. Libby marvelled at how young he looked when he slept, then chided herself for even daring to have such thoughts while they were here with Harry.

She was holding Harry's hand, delighted and relieved that it was still warm. 'You keep doing that, Harry,' she whispered. 'Keep that blood pumping and your hands nice and warm. No more scares. No more drama. Promise us.'

Harry hadn't yet regained consciousness. His colour was what her mother would have described as the same as 'boiled blooter'. Libby wasn't sure what boiled blooter was, but she knew enough to know it obviously wasn't something very pleasant or that anyone would want to be the same colour as.

Wires and tubes ran into him, and wires and tubes ran out of him. His heart rate hit its peaks and troughs on the monitor beside the bed, but they weren't to be fooled that the steady red lines meant everything was okay. Harry was, in the words of the tired-looking doctor who had spoken to them, a 'very sick man indeed'. He'd suffered a major coronary episode. In fact, it was probably only the quick thinking of Mrs Doherty and her CPR skills that had kept him alive at all. He would require a bypass, but for the moment was stable. He was, however, facing a long recovery and he would simply have to slow down a bit. No more 6 a.m. starts in the shop. No more up to fourteen-hour days, six or seven days a week. He needed to take it easy.

He was very much not out of the woods yet, but Libby hung on to the fact that Harry was clearly a fighter. He had made it past the first hurdle and she was going to do her very best to make sure he made it past all the others too.

Both she and Noah had agreed to stay overnight, taking it in turns to grab an hour's sleep on the uncomfortable chair. Harry's children would be arriving in the morning, and Jo had already rounded up a host of neighbours only too willing to keep the shop open, albeit on reduced hours.

The entire experience had left Libby exhausted and wrung out and desperately wishing that the hugs she was sharing with Noah had lasted a little longer.

At times, they slipped back into their easy manner of conversation and gentle teasing and her heart would soar, but Harry's bedside was not the place to confess her feelings. Especially when Harry was still so ill.

By the time morning came and Mrs Doherty arrived to take over bedside watch, both Noah and Libby were beside themselves with exhaustion. Struggling to keep her eyes open, Libby drove back to Ivy Lane, where Noah said he would try and grab a couple of hours' sleep before the lunchtime rush in the pub. She in turn glanced over at the shop and the windows of her flat above it and wished her furniture was all in and fitted and she could simply climb the stairs and fall into bed herself.

She couldn't even go home. She needed to stay close to the shop in case of any problems arising with the fittings.

'Come into my place,' Noah urged. 'No ulterior motive. Just get some sleep – I'll kip on the sofa. You can have my bed. We've both had a tough night, Libby. We don't have to make the day any more arduous than it needs to be.'

Too tired to argue, she nodded and followed him up the iron spiral staircase at the side of the bar into his flat, which was surprisingly cosy and, even more surprisingly, nicely decorated.

'The bedroom is through to the back, second door on the left,' he said. 'Unless you want a decent cup of tea or anything first.'

'I think I'm too tired to even think about drinking tea, never mind going to the effort of actually drinking it,' she said.

'Thank God for that,' Noah replied, 'because I've far from the energy to make it.' He was already sitting on his sofa, taking his shoes off and pulling the teal knitted throw from the back of it over himself. The sofa was much too short to afford him the luxury of stretching out fully, but it would be wrong to invite him into the bed beside her. Wrong and far too tempting.

'Why don't I just take the sofa?' she asked.

'Shush, woman,' he said in a gently teasing voice. 'I'm already asleep here.'

She smiled and turned, walking into his bedroom, kicking off her own shoes and climbing into his bed, where tiredness and the smell of his cologne on his sheets lulled her off to sleep.

* * *

It felt a little strange to be woken by the sound of a man's voice. Libby struggled to open her eyes, desperate for just five more minutes – or five hours, if she was honest. The room was hazy, the bed warm and comfortable, but she couldn't ignore the sound of her name being called by a vaguely familiar voice. Willing herself into consciousness, she looked up to see Noah, bleary-eyed and ridiculously handsome, standing in the doorway, his clothes crumpled, stretching and urging her to wake up.

'Much as I hate to wake you, Jo just said Craig's been looking for you at the shop and I thought you might want to freshen up a bit first?'

It dawned on Libby that she must look a state, and she must smell quite rank too, after the hours spent in a hot hospital, the lack of a shower, or even access to a toothbrush. Her make-up from the day before was still somewhere in the vicinity of her face, she was still in her paint-splattered clothes and she doubted her deodorant was working at an acceptable level.

'I must look a mess,' she muttered.

'Well, to be honest,' Noah smiled, 'you've looked better. Some of us can work that twenty-four hours on the trot look and some of us can't. Don't be jealous.' He sniffed his armpits and pulled a disgusted face before laughing. 'See, I'm fresh as a daisy?'

Libby couldn't help but laugh. 'Do you mind if I freshen up here? Maybe get a shower? The shower's not connected across the street, and I don't have any towels, come to think of it.'

He blushed a little. 'Of course. Take a shower. There are fresh towels on the rail. If you open the bathroom cabinet, you'll see some of Jo's smellies too. I'm sure she wouldn't mind you using them. And there are spare toothbrushes as well. Help yourself.'

'Thank you.'

'You're welcome. Thanks, Libby. For staying last night.'

'It was nothing,' she said.

He shook his head. 'It wasn't nothing. It will have meant a lot to Harry, but it meant a lot to me too. I'm not a big fan of hospitals,' he said. 'Too many memories, and none of them good. My family, you know. How they died...'

Libby felt shame wash over her. She'd been so wrapped up in remembering her grandad, she'd never even thought about the trauma Noah must have been living – the unspeakable tragedy in his life. 'You've been through a lot,' she said, feeling there was nothing she could say that was adequate to provide comfort after such a loss.

'Yeah, you could say that,' he said. 'But, anyway, thank you. Now, hurry up and get in that shower!'

She so wanted to say something more, but she couldn't find the words, so she just nodded and headed to the bathroom.

* * *

Craig had worked miracles with the shop fitting. He had secured the shelves she'd bought in Belfast to the walls as she wanted, and installed a series of new units in different sizes to suit different books. There was even a small colourful corner which had been designed just for children. Libby had plans to bring her grandad's old chair into the shop, reupholstered and refurbished, and leave it in the children's corner so that parents and carers could read to their own children.

The shelving had been installed for the coffee bar too, along with a food display cabinet, and the small kitchen had been fitted with units which matched those she had in the flat.

It wasn't finished, but it was close, and it made her heart swell.

Most of all, Craig seemed really happy with the job himself, telling her it had been one of his favourite jobs of recent times. And although only an occasional visitor to Ivy Lane, he seemed as stunned by Harry's illness as anyone else and said he would do whatever he could. He even offered his teenage daughter's services to man the shop at the weekend. 'She's a good girl. Good with numbers, and she won't spend all her time chewing gum and staring at her iPhone. She'll be glad of the work experience,' he said, while Libby had vowed to slip the youngster a few pounds for her troubles and inwardly thought if she was good enough and interested she may even rope her in to help at the bookshop.

The realisation that her flat would be ready sooner rather than later, and that the wider community was rallying around Harry so much, brought tears to Libby's eyes and as she worked in the shop at a greatly reduced pace due to her tiredness, she thought about how quickly life could change and how nothing was ever promised forever. Not money. Not your health. Not love.

At around 3 p.m., her phone buzzed to life and she swore to herself when she saw the name flash on-screen. Jess! She had promised she would call her back as soon as she got back to Derry yesterday, but in all the fuss and fear of the night before, and with the utter exhaustion of today, she had forgotten to do so. She swore under her breath. What if Jess thought she was being selfish or angry about Ant asking her out? She couldn't stand it if, on top of everything else, she fell out with her best friend again.

Feeling more than a little nervous, she hit the answer button and said hello before launching into an immediate and heartfelt apology.

'Jess, I'm so, very, very sorry. You see, when we got back, well, Harry was sick and we had to go to the hospital with him, because his family is all away and I was there all night and my phone was dead and then today, well, today has just been strange and I'm so tired. But I wasn't avoiding you or ignoring you, I promise.'

'Libby, calm down!' her friend said. 'I knew there would be a good reason. And Harry? That's the wee old man in the shop, isn't it? Is he okay?'

'He's in surgery undergoing a bypass. He's lucky to be here, Jess. Oh, it was awful and scary and how on earth do you do this every day? Deal with life and death and serious illness?'

'Well, thankfully general practice has its fair share of mundane appointments, rashes and manky toes, and then some happy times, like new babies, so it's not all bad.'

'It reminded me of grandad,' Libby confessed, almost in a whisper.

'Oh, pet, that must have been tough for you. But it sounds like Harry's in good hands. If he is in surgery, they must have hope for him.'

'Oh I hope so. He's such a lovely man. It would be hard to imagine the street without him. But, Jess, I need to tell you about his wife...' Libby was just about to launch into the sad saga of Mary when she realised it was unlikely that Jess was calling her to find out about the tragic death of her neighbour's wife, but was more likely to be calling to share news of her own. Libby could have thumped herself for being so stupid. 'But, look, enough about that. You and Ant? Coffee? Did you say yes?'

'I did. I'm seeing him later and I've just been having a bit of a panic that it might upset you.'

'I'm not at all upset. Meet him. See where it goes. If he starts telling you any of my secrets, then, of course, dump him, but I don't think he's like that,' she added.

'Are you sure you don't mind?' Jess asked, and Libby could hear the anxiety in her voice.

'I really don't mind,' Libby said and realised she really, really meant it. The last twenty-four hours had brought that all into focus. 'Life's too short to wait for the right timing for things. Especially nice things. And things being awkward shouldn't stop you taking a risk either,' she said confidently.

'Physician heal thyself,' Jess muttered.

'What?'

'Libby, my friend, did you ever think sometimes you need to listen to your own advice?'

The weeks passed quickly in the run up to the grand opening. They managed, just about, to get everything – including the flat - ready on time. Libby stretched and yawned and slowly opened her eyes, and smiled at just how far she had come. Here she was, having survived, and in fact enjoyed, her first night in her new home. Yes, the flat still needed a few finishing touches, a picture here and there, and her kitchen could be better stocked with kitchen-y things, but she would get a garlic press and a colander in due course.

She'd forgotten just how comfortable her own bed was and was surprised at just how well she had slept. She'd been convinced she would spend the night tossing and turning and worrying herself silly. Instead, once she had enjoyed a soak in the bath and had spent an hour pampering herself in her new boudoir (tastefully decorated in pale grey colours with accents of pink), she'd drifted off under her brand new sheets in her brand new pyjamas and had only woken once in the night to grab a glass of water from her new, beautifully fitted kitchen.

It had been a bit like Christmas Eve, the excitement had

verged on overwhelming. But she was delighted to find that when she woke properly, the daylight doing its level best to peek in around the edges of her blackout blinds, she felt calm. Sitting up, she stretched again and enjoyed the feeling of the day's sunshine warming her windows. Summer was still in full bloom.

Pulling the blinds up, she opened her window and inhaled the morning air, her breath catching just a little as she saw Noah standing at his own bedroom window, looking crumpled and sleepy and gorgeous.

The last few weeks had been mad. Insanely busy. Between trying to get the shop ready, the flat sorted, working the occasional shift at Harry's shop and visiting him in hospital, she had run herself ragged. She and Noah had become ships that passed in the night, but she absolutely longed to speak with him, properly.

She'd visited Harry the day after his operation and while he was still quite weak and poked and prodded with tubes and wires, he had smiled broadly when he saw her approach.

'Bookshop Libby,' he'd said. 'It's nice to see you.'

'It's nicer to see you, Harry,' she'd replied. 'You gave us quite a fright there.' To her surprise, she had felt tears prick at her eyes.

'Well, sure, I have to keep you all on your toes,' he'd said, nodding his head towards the chair beside his bed.

Libby had reached over and kissed his scratchy cheek and then she'd taken the seat and his hand in hers.

'Well, we're so on our toes, we could be ballerinas at this stage,' she'd said gently. 'But, sure, as long as you're okay. Jo and Noah have told you you've not to worry about the shop?'

'They have,' he'd said. 'You are good people.'

'Takes one to know one,' she'd answered.

'I can't thank you enough, you know,' he'd said, his voice cracking.

'Harry, don't be upsetting yourself, it's okay. We're neighbours. We look out for each other.'

'Now, Libby, let me say my bit. Humour an old man! My sons have told me that you and Noah stayed with me here all night. That you never left my side. That means a lot, an awful lot, to an old curmudgeon like me.' He'd sniffed and Libby had felt the tears that were threatening to fall start to slide down her cheeks.

'We wouldn't have left you,' Libby had said. 'We had to make sure someone was with you.'

'You're very good. You're what my Mary would describe as a good egg.'

At the mention of Mary's name, Libby had felt her heart constrict a little, but if it gave Harry comfort to talk about his beloved wife as if she was still here, she was happy to let him.

'Smart woman, your Mary,' Libby had replied. 'Why don't you tell me more about her? How did the pair of you meet?'

Libby and Harry had talked for about half an hour until tiredness had started to overwhelm him again. She had told him she would leave him to sleep but would be back the following day and would check with his sons if there was anything he needed or that she could help with. Harry had nodded sleepily and Libby had stood up to leave. But just as she made to go, he'd squeezed her hand.

'Libby,' he'd said, 'as you know, I'm not one to interfere, but you and Noah? You'd be good together, you know. And I know it can be scary. I'm not a silly old man. I know you young people have a lot on your plate, but I'll tell you this now, you'll never regret taking a chance on the person who could be the love of your life. You never know what time you have with anyone in this world – don't risk losing precious days, weeks or months.'

Libby had placed another kiss on his scratchy cheek and had left, her head spinning.

Later that afternoon, Jess had called her to fill her in on the big coffee date with Ant. She had excitedly told her friend how they had met, talked a lot, flirted a little and decided to make a go of things.

'We're going to take things really slowly,' Jess had told Libby. 'He says he wants to do this properly. So we will.'

'Sounds like a solid plan,' Libby had said.

Within a couple of days, she had vowed to talk to Noah, to ask him out on a date. If Jess could take a leap of faith, so could she. Even though she felt disgustingly nervous at the prospect, she couldn't deny she had butterflies in her stomach. She had watched how the entire community had rallied together for Harry and she knew that Noah wouldn't let her get distracted from achieving her dreams even if they were dating.

It was just unfortunate that no matter how much she tried, the appropriate moment didn't seem to arrive. It wasn't that they were avoiding each other, just that they didn't seem to find themselves in the same room for more than five minutes at a time. She wanted to talk to him properly; not over a quick five-minute chat in the pub, or while discussing marketing in the bookshop or over the slightly out-of-date biscuits in Harry's.

Harry had come home from hospital after ten days, but was on strict orders to take it easy. His sons had been forced to go back to England, to their jobs and families, but they had ensured a care package had been put in place for their father. Harry, however, was proving to be exceptionally stubborn and said there was no way a 'little thing like a heart attack' was going to force him into retirement. In the end, to stop him doing an injury to himself, it was agreed he could spend a couple of hours a day in the shop, along with a shop assistant to do any actual work. Harry could just sit on his newly bought chair and oversee his kingdom.

Of course, now it was the day in which Libby would oversee a kingdom of her own. The doors to Once Upon A Book were due to open at 11 a.m. Libby almost had to pinch herself that it was actually opening day. When she had climbed the stairs to bed the previous night, she had left the shop in waiting – the shelves stocked, the coffee machine finally mastered. She had even managed to figure out how to work the cash register, which would automatically stock-take for her. Bookings had already been taken for the writing nooks and she was well on her way to organising her first open night event. All she really had to do that morning was get up, get dressed, and make sure the champagne glasses currently sitting on the tables in the shop were filled with fizz or orange juice for the non-drinkers. She would take an order of freshly baked pastries at 10 a.m. and the caterers would also deliver some hors d'oeuvres. She had roped Jess into taking pictures of the opening and posting them on Facebook and Twitter and she had invited as many people as she felt could reasonably fit into her shop. Including, of course, the residents of Ivy Lane. At close of business, Noah had promised a 'bit of a knees-up' in the pub and Jo had arranged some live music to play, among other songs, 'Paperback Writer' at the big moment.

A buzz of the doorbell jolted Libby from her reverie and she padded downstairs, still in her pyjamas, to open the door to a massive bouquet of flowers being thrust in her direction by a cheerful delivery man. 'You're a well thought of lady,' he said as she sniffed their aroma.

'Thank you,' she smiled. 'These are gorgeous!' As she made to close the door, he put his hand to it. 'Hang on, that's not the only bouquet for you today!'

He went back to his van and came back with a further two bouquets, both as gorgeous as the first.

Libby grinned, feeling very much like the luckiest girl in the world. Until, that is, she had to try and find enough receptacles to put them in. In the end, they were split between her one good vase and a jug and one of the bouquets was simply left resting in a sink filled with water. Reading the cards, she felt even more emotional. The first was from her mum and dad, telling her how proud they were of her. The second was from Jess and Ant (she made a mental note of the joint signature!), wishing her all the very best – and the third? Well, that was addressed to 'Bookshop Libby' and was signed on behalf of all the residents of Ivy Lane. Her heart full, she dressed and carefully did her make-up, before going downstairs to spend a quiet half hour in the shop before the fuss of the day began.

In the morning light, she breathed in the smell of the books and the wooden fixtures, and the vague aroma of coffee. She watched the sun start to stream in through the windows, casting shadows into each corner. She switched on the cash register and powered it up, running through a trial transaction or two to make sure it was working and then she took a seat at one of the little café tables and thought about how far she had come. She tried her best to swallow down any fears she might have about the future, simply enjoying the fact she had done what she had said she would do. She had kept her promise to her grandfather and she hoped that he was watching over her from wherever he was and that he was proud of her.

Whispering 'I love you' into the stillness of the shop, she brushed away a tear, determined it would be the only one she would shed that day, and opened the door to wait for the delivery of chilled champagne and delicious refreshments. Today would be a good day.

* * *

When there was a knock on the door, Libby assumed it would be one of the caterers arriving. She was surprised, but in a nice way, to see Noah looking at her through the glass panel. He looked less sure of himself than ever before. He was gazing down at his shoes, one hand thrust deep into his pocket, the other holding a parcel wrapped in brown paper and string. There was no denying he was a handsome man – but there was more to him than physical attractiveness, she thought as she walked to the door. He was a good person and that counted for so much more.

'I wasn't expecting to see you until later,' she said as she opened the door, smiled and invited him in. 'But since you're here, you can have the inaugural coffee from my brand-new coffee machine. Sadly, the pastries haven't arrived yet, so if you want a treat with it, you'll have to make do with some chocolate biscuits Harry donated.'

'Out of date?' Noah said with a cheeky smile.

'No! Would you believe it? These ones have a whole nine months left until they expire. I think the hospital addled his brain a little.'

Libby did her best to work the coffee machine, running through all the steps she had been taught at her training course. Even though her heart thumped loudly and her hands shook, she managed to make a very respectable latte.

'What brings you across the road at this hour anyway?' she asked as she handed him his drink. He sat down at one of the bistro tables and Libby sat down opposite him.

'Just wanted to make sure you weren't melting down under the pressure.' He laughed.

She turned and put her hands out in front of her so he could see how they were shaking. 'I'm perfectly calm, can't you see?' she said with a wry smile.

'Yes, of course,' he smiled. 'You do know it's going to be brilliant, don't you? You've done something special here.'

'I hope so, but we'll see,' she said and watched as he brought the coffee cup to his mouth and took a sip. No grimace, that was a good sign.

'That's good coffee,' he declared. 'But you should know I didn't really come here to see if you were okay. I knew you would be. And nor did I come here to con you out of a free cup of coffee.'

'Who said it was free?' Libby teased, sitting down. 'I'm putting it on your tab!'

Noah laughed before his face grew serious again. 'Look, I wanted to do this now. Before the shop opens. I was thinking of doing it when everyone was here, but I didn't want to upset you. I figured it might be a bit emotional.'

She felt her heart sink. What was he at? Was he about to tell her he was seeing someone else?

'Don't look so worried!' he said, seeing her face drop. 'Look, I hope you like this and appreciate why I did it.' He pushed the brown-paper-wrapped parcel in her direction. Flat and A4-sized, she wondered, had he bought her a book, as if she didn't have enough books as it was.

She blinked up at him.

'Open it,' he said.

Slowly, nervously, she untied the string and folded out the corners of the parcel – pulling back the paper to find a picture in a frame. If her heart could have exploded with every emotion, it would have done at that moment. Grief, sadness, pride, love, joy. It was all there.

'I saw the picture in your parents' house when I came to visit,' Noah was saying as she couldn't take her eyes from it. 'I thought it deserved to be here, behind your counter. He deserves to be here.'

Libby couldn't speak through her tears. So much for promising she wouldn't shed another tear that day! Framed and ready to hang behind her counter was one of her favourite photos of all time. She must have been about six when it was taken, sitting on her grandfather's knee, both of them staring into the pages of a book, smiling broadly, discovering a love of the written word, realising what love really meant.

It was perfect.

She looked up, tried to compose herself, just as she saw Noah stand up. 'I'll see you later, Bookshop Libby,' he said softly. 'This is your day. Enjoy it.'

33

Slipping off her leopard-print pumps, Libby rubbed her tired feet and gratefully accepted the glass of wine Jess had just put in front of her.

'This one's from Harry,' Jess said, and Libby raised the glass in the direction of Harry, who was holding court in the corner, his usual pint replaced with a glass of red wine.

'If people keep buying me drinks like this, I'll be seven sheets to the wind in no time at all,' Libby said, gratefully taking a large sip from her glass. 'But, boy, have I earned it.'

'You most certainly have,' her dad said, a proud smile on his face. 'That was a brilliant day, Libby. Just brilliant. You've done yourself proud and all of us proud.'

'I'll second that,' her mum said, sniffing back a tear as she started to drink her third glass of wine, which had her a little giddy.

Despite her aching feet, Libby was deliriously happy. The day had indeed exceeded all her expectations. Everyone had oohed and aahed appropriately and she had shifted enough stock to make her feel fairly confident in the shop's future. She'd also taken a number of bookings for the writing nooks – including one from Jo, who said she wasn't going to put off writing a book any longer.

Still, she was delighted to be able to sit down and relax and, yes, to celebrate. The Ivy Inn was buzzing with customers, all of whom seemed intent on buying her a drink and wishing her well. It felt a little like a wedding, and she tried to make sure she spoke to everyone to thank them all for their support.

But there was, of course, only one person she really, really wanted to speak to. Looking across the bar, she could see him now, chatting to a customer as he took their order. Her eyes were continually drawn to him and while she tried to make it less than obvious, she knew she was making a very poor job of it.

That was confirmed by Jo, who, sitting down beside her a short time later, whispered in her ear: 'A bit like writing my book, sometimes you have to make things happen. Find the time. Steal the time if you have to.' Jo nodded in the direction of Noah and, feeling emboldened by two large glasses of wine, Libby told her she was absolutely, one hundred per cent right.

She wriggled out from behind the table and walked towards the bar, getting as close to Noah as possible.

'Your order?' he asked her, his eyebrow raised.

'Actually, I need a word. Would you mind if we had a quick chat?'

'Of course not,' Noah said, lifting the hatch on the bar to allow her through and directing her towards the office, where Paddy immediately jumped up to show her he was happy to see her. That was enough to break the ice. This all felt natural and normal. All nerves were gone.

She didn't even feel nervous as she closed the office door and found herself alone with Noah. He leant back against his desk, just a few feet from her.

'Well, Bookshop Libby, what can I do for you?' There was a cheeky smile on his face, one that made the butterflies in her tummy take flight.

'Well, Ivy Inn Noah, I've been thinking about this a lot. And I do mean a lot. What you can do is take a chance on me, with me. You can help me find proper happiness. You can keep on making me laugh. You can keep on being a good friend and a damn good businessman. You can keep on taking me for road trips in your van. You can keep being you.'

Noah glanced briefly downwards before he looked right back at her, his eyes twinkling – his face more serious. 'Anything else?'

'Just one little thing,' Libby said, taking her future entirely in her own hands. She started to walk towards him. 'Ivy Inn Noah, you can kiss me.'

And he did.

Libby sat back on the ercol rocking chair she'd picked up for a song at the latest Belfast market. At her feet a group of children, ten of them in total, sat on coloured cushions and beanbags, their eyes were very firmly on her.

Her Saturday morning Reading Club was proving to be extremely popular, not only with the children but also with their parents who could relax with a coffee while she took their children on a magical journey each week – opening their minds to new worlds, new stories and a love of reading.

This week was a little different though. This week she was going to start telling a very special story – and she only hoped it would keep the attention of the children in front of her.

'How do we begin a story?' she asked the children.

They smiled before parroting in unison: 'Once upon a time!'

She grinned back at them. She loved starting her sessions just like this, inviting the children into the story with her.

'Good job!' she told them. 'So, once upon a time there was a very wise and caring king called Ernie. And he had a very inquisitive, and sometimes a little messy, granddaughter called Princess Libby.'

The children giggled at the use of her own name.

'Together King Ernie and Princess Libby decided that every child in the land should have no homework ever.'

The children cheered.

'But instead, they would get to read as many stories as they wanted and their parents absolutely had to read them a bedtime story at night!'

The children cheered again.

'They worked very hard to make sure everyone obeyed their rules. They worked so hard that Princess Libby very rarely had time to go out and play with her friends. Or, as she got older, to meet a handsome prince. Then one day, quite unexpectedly, a visitor came to their castle. Princess Libby didn't have very much time for him at first because she was so very busy tidying her books and writing stories for the children of the land to read. But very slowly, their visitor, Prince Noah, nudged his way into her heart...'

Libby knew the story was a bit cheesy, but she had always believed in happy endings and six months after Once Upon A Book had opened she was fairly sure she had finally found hers.

The bell above the door of the shop tinkled and all eyes turned to look at Noah walking in – coming over for his morning coffee as he normally did. A few of the children giggled when they saw him. They all knew Noah well by now. He was a frequent visitor to the bookshop, just as Libby was a frequent visitor to the Inn.

'Ah!' Libby said. 'Here is our brave prince, come to tell you how he slays dragons and wins the princess.'

Noah stood proudly, his hands on his hips in a superhero pose. 'Prince Noah at your service,' he said. 'Or I will be, just as soon as I get a cup of coffee!' He pulled a silly face, before walking across to Libby and giving her the softest of kisses on the cheek. The children made 'ooooh' noises and laughed, before Libby guided them back to the story of the princess who found her happy ever after.

ACKNOWLEDGMENTS

With thanks to Caroline Ridding and Nia Beynon and all at Boldwood for taking a chance on Libby Quinn and her hopes and dreams. I'm delighted to have joined such an innovative and passionate publishing house. Special thanks go to Jade and Shirley for their insight during copy-editing and proofing.

Thanks also to my agent, Ger Nichol, who insisted this book did not rest in a drawer but instead was sent out to the world to find an audience. It has been lovely to delve into the world of romance again.

Writing this book was initially an exercise in distraction at a time when it was nice to write about nice things happening to good people. It was also written with the encouragement of many writer pals, most notably Fionnuala Kearney, who is my most trusted beta reader. Thank you, Fionnu – as always x

Thanks also to Michelle Gorman, Marian Keyes, Melissa Hill, Louise Beech, Sheila O'Flanagan and John Marrs and all the many writers who make this business nicer. There are too many lovely writers to mention, so I hope this is seen as a catch-all.

Thanks to all the bloggers, readers, reviewers, booksellers,

Twitter friends and media champions who prove time and time again that women's fiction is still as strong as it ever was, and without whom writers would be lost.

On a personal level, thank you to my family and friends, my husband and children and all those who allow me to make up stories for a living and encourage me to keep dreaming.

This book is dedicated to the original Grandad Ernie – who passed away in 1993 when I was just sixteen. He was the special kind of grandparent who could find magic in the mundane, who encouraged silliness and ambition and who I'd like to think would be proud as punch of all of his grandchildren. These stories are for him.

MORE FROM FREYA KENNEDY

We hope you enjoyed reading *The Hopes and Dreams of Libby Quinn*. If you did, please leave a review.

If you'd like to gift a copy, this book is also available as an ebook, digital audio download and audiobook CD.

Sign up to Freya Kennedy's mailing list here for news, competitions and updates on future books.

http://bit.ly/FreyaKennedyNewsletter

ABOUT THE AUTHOR

Freya Kennedy lives in Derry, Northern Ireland, with her husband, two children, two cats and a mad dog called Izzy. She worked as a journalist for eighteen years before deciding to write full time. When not writing, she can be found reading, hanging out with her nieces and nephews, cleaning up after her children (a lot) and telling her dog that she loves her.

She has met Michael Buble and even kissed him. It was one of her best ever moments.

She believes in happy ever afters.

Freya Kennedy is a pen name for Claire Allan, who also writes psychological thrillers.

Visit Freya's website: http://www.claireallan.com/freya-kennedy

Follow Freya on social media:

 facebook.com/ClaireAllanAuthor

twitter.com/claireallan

 instagram.com/claireallan_author

bookbub.com/authors/freya-kennedy

ABOUT BOLDWOOD BOOKS

Boldwood Books is a fiction publishing company seeking out the best stories from around the world.

Find out more at www.boldwoodbooks.com

Sign up to the Book and Tonic newsletter for news, offers and competitions from Boldwood Books!

http://www.bit.ly/bookandtonic

We'd love to hear from you, follow us on social media:

facebook.com/BookandTonic

twitter.com/BoldwoodBooks

instagram.com/BookandTonic

Printed in Great Britain
by Amazon